I0777500

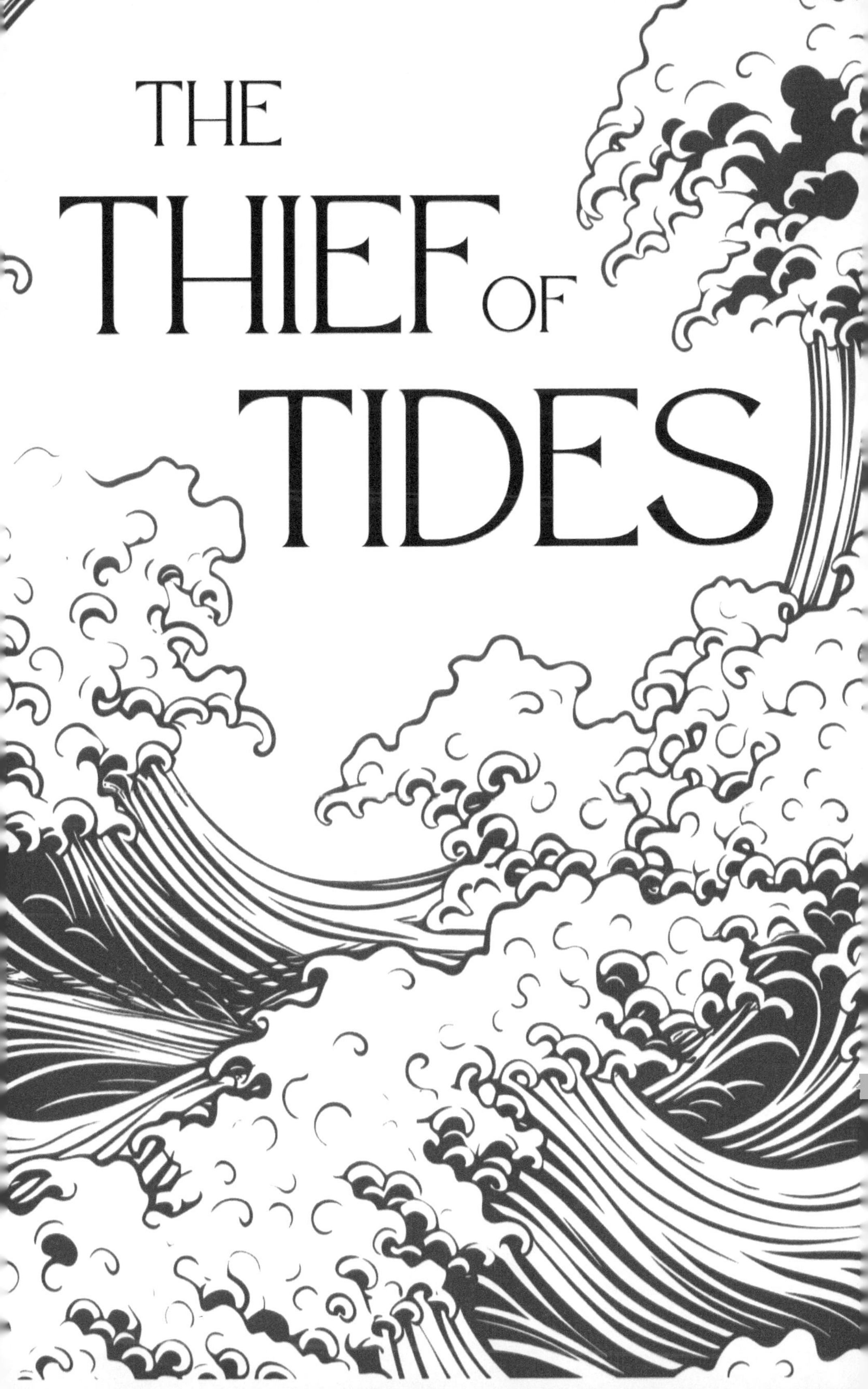

THE
THIEF of
TIDES

Names: Olivia Harlow.
Title: The Thief of Tides.
Description: First Edition: September 2024
Identifiers: ISBN 979-8-9913235-0-5 (hardcover)
ISBN 979-8-9913235-1-2 (paperback)

Dust jacket art by the author.
Cover and interior art from Canva.com.

For those who need to rest their mind somewhere else.
Get comfy and unbind your imagination.

Adventure awaits.

Chapter One

One of the ten rules of assassination is that you should never execute a hit without proper observation. Going into a job with minimal knowledge of your target is like dipping your toes in alligator-infested waters. You might be fine, or you might be chomped by a sharp-toothed reptile and dragged beneath the water's surface. It's a total crapshoot.

A risk I would normally never take. Which is exactly what I told Mother when she assigned me to this job. Yet here I am, sweating my ass off in a tight black jumpsuit outside of a brothel window, waiting for an old man to fall asleep so I can kill him.

Usually, I'd spend at least a few days following a target.

"The client paid three times our usual fee on the condition that it be done tonight," Mother said this morning from her usual place behind her desk. Her office, which always smelled of leather and dust, was cluttered with boxes of mysterious documents. Various treasures from my travels decorated wooden shelves. While hunting, I tended to keep an eye out for small souvenirs, mostly because I knew it annoyed her. She'd complain that she had no use for it, then display it regardless.

"Only a complete idiot would walk into a hit with no information. You taught me that," I replied.

"I did. Now I'm telling you to complete this job as the client requested."

I rolled my eyes. She handed me a rough sketch. It was a man, maybe in his late seventies, with thinning hair and loose skin.

"A strong gust of wind could knock this guy over. The client is better off waiting for him to die." I slid the paper toward her, but she stopped me and shoved it back. I straightened and crossed my arms, leaving it on the desk. "I'm not going to take out an old man."

She scoffed and stuffed the drawing back into her large leather book. I'd always suspected that the black book contained a ledger of past transactions written with invisible ink. Not that I'd ever get close enough to check.

"The high and mighty thief." Her cold gaze searched my face.

"Pirate," I corrected. "Can't one of the other girls do it? What about Savina?"

"She's been detained."

My stomach flipped. I'd never been Savina's biggest fan, but it was useful having her around. She was always assigned the hit jobs, which allowed me to focus on hunting and trading. Now she was in the king's hands, which meant a swift execution.

"Was she captured? Or . . . ?" The unspoken question hung in the air between us.

Or did you turn her in?

If Savina violated her contract, Mother would've had no choice but to hand her over to the knights. If she didn't and was caught, we'd all pay the price.

She leaned back in her ancient chair, which groaned despite her small frame, and steepled her fingers.

She wasn't my real mother. With my skin being six shades darker than her powdery complexion, we weren't fooling anyone. But there were no allies in the mercenary business. Information was a weapon. While truth wearables were extremely rare, it wasn't unheard of that one, if not all of us, would be subjected to questioning by someone who had one. I considered myself an excellent liar, but even I would be forced to tell the truth.

If someone asked me who she was, I could say that she was my mother, and she adopted me when I was seventeen. All of that was technically true. Her 'children,' a.k.a. employees, didn't know her real name. It was safer that way. We would only be in trouble if the person using a truth wearable knew the right questions to ask.

Ignoring my question, she reached into her desk drawer and pulled out three large velvet satchels. Its contents clinked when she dropped them heavily onto her desk. "I'll up your share to 20 percent."

"Thirty, and I want you to fix the broken window in my room," I replied without hesitation.

Her lips tilted into a satisfied smile. "Deal."

On my way out, I paused at the doorway and asked over my shoulder, "Why?"

Mother knew what I was asking, but gave me the same answer she'd always given. "Does it matter?"

At first, I only accepted hits on criminals. Then it was abusers, then men only, until eventually I stopped discriminating and accepted the jobs I was given. The line between right and wrong dissolved long ago. It was easier not to know the reason a client wanted a target dead. Savina's arrival was a relief. I was happy to hand the hit jobs over to her. I was more useful on the water anyway.

Laughter from a passing group of women echoed against the stone walls of the shadowed alleyway where I was hiding. I lifted my braids to let the gentle breeze cool the back of my damp neck.

The lamplight in the room where the target was staying had been snuffed out an hour ago. I couldn't help but have some respect for a seventy-something-year-old man hanging out in a brothel, but he was likely asleep by now.

My knees popped and groaned in protest as I stood from my hiding spot behind some abandoned wine barrels. Most mercenaries retired from physical work by the time they reached thirty. At thirty-two, I fully intended to keep working until I was good and dead. Which, in this line of work, could be any day.

The barrels were stable enough to stand on. I hoisted myself up and peered into the second-floor window. The thin white curtain was transparent enough that I could tell there was no movement, but not enough to make out any figures.

"This is so stupid," I grumbled. I unsheathed my thin dagger and carefully wiggled it into the worn seam between the window panes. The wood trim was swollen and rotting from years of rain and neglect. Each creak made me wince. I wiggled my fingers into the crack and gave it a gentle tug.

I lifted the gauzy curtain and peered inside. Across the dark room, a lumpy shape lay on a small bed. He was tucked under a thin sheet and turned away from me on his side. I watched his shoulder rise and fall with each slow breath. I lifted myself and slipped through the window with ease. For as tall as I was, my movements were impressively silent.

Without the gentle summer breeze, the stagnant air in the room pressed in on me. The black fabric mouth covering I wore to hide my identity was suffocating. The nagging pressure on my neck and tingling across my skin worsened.

I paused.

This was a bad idea. Sure, he was an old man. But if living with a sixty-two-year-old retired assassin taught me anything, it's to never underestimate anyone.

In one fluid motion, I replaced my small dagger with a larger one. It would be a quick death. One clean slice to the neck and he'd bleed out in three minutes. At his age, it would probably be quicker.

My eyes steadily adjusted to the darkness. I needed to see his face. Creeping to the front of the bed, I peered over him. The thin hair and skin matched the drawing, but I couldn't make the kill without officially confirming his identity. Regretting not taking the drawing with me, I pressed myself closer to the wall and leaned over him further.

Being this close, he would eventually sense my presence and wake up. I didn't smell alcohol on him, which meant there was a higher chance of him waking.

His face was still partially obscured. Maybe waking him up was the best option. I was fast enough to attack before he could make a sound. All I needed were his eyes locked on mine.

I reached toward him and gently stroked his head. A chill only the dead can create met my fingers, and I recoiled.

White-hot pain splintered my left shoulder, and I cried out. A knife clattered against the stone wall past me and I spun to the door, angling my dagger at the attacker.

Black slicked-back hair. Four fingers on his left hand. The king's seal glinting from the medal on his chest.

Standing there, sword at the ready, was the man I would give anything to rip apart. The man I despised more than any other with a head I wanted to proudly display on the bow of my ship.

Commander Nathaniel Bartholomew.

Chapter Two

Ice-cold hatred shot through me. He arched his arm, faster than I remember, and swung the sword downward. I twisted my body out of the way with ease. When I tensed to charge at him, knights thundered into the room and filled the space. Men blocked both the window and the door, cutting me off from my only exits. Their swords were drawn, each sharp tip pointed at me.

I froze.

Nathaniel's cruel gaze locked onto mine and I slowly straightened, putting my hands up in surrender. I forced my body into a relaxed stance while every escape scenario flashed through my mind.

"I'd hoped our reunion would be more intimate." I lowered my mouth covering and granted him a disappointed frown.

"Lou-Ann Aurum,"—I flinched at my full name—"you are under arrest for the murder of the king's royal courtesan and honored knight," Nathaniel spoke in a firm and professional manner. I almost laughed at the pretense.

"Doesn't ring a bell." I flicked my eyes over the eight men that surrounded me.

"You are now under the custody of King Francis."

"Your one true love. I've wondered how far you've crawled

up his ass. Now he's got you cleaning up his messes. You're a perfect pet for him."

His scowl deepened, and a dark eyebrow twitched. "You're ordered to come with us. If you don't come willingly, we will take you by force."

"Don't threaten me with a good time, *Commander*."

Red crept up his pale neck. He nodded to his men without taking his eyes off me. One of them stepped forward and grabbed my wrists, forcing them behind my back. The skin stretched in my left arm, sharpening the pain from the bloody gash in my shoulder.

I blocked it out. It was hardly the worst wound I'd ever received. It would be a lovely addition to the many scars that already marred my skin.

I let the knight take the dagger from my hand and the smaller one from my belt. He handed them to another man. Cold iron weighed on my wrists as the knight locked the shackles in place.

He patted me down briskly, searching for any other weapons that might be hidden in my jumpsuit. When he reached the upper part of my inner thigh, I jerked away.

"Careful, boy. I'm sure you wouldn't want to lose that hand." My voice was low and dangerous. The younger man swallowed and glanced at Nathaniel. The commander stepped forward and raked an assessing glare over my body. I tensed under his sharp stare and avoided his dark eyes. Satisfied, he turned on his heel and walked to the door.

"She's clear. Let's go," he addressed the man beside me.

The knight shoved me forward.

I glanced back at the dead body. A sleepy old cat crawled out from under the bed sheet, explaining the gentle rise and fall that I mistook for the man's breathing. It stretched lazily, and I threw it a glare before being shoved into the hallway.

We clomped down a set of creaky, old steps that led to a rowdy bar. The floor was sticky. Prostitutes were either draped over men's laps or serving drinks. Some laughed at jokes that likely weren't funny, strategically leaning forward to reveal what was hidden beneath their loose night dresses.

That could've been me had Mother not contracted me. As nasty as my job could be, I'd never trade it for this. Letting men touch me with their sweaty, greedy hands would be enough to drive me to madness.

The knight shoved me onto the crowded street. A horse-drawn cart with an iron cage took up most of the narrow road. They could've hauled me in something less conspicuous, but I suspected Nathaniel preferred to humiliate me.

A few people glanced our way, curious about the commotion. Most merchants were likely unnerved by the knights' presence. If they decided to raid the stalls, they'd find enough enchanted contraband to arrest the entire market.

A knight opened the creaky cage door. I prepared myself as they pushed me closer.

Three . . . two . . . one . . .

I swung my leg out and kicked against the bars, lifting myself into the air. I threw my body upward over the knight who held me. He startled and I flipped over him, breaking his hold and landing on the ground behind him.

The knights that followed behind us surged forward, but there were too many. Two swung their swords at the same time. I ducked and there was a sharp *clang* as their blades collided.

Nathaniel cursed and charged at me. His swordsmanship had improved since his last attempt to arrest me, but his speed still left much to be desired. He swung and I spun out of the way. The blade nearly skimmed my chest.

I charged forward and used his chest as a launching pad. I kicked off and threw myself on top of the cage, landing roughly on my stomach. Before I could pull my legs up, Nathaniel grabbed my ankle and yanked me downward. I spun and slammed my boot into his face.

The sweet sound of his bones crunching warmed my heart. He cried out and stumbled backward, covering his nose with his hands. I didn't pause to watch the blood spill between his fingers.

The knights grabbed at the cage. I balanced on the iron bars and jumped into the front. I locked eyes with the poor driver just as my boots knocked him from his seat. While the knights clumsily reached for me, I hopped onto the horse's back. The animal reared and shot forward.

"Get her!" Nathaniel shouted.

The horse crashed through the street. People dove out of the way, narrowly missing the large cage, which wobbled dangerously behind us. Hands bound, I clenched my thighs and leaned forward to keep myself on the saddle.

We rode over a large broken stone and the cart sailed upward. When it crashed down on the stone road, the wooden wheels splintered and the harness snapped. I turned long enough to watch it crash into a merchant's stall, blocking the narrow street. The knights, who were chasing us on their horses, skidded to a halt.

I kicked the horse. It replied with an aggravated snort and charged forward, carrying me safely toward the edge of town. I firmly gripped the back of the saddle to maintain my balance.

When I finally reached the last few buildings, the stone street softened to a worn dirt road. The soft glow from the town faded, replaced by moonlit darkness. I grabbed the reins with my teeth and yanked them, ordering the horse to stop, and slid off its back.

I wasn't familiar with the surrounding woods, but it would be safer than staying on the road. His men would eventually catch up. I couldn't outrun them forever, especially with my hands bound.

Nathaniel would suspect that I'd continued north. He would search the surrounding area first, but his fears about me boarding a ship would eventually send him to the northern coast. Until then, I'd head west into the woods as deep as I could, then move south. Once I was confident he'd moved on, I would cut east to return to Bangor.

Once the rush calmed, my giddiness at evading him

evaporated. Mother sent me into a trap. The chance that she did it on purpose was slim. Regardless of whether she knew or not, she still sent me to a job with a high likelihood of failure. The woman needed a reality check. One I would gladly give once I returned home.

Chapter Three

A few hours after leaving Bangor, I came upon a moonlit meadow that had not survived the summer heat. The dry brush crunched beneath my boots. After pulling the reluctant horse through the forest, my calves burned and my shoulders ached. Once I released the reins, it happily trotted away to find something green to eat.

The shackles that bound me were outdated. Knights typically used a smaller set for women. Though it would be extremely painful, it was possible for me to slip my hands through.

I sat on a stone at the edge of the woods and gritted my teeth. Leaning back to pin the chain beneath me, I bunched my fingers together and pulled. I wiggled and twisted. My skin burned, and the small bones in my hands crunched. The gash on my shoulder split further from the effort, and I growled in pain.

The slickness of my sweat worked in my favor. After a few agonizing moments, my right hand released, then my left. I dropped the shackles and slumped forward. Tears burned and slid down my cheeks. I moaned and cradled my fractured hands in my lap.

Mother had a hidden supply of enchanted tinctures that would heal me in minutes. I'd have to wrap my wounds until then. It took a few shaky tries to untie the mouth covering from my neck and wrap my right hand. I used a damp sock to tie the left, and the other sock to wrap the leaking cut. I carefully unzipped the jumpsuit and stripped it, using the fabric to wipe myself down. I spread it on the rough ground and laid on top of it.

The moon was nearly full. Misty charcoal clouds obscured some of the stars. It's said that centuries ago, the stars were fixed in the sky. Sailors could use the night sky to navigate the seas, tracking their positions by following the same stars and the moon.

Legend says the sky shifts were the gods doing. They grew bored with the same sky each night and made a game of it. The powerful god Lex would entertain his friends by scooping the stars into a cup, shaking it, and then tossing them into the darkness to create new patterns. He would find shapes in the chaos to honor the virtues of the proud and vain immortals. These patterns would change upon each roll of the stars, creating endless constellations, never to be repeated.

When my father first told me this story, I was immediately skeptical. I'd turned ten and, much to my parents' dismay, started to question everything adults said. It sounded like a fun game, but wouldn't the gods eventually get bored of playing with the stars?

Nobody I knew believed in the gods. It was mostly the older people in town who would pray or mention them in passing. "Thank the gods you're okay," they'd say. Or, "I'll pray to the gods for a bountiful harvest this year." Personally, I found it hard to believe, but what did I know?

On every clear night for seven years, I tucked a blanket under my arm and snuck out my bedroom window. There was an open field next to our small farmhouse where our goats grazed. I'd climb up a small grassy hill and sit cross-legged, paper and pencil in hand. Night critters kept me company during the sweltering summer months. In winter, I'd shiver under a pile of blankets until my fingers and toes went numb.

Throughout those years, there wasn't a single moment I wasn't in awe of the velvet sea spattered with winking lights.

Sometimes one of the stars would streak across the sky, brilliant for a moment before disappearing. It was there in that field that I found my gods.

The stars and moon rearranged themselves irregularly, known as sky shifts. Sometimes it would be different each night. Other times, the stars would remain fixed in their positions for weeks. The longest recorded sky lasted for twenty-nine nights. After years of watching the sky, I noticed repeating patterns. Two more years of observation confirmed my suspicions.

The stars weren't randomly rearranging themselves. The sky was.

Thirty-two skies were shuffling at irregular intervals. By creating my own constellations, I was able to track the changes. Most skies had different constellations, often in new positions, but it became clear that they indeed were the same shapes I'd noticed during other sky shifts.

Despite the evidence I'd collected over years of observation, I still doubted my discovery. I was only sixteen. Surely an adult had figured this out. My school's library and town archives had little information on astronomy. After a lot of begging and extra chores, I finally convinced my parents to let me check the libraries and archives in the surrounding villages and towns.

I searched through many dusty shelves and moldy corners until I found field guides, maps, and a few academic papers. Through those, I learned as much as there was to know about how the heavens worked and what the stars were. None of the texts mentioned the patterns. As I got older, I learned that the king had taken the funding allocated for research and used it to fund the construction of more warships.

The sky shifts marked the end of intercontinental trade. Our country, the Oceana Empire, was forced to become completely self-sustaining. When the king and queen divorced and the empire was divided, we lost a great deal of farmland. We were on our own, forced to rely on whatever resources the coast could provide.

Sailing at night was treacherous. If someone decided to take a chance on straying too far from the coast, hoping the sky would be the same the next night, they were often never seen again. While a compass was vital for sailors, inconsistent weather conditions, currents, and other factors complicated longer voyages and made straying too far from the coast extremely dangerous.

Unless you had a secret star map.

Not only could I track my position, but I could predict the wind and currents, which were consistent with the shifts. Shift number 9 had strong winds, while shift number 30 meant still, calm waters.

My ability to sail at night using my constellations is what earned me the title of the Ghost of the Sea. I could sail further from the coast than any other ship, appearing as a faint smudge on the horizon. This, combined with skilled stealth and evasion, made it almost impossible to catch me.

Pirates and royalty alike coveted my secret. It wasn't long before I became a target. Even the king tried to have me taken into custody for questioning many years ago, but without evidence, there wasn't much he could do. I'd burned the pages of my notebooks long ago. Everything I knew was tucked safely in my mind.

Tonight was Bonny's time to shine. The constellation reminded me of my favorite goat from my family's farm during my childhood. Bonny was feisty, and she followed me wherever I went. My mother had to lock her in the barn whenever I left for school to stop her from tagging along. Some nights, I'd sneak her into my room and let her sleep with me in my bed.

I traced the shape with my sore finger. She was upside down. Sky shift number 16. She could be found in four other shifts, facing in different directions.

She was my favorite, not only because the constellation was easy to spot, but because it reminded me of those pure nights spent in that grassy field. If I followed her tonight, I'd be heading north-

northwest. The waters would be choppy and the breeze would be strong.

But the sky brought me no peace tonight. I turned onto my side and listened to the chirping and buzzing of the restless bugs and critters hiding in the meadow.

It had been almost three years since I last saw Nathaniel. He'd been hunting me for almost a decade, desperate to see me rot in the king's dungeon. While I consistently had a bounty on my head, the king didn't put pressure on capturing me or any of Mother's contracts. He had bigger things to worry about, such as preparing to go to war against the Kingdom of Laila to the west, ruled by his ex-wife, Queen Lenora.

There were times, such as with his courtesan, when he needed a job done discreetly. In exchange for our services, he looked the other way and left us alone. Nathaniel's supplies for this hunt were outdated and worn, which told me that my capture wasn't an order from the king.

Nathaniel's loyalty to the king was outmatched only by his obsession to capture and imprison me. He mentioned once that it was his sense of duty that fueled his pursuit, but I knew better. His hatred for me was far deeper and more personal than he'd ever admit.

We met in middle school and spent almost every day together. Lounging at the swimming hole. Eating lunch together. Exploring the woods. He went along with pretty much anything I suggested. He was very different back then. Gentle, kind, and thoughtful. We were close friends before we became lovers.

Though he didn't share my fascination with the skies, he would meet me in that grassy field from time to time to keep me company. I never mapped the sky while he was there to ensure that he never learned my secret. Nathaniel was my closest friend, but I wasn't eager to share what I'd learned. One night, a year before we were arrested, we became something more.

We were lying on a blanket, watching an unusual cluster of

shooting stars slash across the sky. He had been acting weird all day, but when I asked him what was wrong, he simply shook his head.

His warm hand closed around mine. When I turned to him, he was watching me closely with a strange expression.

"Lou-Ann, if I kissed you right now, would you hate me?"

I'd only ever kissed two other boys on a dare. Never because I wanted to. I almost said no. I hadn't thought of him that way before. But considering his pleading stare and the glorious leaping stars bearing witness, it felt wrong to say no. It was as awkward as any first kiss could be. Before he went home that night, he asked me if I would be his girlfriend, and I agreed.

I already loved him as a dear friend, and it wasn't long before that love turned into something more. He was my first everything. First boyfriend. First love. First lover.

The night we had sex for the first time was both terrible and amazing. Since we both lived with our parents, we did it in the field on a scratchy blanket. It was painful, which I'd expected. When he saw my tears, he stopped right away and pulled me into his arms. He rubbed my back and mumbled comforting words into my hair.

His warm embrace was my safe place.

Sometimes he would come to school with scratches and bruises. He would wear a haunted expression and spend entire days lost somewhere in his mind. He never told me what bothered him or where the injuries came from. One day, when I surprised him at his house, I learned the truth.

We both lived on a farm, though his was smaller and closer to town. I'd only been there a few times, and only when his father wasn't home. On the day I surprised him, I'd traveled there on foot. It was a sweltering summer morning, and even though I'd left before dawn, I deeply regretted not taking a horse.

When there was no answer to my knock at the door, I made my way to the barn. As I approached, a deeper male's gravelly voice, possibly belonging to his father, drifted from inside.

"Let's try again. Where were you last night?" he asked. His tone was even, and his words were slow.

"Asleep in bed." I recognized the second voice as Nathaniel's, but there was an emptiness in his tone that sent a chill over my damp skin.

The sharp sound of a slap echoed from inside the barn and I jumped, covering my mouth to muffle my gasp. Hastily, I ducked behind some hay bales that were stacked beside the open barn door.

"No. You were up late with me. We played cards, then you went to bed around two a.m.," his father said. "Again. Where were you last night?"

Nathaniel's voice shook this time. "Awake with my father, playing cards. I went to bed around two a.m."

"Good. Have you ever heard of a man named Johnny Thoren?"

"No."

"Are you aware of anyone who might want to hurt Johnny Thoren?"

"No."

"Are you aware of any business your father might have with Johnny Thoren?"

"No. My father has no business with anyone named Johnny Thoren."

"Correct." There was a light shuffling sound of someone moving on a hay-covered floor. His father's voice lowered, and I heard Nathaniel whimper.

"Are you going to try to take the ring off again?"

I couldn't hear Nathaniel's response. His father continued, "Good boy. Go wash yourself and burn those clothes."

The footsteps that followed were muted by the hay. I jumped when Nathaniel's father, Victor Bartholomew, breezed past my hiding place. He had a thin, wiry frame and dark, greasy hair. He made his way to the house, and once he was gone, I slipped into the barn. When I saw Nathaniel, my heart dropped into my stomach.

He was on his knees.

Covered in blood.

I rushed to him. "What happened?!"

It wasn't until I cupped his face that he registered my presence.

"Lou, what are you . . . "

"I came to see you. Tell me what happened." I forced him to look at me. The dark fog in his eyes slowly cleared, replaced by a shiny wetness.

"I did something bad—"

His body convulsed, and he screamed in agony. I reached for him, but he swatted me away, clenching his body against the pain. He slammed his right hand over his mouth to muffle the sound. After a few cruel moments, he stilled and collapsed on the ground.

I gingerly lifted his head and placed it in my lap. He lay there, limp and exhausted. Fat tears fell silently from his red, vacant eyes. My own tears burned, and I held my body as still as I could while brushing his soft hair with my fingers.

Using what little information Nathaniel shared with me and my research, I pieced the truth together over the next few weeks. The red ruby ring he always wore wasn't a family heirloom. It was an enchanted artifact known as a corpus imperium.

His father was using it to control his son's body, making him do terrible things on his behalf. Nathaniel had no choice but to do what he was told. He had been ordered to never remove the ring. If he tried to tell anyone about it, he'd suffer extreme agony. The same would happen if someone else tried to remove the ring for him. He'd writhe in pain, riding the excruciating waves until it was over. The night before I found him, his father commanded him to kill someone he owed a debt to.

While worn, there was no escaping the corpus imperium's influence. The power was in the ruby. Imbued with the blood of an enchanted creature, artifacts were extremely powerful, old, and rare.

There were few known artifacts left in the world. Since most enchanted creatures had been poached into extinction, their value was astronomical.

Why his father hadn't sold the ring, I'll never know. Maybe he became addicted to the power, as he had with booze. Maybe he didn't fully understand what he had in his possession, which wouldn't surprise me. From what I could tell, he wasn't the brightest.

Unlike artifacts, items such as truth wearables were powered by transferring enchanted blood from one item to another. Items were much weaker than artifacts since the blood was diluted during the process. Alchemists activated the power. From what I understood, the process involved reciting incantations. Alchemists were rumored to hide themselves for fear of being captured and abused for their skills. For as long as I'd hunted enchanted items, I never met anyone who knew an alchemist.

Enchanted items were illegal, but newer kings and queens turned a blind eye since they secretly used them. They were typically sold on the black market by thieves and pirates. Myself included.

When I found out what Nathaniel was forced to do, I was livid. I'd rant and rave on his behalf, hatching escape plans to free him from his servitude. While I was furious for him, he had already resigned to his fate. His father would hold him hostage until his death.

After a particularly cruel order to burn down the home of another debt collector with his family still inside, I saw the first spark of fury in him since I learned his secret. I urged him into action, convincing him to go against his father. Nathaniel was eighteen and nearly a foot taller. If the fight got violent, he would be able to defend himself as long as his father couldn't issue a command.

He finally agreed and went home to demand his freedom.

A decision that would spill blood and condemn us both. A life of crime for me, and servitude to the crown for him. No trauma could excuse his actions or ease the ache of that red-stained night.

I'd practiced not thinking about it or the horrible months

that followed. It took several years for the nightmares to end. I experienced it over and over again, as though I was still there.

The sound of shredding bone. A soulless body. The weight of it. The splash it made. The panic. The tears. The begging. The blood.

My love for him spoiled into an oily, sick hatred that made my stomach burn and my chest tighten. Imagining Nathaniel's death brought me great comfort.

The world would be a better place without him in it.

The horse had wandered to the tree line, searching for some fresh foliage. I settled into the sharp grass beneath my favorite sky and sank into an achy slumber.

Chapter Four

Five days later, after confirming that the knights had abandoned Bangor and selling the horse to a nearby farm, I returned home. My survival skills and sheer willpower kept me alive during that time. My stomach cramped from hunger, and my dry throat burned as though it was coated with sharp gravel. The stabbing pain that pounded against my skull for the past few days only intensified my foul mood.

The breeze was cooler than it had been lately, but my filthy long-sleeved black attire clung to my sweat-soaked body. I'd stripped it in the woods, but walking through the streets naked was certainly worse than looking completely out of place. I ignored the stares from nosy shoppers and stomped toward the boarding house.

A wobbly voice pleaded to my right. An old woman sat on the dusty stone ground in the shade of a building, wiggling a dirty jar at passersby.

"Please spare some coins. Please, can you spare some coins?" she begged.

I watched her repeat the same plea for a few minutes with my arms crossed. A woman and her child paused. The woman brought a hand to her chest and bent toward the old woman.

"Oh dear," she said with sincere concern creased on her face. "Are you all right ma'am? Are you hungry or thirsty?"

The old woman struggled to sit upright, then slumped back against the wall weakly. "What a sweet girl you are," she rasped. "I've been given food and water, though I truly appreciate the offer. I only seek a bed for the evening. Would you be able to help me?" She nudged the jar toward the woman, who hesitated for a moment. The child, maybe six or seven years old, tugged on the woman's skirt.

"Mama, can you help?" the young boy asked.

The mother sighed but nodded, fishing a few coins from her purse and dropping them into the jar. The old woman smiled and bowed her head in thanks.

"May the gods smile upon you both."

The woman nodded and urged the child to resume their stroll through the market. Another throb of pain stabbed my head. I scoffed and approached the woman. When she noticed me, her gentle face hardened, but she spoke with the same fragility.

"Hello, dear. Care to spare a few coins for an old woman?"

"You believe in the gods?" I asked.

"I do, and so should you. You look like you could use their favor."

I smirked and swiped the jar from her wrinkled hand. I peered inside and counted five silver coins. Enough for a comfortable place to sleep and a warm meal.

"You've done well for yourself today, *ma'am*. So many generous people in this town. The gods must be pleased with you." I tilted the jar and spilled the coins into my palm, then stuffed them into my pocket. The old woman's jaw dropped.

"Hey!" she exclaimed. I gently rested the jar on the ground and lowered my voice.

"Consider it reimbursement."

I smiled and continued on my way. My back burned from the old woman's glare, and I heard someone approach her to ask if she was okay.

My momentary satisfaction dissolved into something closer to violence as the boarding house came into view. Several minutes later, I was bounding up the stairs of the house, stomping through the hall, and shoving Mother's office door open. It crashed into the stone wall behind it with a loud crack.

She sat in her chair and glanced up from her writing. I marched to her desk, and with one violent swing, I swiped all of her papers and trinkets off its surface. Everything clattered to the ground. Something made of glass shattered. Pain pulsed from my wounds, which I ignored.

I leaned across the desk, seething.

"You fucking bitch," I hissed.

"Louie," she sighed.

I stepped back and swiped a sharp letter opener that fell to the ground and sent it flying at her head. In one fluid motion, she caught it midair and stood, twisted her body, and sent it flying back at me. It sliced into one of my braids, lodging itself in the thick twist of hair before I could blink.

If she wanted to kill me, she could have. She would if I tried to come at her again.

"Sit. Down." Her voice was low and her command was absolute. I huffed and slumped into the seat across from her, tossing the letter opener onto the floor. She settled back in her chair and kept her stony gaze locked on me.

"Are you finished with your tantrum?" she asked, eyebrow raised.

"It's a perfectly understandable reaction to you sending me into a trap."

"You think that was on purpose."

"Was it?"

"And waste my most talented employee? Risk you spilling all of our secrets to the king's inquisitors? I think not."

"You should've listened to me. The job was sketchy from the outset."

"You're right."

It took a moment for her words to register. "I am?"

She sighed and roughly brushed her short, wavy silver hair from her tired face. "We aren't in the position to be turning down work, but I should've known the quick turnaround was suspicious. Even I make mistakes, Louie."

Her admission knocked the wind from me, cooling my anger. If she was sharing this, then her financial position was grimmer than I figured. I had no idea what she spent her coin on and didn't care enough to ask. As long as I got my cut, the rest wasn't my business.

"I'll make it up to you." She steepled her fingers as she always did when making a deal. "We've received a new job that I think you'd be perfect for."

"I'm not interested in any more hit jobs if that's where you're going with this."

She shook her head. "I assume you've heard of the Sands of Time."

A chill prickled over my skin.

No freaking way.

Mother read my face and smiled. "Ah, that's what I thought."

"You're not serious."

"I am. There's a lead on its location, and I need you to find it."

"You believe it's real?"

"Maybe. It wouldn't be the craziest enchanted artifact to exist. More importantly, our benefactor believes it exists and is willing to pay twenty times our usual rate."

I leaned forward in my chair. Sweat dampened the wraps around my palms. "If there's a lead, that means every hunter will be searching for it."

"I have reason to believe that this information has not been leaked."

"Does this mean that I can sail?" I held my breath.

"Louie Aurum, due to these extenuating circumstances, I hereby announce that your probation is officially over."

I jumped up from the chair and pounded my fist in the air.

"Yes, yes, yes!"

Mother watched with a small smile. I spread my aching palms on her desk and leaned toward her.

"When can I go? Can I go now? What about my ship? Did you sell it or not?" I was vibrating with excited energy. She leaned away from me.

"Calm yourself. I did not sell your ship." I danced around the room, and she shooed me away. "You'll find it off Gallow Harbor. From there, sail to Port Roche to locate the lead. Our benefactor made it clear that we could use any resources necessary to make this happen, no matter the cost. I'll have more information for you soon. Gather your crew. You leave in a week." She reached into her drawer and pulled out a small vial of dark liquid. "Take this." She tossed the healing tincture, which I caught with my sore left hand.

"Thank you! I'm sorry I called you a bitch!" I said over my shoulder as I raced from her office. I took the stairs two at a time and nearly collided with a figure entering the house.

Kendra shoved me and slammed the door shut behind her. She glared and shook her empty jar at me, still wearing her old woman prosthetics.

"Can you not be an asshole for once in your life?" she spat.

"Not with you, I can't." I smiled. Even Kendra couldn't ruin my mood. I was setting sail. I would board my ship again. Nothing could bring me down.

She scoffed and carefully removed her wig. Her light brown hair was plastered to her head underneath a sweaty cap. I followed her up the stairs, and she squinted at me over her shoulder.

"You're too happy. It's creeping me out."

"Guess who's probation is over early?"

She whipped around to face me. Her round, dark blue eyes

grew wider. "You've got to be fucking kidding me."

"Nope." I beamed.

She shoved her bedroom door open with her foot and entered, tossing her wig on her makeup table.

Her room was about the same size as mine, though more cluttered with tchotchkes she'd 'collected' over the years. The other girls' rooms were similar. Mine was on the other end of the hall and nearly barren. I could fit my things in one bag and nobody would ever know I was there.

Unlike me, Kendra was raised by Mother from the age of ten. Her real mother sold her to a traveling theater troupe when she was four. Years later, Mother bought her to raise and train the perfect mercenary. Kendra's ability to alter her appearance and talent for espionage proved to be a fruitful investment for Mother.

She kneeled on the floor and pried up a loose floorboard. She retrieved a fat satchel from the hiding place and filled it with handfuls of coins from the many pockets of her worn clothes.

She took a seat on the stool at her table and carefully peeled off her prosthetics. Rubbing them with a cleaning solution, she laid each piece on a rag to dry. Gradually, her round face was revealed. She appeared younger than twenty-nine, which was useful for a 'master of disguise', as she often called herself. Her full lips parted in concentration. I'd say she was beautiful if she wasn't so damn annoying.

"You smell like shit," she said as she worked.

I sniffed myself discreetly. "Sleeping and starving in the woods for a week will do that to you. Not that you even noticed I was gone."

"Oh, please. It's not unheard of for you to disappear for days at a time."

"If I died, would anyone even know?"

"It would be quieter here, so yes."

I leaned against the doorframe and crossed my arms, careful

not to put too much pressure on my hands. "How much time is left on your sentence?" I mocked. She frowned.

"Fuck off."

"Jealous?"

"Not in the slightest." She kept her eyes fixed on the mirror, but the twitch in her eyebrow betrayed her annoyance.

"I'm setting sail at the end of the week. It's a shame you can't join me."

"I'd rather swallow glass than be stuck on a ship with you."

"You would be lucky to sail with me. After all, I am the—"

"Ghost of the Sea. Yeah, I know." She turned toward me with mock confusion. "Or is it Lost Louie now?"

I clenched my jaw. *Fucking Benny.*

While I didn't know for sure, I'd bet anything that 'Blackjack' Benny spread that nickname. Fucking asshole.

She smirked at my irritation. "Where will you store your ego on that tiny ship of yours?"

"Tiny? Please. It's aerodynamic. Or something like that."

"What's the job?"

"None of your business. I need to get started, though. Have fun with your begging." I waved and left.

When I first arrived at the original boarding house in Templan, the wealthy capital situated along the northern coast, Kendra greeted me with the jealousy only a fifteen-year-old girl could manage. I was older by two years, taller, faster, and stronger than she was.

At first, our relationship was a one-sided competition. I was secretly grateful for her constant need to one-up me. It was a nice distraction from the catastrophic ending to my normal life and any hope I had for a peaceful future.

We went back and forth torturing each other. She'd steal and sell my daggers. I'd given her a false lead that sent her a full day's journey north. She switched out some of the coins hidden under my mattress with chocolate ones, which melted. I spread rumors around the market that she had 'the itch.' She sabotaged the few dates I'd planned by sneaking a nausea tincture into my drink. I was stuck in the bathroom for hours.

The pranks were one thing, but after we were put on probation, she started stealing my jobs. She would disguise herself and prowl the night market to eavesdrop for leads on enchanted items to sell to other mercenaries. She nearly undid a decade of work establishing Bangor as my territory. When I found out, we had a not-so-polite confrontation that left me with a split lip and her with a chipped tooth and a sprained ankle. She's lucky I went easy on her.

In short, we never got along.

Three years ago, Mother put us on a five-year probation for the accidental murder of a knight. We'd been contracted to kill one of the king's courtesans. It was supposed to look like an accident, but I had to eliminate the knight who witnessed us leaving the woman's quarters. The poor guy happened to be in the wrong place at the wrong time.

It was the first and only job Kendra and I worked together. A bounty was placed on our heads, even though the king ordered the hit. We had to flee Templan. Mother eventually paid off the bounty with our wages. She was furious. She ordered that I remain on land, and Kendra was forbidden from leaving Bangor. If we dared to defy her orders, she'd turn us in for violating our contract, as she had with Savina.

Kendra asked me once about my past. It was a cool spring night a few years after I arrived. We walked through a swanky market in Templan. She'd insisted on tagging along, hoping to swipe a coin or two from my pocket when I wasn't looking. A habit she'd thankfully grown out of.

We walked side by side through the crowded street when she asked, "How did you get here?"

"I walked. Are you stupid?"

"I mean with Mother."

My stomach flipped, but I kept walking. The question caught me off guard. The only people who knew of my sentence were my parents and Mother, who was briefed on my crime when she signed my contract.

And Nathaniel, of course.

"None of your business." I picked up my pace, but she fell into step beside me, despite my legs being considerably longer than hers.

"Come on. It must've been bad if you ended up as an Undesirable. What was it? Kidnapping? Torture?" She moved closer to me and lowered her voice. "Murder?"

I halted and spun to face her. She flinched at my scowl.

"Shut your fucking mouth before I shut it for you," I warned.

"Ah." She looked up at me in awe. "A murderer. Who would have thought?"

Rage blurred my vision, and I shoved her harder than I meant to. She tumbled to the hard ground and yelped in pain. Her hand went to her shoulder, and I could tell from the way it hung limp against her that she was hurt. Onlookers stopped and stared, whispering to one another. I scooped her up and carried her in my arms back to the rented boarding house. She whimpered but forced a wry smile.

I'd recently started my sailing training, still a mentee learning evasion techniques. I'd been bragging about it, saying I'd be the sneakiest pirate of all. That night, while I carried her, she gave me the moniker that stuck to this day.

"It's a shame you aren't a man," she said. "Serving in the king's navy would've been a more appropriate sentence for the Ghost of the Sea."

That's the way it was in the Oceana Kingdom. A woman convicted of a Class One crime was either hanged or declared an Undesirable and cast from society. Unmarriable and unhirable, the only way for an Undesirable to survive was either prostitution or crime.

To be released as an Undesirable, another citizen had to pay for the criminal and sign a contract stating that they would assume all responsibility for that person. This is what Mother did for all of the women she employed. Including me. A woman claimed by a contract would be branded on their chest with a mark identifying them as an Undesirable. A circle with an X through it, about the size of my palm.

It was different for men. Multiple Class One crimes meant death. But if it was a one-time crime, and if the inquisitors believed the man was repentant, they could choose between ten years in the dungeon or joining the king's forces. They would receive the same compensation and accommodations as those who entered the king's service willingly. The punishments were unbalanced, but that was the way it had been for centuries. Even more so since the royal divorce.

My theory was that the king wanted his forces strong and the brothels stocked. He didn't want women 'distracting' his knights. Or maybe he was simply a misogynist. I'd never know for sure, nor did I care. What did it matter? Dwelling on it would only infuriate me, and I'd probably do something with my daggers that I would regret. My fate was sealed. There was nothing I could do for the other condemned women, except hire them. Or murder the king and take the throne. But even I'd admit that I'm unqualified for such a task.

After gulping down enough water to make me nauseous, I bathed and applied the healing tincture to my wounds. Once I'd shoved nearly a whole loaf of bread down my throat, I skipped out the front door onto the street, donning fresh market-appropriate clothes.

The giddiness from earlier surged again and I ducked between shoppers and sellers, weaving through the streets toward my destination. Lyonel would be surprised to see me, no doubt. The poor man was startled by just about anything.

Freedom was a week away. While I doubted the existence of

the legendary Sands of Time, the opportunity to hunt again made me dizzy with elation.

  The sea awaited.

  I was almost home.

Chapter Five

Lyonel was indeed startled to see me. He opened the door after my gentle knock and gasped, clutching his chest as though I were an actual ghost.

"Hey! Miss me?" I smiled wide. He steadied himself and stepped aside to let me in.

"Louie! You can't sneak up on an old man."

"Apologies. Next time, I'll send a note before I arrive so you can mentally prepare."

He nodded gratefully as though it was a serious offer.

Lyonel was a brilliant but anxious sixty-three-year-old man. What endeared me more than his wiry gray hair and perpetually bunched brows were his large round glasses. The lenses were thick enough that his eyes appeared twice their real size. He was nearly blind without them.

He wrung his hands together and led me to his small kitchen. The house was tucked in a side street at the southern end of town. He owned the first floor, which consisted of a small kitchen, a living space where his small bed sat, and a tiny workshop that overflowed with his projects. I assumed there was a bathroom tucked in there somewhere, but I had yet to see it. He usually had lanterns lit regardless of the time, since there were only two windows that revealed the street. He kept his small curtains drawn, wary of passersby.

We sat on his worn wooden dining chairs.

"I haven't seen you in ages. You look well, though your smile is making me nervous," he said.

I chose not to point out that he was always nervous and cut to the chase. "I'm setting sail again, and I want you to join me."

The permanent line between his brows deepened. Before he could reply, a tall, lanky teenager with wiry light brown hair popped his head out of the workshop.

"Sir?" he asked while eyeing me warily.

"It's okay, boy. Come sit; this concerns you too."

My body tensed as I made a quick assessment. No scars or calloused hands. Maybe fifteen or sixteen years old. Hardly a threat.

The boy sat and narrowed his eyes to assess me in return. His gaze locked on my brand. I was used to people staring at it and my scars, which slashed jagged lines across my dark arms. The worst ones were hidden under my clothes. Fighters usually aimed for the midsection. It's an easier target, and it took me a few years before I became fast enough to dodge most knife attacks.

"Finny, this is Louie, an old . . . "

"Employer," I offered, smiling at the boy. The introduction did little to relax him.

"It's been three years. Your ship should still be in decent condition. I can check on it, but I can't sail with you," Lyonel said.

I'd expected this. He usually declined my offer on the first try. I glanced around the space. The paint had faded from the walls, and there were water stains along the wooden floorboards beneath the windows. Lyonel's and Finny's clothes were worn and patched here and there.

"This isn't an ordinary job. We're hunting something rare. The benefactor is paying twenty times our usual rate."

Lyonel's bug eyes grew rounder. Finny looked back and forth between us, having no point of reference for what our usual rate was.

"I'll pay you your usual percentage." I leaned forward, and

my voice softened. "That's enough for you to retire on. Comfortably. Maybe you can get a bigger place with a nicer workshop." I gestured to the pile of random materials that spilled out into the living area.

Lyonel shifted in his chair. "How long?"

"I don't know."

"I'd ask what you're seeking, but I know you won't tell me." He sighed. "How much time do we have?"

"A week."

His face relaxed a fraction.

"But I want some upgrades."

The tension returned, and he gripped the table. "What kind of upgrades?"

"I want more hidden doors and spaces on the deck, large enough to hide weapons. With proper drainage too, of course. And this."

I unfolded a crude drawing I made shortly before becoming landlocked. It was two sails, one on each side of the ship, that unfolded similar to bat wings. Adding side sails would give me an extra speed boost if needed.

He scoffed. "We can't. I'd have to engineer this to withstand the gusts and be adjustable. A week isn't enough time." Lyonel set the paper on the table. Finny picked it up and squinted at it.

"I can do it," he said. We both turned to him, eyebrows raised.

"You're not going," Lyonel said firmly.

"Why not?" he asked.

"You've only been shadowing me for two months. This isn't some fun week-long adventure." Lyonel looked at me, and I nodded in agreement. "I'm sorry, but it's not safe."

"What good are we sitting inside all day? And the coin . . ." he trailed off, and Lyonel's expression softened.

"What's better than on-the-job experience?" I offered. He

ignored me.

"You've barely even seen a ship." He snatched the paper from Finny, sliding it back to me.

"If anyone can make this, it's you." I tapped the paper. Lyonel was not immune to flattery.

"One week!" He rubbed his forehead as though to ward off a headache.

"If we have enough people, I think we can make it happen," Finny said.

I clapped my hands. "Sounds like we've got a deal!"

"A week is hardly enough time to make minor repairs, let alone design *this*." He glared at the paper. "Plus, it'll need a fresh coat."

"Blue-gray wax this time."

He lowered his head and squeezed the bridge of his nose beneath his glasses.

"Louie—" he started, but I cut him off.

"You'll have as many hands as you need. Our benefactor was clear about that."

"Even with a full-time crew working without sleep, this would be impossible."

"Haven't we achieved the impossible? More than once?"

Lyonel opened his mouth to argue but sighed instead, slumping back in his chair. "Okay."

Finny's pimpled face brightened, and I smiled at both of them.

"Great! Welcome back to the crew, my dear friend." I rose from the table. "Joining a pirate crew in your first two months? Very brave, Finny. Very cool." I patted him on the shoulder and watched the color drain from his face.

"Pirate?" he asked weakly. I laughed and gave them a wave before letting the door fall shut behind me.

I brought Lyonel with me on almost every journey. He was the ship's original architect. No matter my request, he always made it happen. Hidden doors that led to secret passages below deck. Discreet weapons storage. Now, my batwing sails.

He was also the only person I wanted leading the repairs if something went wrong, along with my carpenter, Eve. My crew knew the ship's secrets, of course. It was outside contractors that I was wary of. I had copies of his plans as a backup, but trust wasn't something I was eager to spare.

The possibility that something could happen to him was concerning. I'd been planning on suggesting that he train someone reliable, just in case.

I spent the week seeking out my old crew. Each readily agreed once they found out how much the job paid, except for Eve, who had the nerve to negotiate. I wouldn't share what we were hunting until we left Port Roche, if at all. The fewer people who knew about the Sands, the better.

The chance that the Sands were real was slim at best. I'd been hunting for a decade and never came across an enchanted item that contained anything close to that kind of power. It was difficult to imagine that controlling time would be possible.

It was even harder to think of what someone could do with that power.

I didn't share Mother's confidence that rumors of the artifact would remain secret. It was only a matter of time before we'd run into other pirates and the king's men. The idea only intensified my excitement.

They could try to claim the treasure before me. They could attempt to take me down, but their efforts would be in vain.

If the treasure did exist, it would be mine.

Chapter Six

Slick wetness gathered in the creases of my bent knees and elbows as I jostled in the back of a transpocart to Gallow Harbor. The midday sun was pressing on the canvas walls of the cart. Without a breeze, the air was hot and stagnant.

One of the other passengers forgot to bathe. The horse pulling the cart must have eaten something particularly foul, and we were all subjected to its frequent bowel movements. The woman next to me kept making a strange phlegmy sound in her throat. But I didn't care.

My heart thumped harder when the steamy air became damp and salty. I wiggled on the wooden bench, garnering glares from the few irritated travelers around me.

The cart was closed on the sides and top, but open in the front and back. I leaned over the young man in front of me and tried to peer around the driver and horse. All I could see were slivers of the worn gray wooden buildings and stalls selling fresh seafood. The boy glared at me and scooted closer to the woman next to him, who he had been glancing at shyly for the entire two-hour trip.

The sounds of bustling merchants and fishermen filtered in, growing louder as we traveled deeper into town. The shush of the waves slapping against the creaking docks made the last few minutes of the ride almost too difficult to bear.

I didn't wait for us to come to a complete stop. I roughly tumbled past the people sitting behind me and jumped out of the back of the cart, ignoring their shouts and curses. The thick salt breeze was an instant relief. Weaving between shoppers, I rushed to the water. I brightened with fresh elation when my ship came into view.

It was smaller than the others, but the unique tinted wax made it stand out against the drab merchant and fishing ships. The colored wax was something I'd wanted to do for a while but never got the chance. Evasion was one of my strengths for a reason. The blue-gray color would make us much harder to spot, especially since I tended to sail further from the coast than most.

Warmth spread through my chest as I neared the shining ship. Fond memories of past adventures, battles, and explorations flipped through my mind. Mercenary work was all well and good, but this was where I thrived. My true talents were on the water.

It was a two-mast ship with three levels below deck. The first housed the sleeping quarters, kitchen, a small forge, and the infirmary. The second level contained an additional smaller sleeping area, the ship's mechanics, rope, and weapon storage. The bottom level was where we stored the barrels of food and water, a tiny cell just in case we were forced to capture someone, and a bathing room with a water pump and drainage. Two jolly boats were suspended from either side of the deck to ferry us to shore. I'd had an upper deck built at the stern as well as the bow.

There were a few enchanted items on board. The lanterns were set to illuminate only when someone was in the room, which helped prevent fires. The enchanted food and water barrels would keep our supplies fresh. My favorite was the pump in the bathing room. No pooping in a hole on deck for us, and we could all bathe. There were few things worse than spending weeks at sea with a bunch of stinky, poop-crusted pirates.

"Louie, welcome home!" a deep voice called to me from

above.

Velo, my quartermaster and mentor, waved at me from the deck. I smiled and resisted the uncool urge to skip up the gangway. He met me at the top with a wide smile and nodded his welcome.

Mother hired Velo to be my mentor twelve years ago. I learned everything I knew about being captain from him. He was once a feared and skilled pirate who dominated the sea. Vicious and unyielding, he was undefeated. If a ship had something he wanted, he'd take it. If there was a treasure to be found, he'd find it.

Then his crew mutinied. They tied Velo to the mast, keeping him alive to collect his bounty. His daughter, Victoria, was on board. They forced him to watch while they sent her and his helmsman overboard.

Shortly after, they were overtaken by a violent storm. Without the guidance of the helmsman, the ship was destroyed. Velo was found floating on a piece of the hull ten days later. He retired shortly after.

At first, I thought it would be awkward to have my teacher as my quartermaster, but we fell into stride right away. His many years of experience as a captain made him an effective second-in-command. He kept an eye on the crew, making sure everyone did their jobs while vigilantly listening for any whispers of a mutiny. I always valued his advice. He'd shown me nothing but respect over the past decade.

His brilliant smile was contagious. The muscles along his dark exposed arms curved and dipped when he put his hands on his hips, sizing me up.

"You look good, duckling. No fresh scars, I hope," he said.

When we first started our mentorship, I followed him everywhere he went. I warmed with nostalgia at the nickname.

"You look well too. Though I miss the braids." I gestured to his shaved head, and he ran a hand over the smooth, dark skin.

"Time has not been kind to my hairline. This is preferable, trust me." He waved for me to follow. "Come, I'll take you to

Lyonel. The improvements are incredible, by the way."

We found Lyonel near the bow. He was shaking hands with some of the contractors while Finny stood next to him, scribbling something in a notebook.

"I hear you've outdone yourself," I said to him as we approached. Lyonel startled at my voice. I could send him a letter a day in advance to announce my arrival and it would still surprise him.

"Louie, yes, hello, hi," he stuttered.

I nodded to Finny. "Welcome, young man." I spread my arms wide. "What do you think?"

"It's incredible. I've never seen a ship as unique as this before." He moved closer to me, holding out his notebook. "We've managed to design the . . . " He glanced at Velo. "The things you asked for. I'd love to show you."

"It's okay. You can speak freely in front of Velo. Most of my improvements are to keep us all safe. The crew should know about it." He nodded. I glanced around the sides of the ship. "Did you manage to bring my drawing to life?"

"I'd hardly call it a drawing, but yes. Your 'wings' have been installed." Lyonel nodded to the left and right sides of the ship. Inconspicuous posts wrapped in canvas were tucked against the railing.

Lyonel explained how they worked and warned me that they might not survive in high winds or rough seas. "It's not perfect, but we did what we could with what little time we had." He emphasized the last part.

"Mr. Gendy's work never ceases to impress me. You've got a brilliant teacher, boy," Velo said.

"It was Finny who designed the sails. He was up for two days straight working on it. He barely ate." Lyonel gave Finny an awkward pat on the shoulder. "I apologize for doubting you."

Finny smiled shyly and hugged his notebook to his chest.

"Since this is your handiwork, you should explain it to the

crew." I urged him toward our shipmates, who were catching up with one another and unloading their gear. Finny pushed back against me.

"I can't. Mr. Gendy would be better at that." His voice cracked, and I bit my lip to stifle a laugh.

"Head up, chest out, you can do it. They're not as mean as they look."

That was a lie. Some of them had soft hearts, but most spent their time surviving on petty crimes. Others were scarred and bruised from regular bar fights. But none would dare harm someone on this ship. I didn't enjoy leading with fear, but the kindest punishment for breaking my rules was a watery grave.

"Friends, listen up." The crew silenced and turned to face me. "Welcome back. This," I gestured to Finny, "is the brilliant mind behind our new advancements."

He remained rooted to his spot and sweat shimmered on his forehead. I shoved his shoulders back, lifted his head, and pushed him forward.

"You may have noticed . . . " he stammered.

"Louder!" one of the crewmates, Jerma, called from the back.

Finny cleared his throat and tried again. "We've designed new collapsible sails, per Captain Louie's request. They require two pcoplc to operate."

He gestured to the two hidden hatches on either side of the deck. They blended seamlessly into the floor. "We've also added two hatches that connect to the existing passages below deck. There's a small gap, big enough to fit your fingers into, to pull the door up." When he was finished, he glanced at me and I nodded.

"Our wonderful king has invested in making his ships more streamlined," I said. "They are faster and yaw with impressive precision. As amazing as you all are, we can't underestimate his fleet or our fellow pirates." The crew nodded as I spoke. "We're going to review our emergency procedures, including a few new ones since it's been a while."

I pointed to the two hidden doors that Finny mentioned. "If we're taken over or you hear the bell while on deck, duck into these and wait for my command. You'll know it's safe if you hear me say, 'I'm the greatest pirate ever.'"

The crew chuckled. If we're dealing with a dangerous situation, we might as well have fun with it.

"These compartments lead to the lowest deck. If I'm not on the ship for some reason, wait until the invaders go to sleep, then do your thing." I winked, and some of my more violent crew members smirked.

I stepped back and let Velo take the stage.

"You're going to want to write this down," I said, nudging Finny.

He nodded and fumbled with his notebook, scribbling down Velo's overview of our safety protocols word for word. When he finished, I gestured to Finny and Lyonel.

"These gentlemen will show you how to work our new sails once we're far enough from the harbor. Stash your things. We set sail in twenty minutes." The crew nodded and dispersed. Some checked out the compartments while others carried their things down to the sleeping quarters.

I followed suit and carried my pack to my private quarters. It was a small room made up of a desk and a small bed. It was the same as I left it, except for the familiar figure lounging in my chair with her feet resting on my wooden desk. My good mood sank like an anchor.

Light brown hair. Deep blue eyes. That annoying smirk.

"No."

"Yes." Kendra smiled.

Chapter Seven

"No," I repeated, shoving her feet off my desk.

"A master of disguise is a valuable addition to your crew, don't you think?"

"What happened to 'I'd rather swallow glass than be stuck on a ship with you?'" I imitated her higher voice. She waved her hand as though swatting away a fly.

"That was then, and this is now."

"You found out about the artifact."

She leaned forward. "I did, no thanks to you. How could you not share that you're hunting the Sands of Time?"

"Why would I tell you?"

"Who are we meeting at Port Roche?"

"*We* are not meeting anyone. You're staying on land where you belong."

"You're missing the bigger picture. I can help."

"I'm not sharing my cut with you." I folded my arms.

"You don't have to. I'm getting the cut reserved for a navigator, which you don't have. Why is that?"

"Because I don't need one." I dropped my sack on the desk. "Get out of my chair."

She ignored me and leaned forward with her elbows on the desk. "No navigator. And these are outdated." She tapped one of the unfurled maps that had previously been stored in one of the desk drawers.

"You went through my stuff?"

"You've got a reputation for excellent nighttime navigation. How is that possible?"

I moved to knock her off my chair, but she stood before I could reach her with her hands up in surrender.

"That's none of your business. Now get off my ship, or I'll throw you over my shoulder and carry you off."

"No." She stood facing me with her hands on her hips.

I stepped closer, daring her to back away. "Are you sure about that?"

She flashed a challenging smile and shrugged one shoulder. "Yes."

I clenched my fists, then shot my arm out to grab her. She spun out of my reach. I lunged forward and she dodged again. She jutted her foot out in front of mine to trip me, but I hopped just in time. I used my momentum to swing my leg low, knocking her off balance. She stumbled backward toward the desk. I looped my arm around her waist to catch her before she crashed into it.

We locked eyes. Pink crept up her neck and she shoved me backward. I grabbed her roughly by the collar.

"Should I get my daggers? Or will you get the fuck out?"

"I'm not fighting with you. We're on the same side. You're going to need all the help you can get to find the Sands before the king's knights. Other pirates will also find out about it soon enough."

"Mother will make your probation permanent when she finds out. Or worse."

"She's the one who sent me here. She thought this would be a better use of my talents."

She wasn't wrong. Kendra was an extremely skilled spy and a fantastic actor. Begging and thieving were a waste of her talents. Not that I was about to admit that. Mother likely kept this from me because she knew I'd argue. The decision had been made, but I took my time pretending to consider it.

"Fine," I groaned and released her. Her face lit up, and she saluted me.

"Thank you, Captain. You won't regret it."

"Yeah, sure. Go find Velo. There's a lot to remember about our processes and procedures. Pay attention, or you might end up dead. Got it?"

She nodded and wiggled with excitement. "Yes ma'am."

I wrinkled my nose and waved her toward the door. When she was gone, I rolled up the maps and tried to shake off my disappointment. This was the most dangerous job we'd ever accepted. Even though Kendra was likely telling the truth about why Mother sent her, I couldn't help but think that she was trying to keep an eye on me. As though I wasn't capable enough to find the Sands on my own.

I shook the thought from my head. They didn't call me the Ghost of the Sea for being an insecure little bitch. Kendra would prove to be useful, or I'd ditch her at the nearest port.

Chapter Eight

We set sail shortly after three o'clock. The breeze cooled the heat from the strong afternoon sun. Before I walked upstairs to the deck, I tied a red strip of fabric over my hairline to keep my braids out of my face. I'd also found some of my favorite hair adornments in one of my desk drawers. Gold rings that clasped around the braids. These were the only pieces of jewelry that I owned. Necklaces, rings, earrings, and other types were dangerous for hand-to-hand combat.

I vaguely wondered how Kendra and Finny would fare in the blistering summer sun. They weren't the only lighter-skinned people on my crew, but it was likely they weren't accustomed to this much time in the sun. I made a mental note to assign them jobs inside. A knock tapped gently against my open door, and I turned to see Finny standing there, clutching his notebook against his chest.

"You don't have to carry that around with you. No one will steal it."

He nodded and straightened his posture under my gaze. The boy was a quick learner.

"The crew is hard at work, but I'm not of much use. I was wondering if you can give me a job to do?" His voice wavered. He was afraid of me, that much was clear, but his endearing awkwardness made it impossible to tease him about it.

"Showing initiative. I like it." I stepped around him and motioned for him to follow me up to the deck. I squinted against the sudden brightness.

"I want you to study the ship and learn how to fight from Kendra. She's your sailing buddy. I also want you to meet with Noala. If these sails need repairs, you should know how that works. Got it?"

He nodded.

Kendra was standing near the bow with Noala, laughing at something she said. Noala was gesturing and leaning in too close. She was a flirt. I knew that about her. She'd slept with almost every woman on my crew.

The wind whipped Kendra's hair, and Noala reached to tuck it behind her ear. I frowned and clenched my fist. Less than an hour at sea and Kendra was already pissing me off.

We approached, and Kendra straightened.

"Noala, this is Finny. He's Lyonel's apprentice. I need you to give him a rundown of what you do and how you make repairs. Afterward, he'll train to fight with Kendra."

"Excuse me?" Kendra folded her arms.

I ignored her and gave Finny a gentle nudge. "Go on."

Noala led Finny below deck.

"Why am I training him? Did I miss something?" Kendra asked.

"I need you to watch over him."

"You're kidding."

"I'm not. He's young and—if I had to guess—easily manipulated. He's a target."

"I think you're overthinking it."

I raised an eyebrow and stepped closer. "I've survived this long because of 'overthinking.' I need someone I can trust to watch over him. Plus, you can teach him how to fight."

"You trust me?"

"I don't have a choice.

"I know you're mad that I'm here, but—"

I cut her off. "I'm not mad. Mother was right to put you on this job."

She raised an eyebrow. "Was that a compliment?"

"No. We need all the help we can get. Keep me posted, and watch him when we dock. I can think of a few people who would gladly capture someone from this ship. When he's finished with No-ala, I want you each to make an updated map. You can use my quarters."

"Why? It's not like you need it."

"It's not for me."

She opened her mouth to reply, but I was down the stairs before she got the chance.

Once the sun had set and the stars revealed themselves, I took to the deck. I didn't need to chart our course for the short trip. Lorelai, my helmsman, could sail to Port Roche with her eyes closed. We would arrive around eleven p.m. The sea was calm, and we stayed within sight of the coast. The new wax and dim lights would make us difficult to spot unless someone was specifically searching for us, which I doubted.

I shouldn't have doubted.

An hour later, a black ship had crept up behind us.

Velo found me lounging in my bed, trying and failing to take a nap. He burst into my room, and simply said, "Benny."

Chapter Nine

I instructed him to ring the warning bell and hide the crew in the compartments on the deck. My best fighters would need to stay on deck to not rouse Benny's suspicion.

This was not the first time he'd found me and boarded my ship without permission. But in all of his visits, he never hurt any of my crew. Each time, he demanded the same thing. The one thing he couldn't have.

His obsession with learning my secret to sailing at night had only intensified during the past seven years that I'd known him. The more I denied him, the more he wanted it.

Benjamin Russell, also known as Blackjack Benny, was a thirty-six-year-old pirate with a gambling addiction. What he failed to accept was that he was terrible at it. His piracy funded his lifestyle, but it was never enough for him.

We met seven years ago on a hunt for an enchanted item on an island far south. It was my first time near an active volcano. It was in a constant state of eruption, bubbling and leaking far enough from civilians to not be dangerous but close enough to be a draw for tourists.

Souvenir shops had opened near the base of the mountain. It was rumored that the shops were a front for enchanted dealings. Mother had a lead that someone was enchanting volcanic rock with dragon's blood. There have been no known sightings of dragons on our side of the world for centuries, so naturally I figured we'd run into other hunters.

When I arrived at the shop, Benny was already ransacking the place. He was not known for his patience or tact. I confronted him and we fought. He relied on the skills he'd learned growing up on the streets of a poor fishing village. He was fast, but he was no match for my formal training. I retrieved the enchanted item from the terrified shopkeeper, which turned out to be a fake. I went on my way, leaving Benny and his bruised ego behind.

We ran into each other semi-regularly after that. It was unclear how he was getting the same tips as we were. It wasn't a coincidence that he was hunting for the same items at the same time I was. I asked Mother to investigate further, but I don't think anything came of it. Or if it did, she never shared it with me.

As I settled into my desk chair, I wondered if his arrival was a coincidence or if he had, yet again, found out about the Sands from a mysterious source.

"I'm too tired for this shit," I grumbled to myself as I rubbed my eyes.

About fifteen minutes after Velo left my office, heavy footsteps rumbled above me. A moment later, the door to my room crashed open, revealing the pirate.

He was a few inches taller than me with tanned, taught skin and wavy brown hair that curled over the top of his ears. He had a strong jaw that was dappled with soft stubble and violent green eyes that made it almost impossible to look away. Frankly, his good looks were wasted on him.

One thing I tried to forget was that Benny and I slept together. It was only once four years ago, and I've regretted it ever since. I certainly wouldn't admit that it was the best sex of my life. I try not to judge my younger self. I was lonely, and he was impressively suave when he wanted to be. But that didn't stop me from cringing every time I thought of that night.

"Miss me?" He smiled.

He was also the most egotistical and irritating person I'd ever met.

"Not in the slightest." I leaned back in my chair and folded my hands in my lap. He stepped inside the room and a few of his men followed. One of them held Finny against his chest with a knife pressed against his throat.

I froze, but I kept my face as neutral as possible. Finny was trembling. His chin quivered, and his eyes were wide and glassy. Poor kid. Not even a full day on a pirate ship and he was already in danger. I sighed.

"Is that necessary?"

"I've tried to be cordial and communicate like adults, but you didn't want to cooperate." Benny plopped down in the chair on the other side of the desk facing me as though he owned the space.

I glanced down at the maps spread on my desk. He clocked my gaze and smirked. I slapped my hands onto the paper, but he was too quick. He yanked a large map out from under me.

"What is Lost Louie hunting this time?" He skimmed the paper, observing the notes I'd made about our journey and plan. I swallowed, but my mask of indifference held.

"None of your business. Though I am surprised you decided to venture this far out at night. How brave," I mocked. He didn't bother hiding his frown.

"It would be much easier if I had the same information you have. Care to share your secrets?"

"With you? Never."

I'd lost count of how many times we had this conversation. He might fool others, but I could see the mounting desperation in the creases of his face. Piracy was becoming more competitive every year, and he was losing his edge. My star maps would change everything for him. He could hunt at night and eventually sell the star maps to the highest bidder, which would likely be King Francis.

I leaned back. "Tell me what you want. Other than the obvious."

"So curt. You could at least chat with me for a while. It's been years. How was your probation?" He smirked, and I clenched my fists under the desk. Somehow, he found out what happened with the king's courtesan. It wasn't a surprise that he was rubbing it in my face.

"Fuck off."

"Don't be so cold. I missed you." His gaze drifted down my neck, chest, and lower.

"Tell me what you want before I kill you."

The man who held Finny increased the pressure of the knife on his neck. Finny whimpered. Benny glanced at him.

"Your new boyfriend?"

"Don't be gross."

He put his hands up. "Apologies. I've been around scoundrels for too long. I've forgotten my manners."

"How are the card games? I heard you were chased out of every salon in Templan."

Benny's smile faltered. He relaxed into the chair and draped a toned arm across its back. "You win some and you lose some."

"More losses than gains, from what I've heard."

"I also heard that Commander Bartholomew paid you a visit. That must have been an awkward reunion. I would've loved to have seen it."

A feverish chill rushed across my skin, and my heart thumped harder in my chest.

He knows.

He must've snooped through the royal archives and found my record. That was the only way.

"If you want a civil conversation, let the boy go," I said, firmer this time.

He leaned his elbows on my desk. The smell of salt and

tobacco wafted toward me.

"You know what I want," he said in a low voice.

"Can't you accept that I can sail at night because I'm better than you?" I smirked, which he returned. He loved our cat-and-mouse game. He relished the chase. He might be attracted to me, but it was his greed that kept him hunting.

He settled back into the chair and flicked his hand at the man who held Finny. He tensed, ready to rip the knife across his throat. I stood and hurled one of my thinner daggers, which lodged into the man's eye before he could flinch.

Liquid splattered across the side of Finny's face and he shrieked. The man wobbled for a moment, then collapsed on the ground. Finny sobbed and made a beeline for the door, scrambling up the steps. Benny's men gaped at the body, then glanced at each other before following, desperate to return to their ship to live another day.

I scoffed. My crew would never run.

Benny whipped around to face me with unmasked vexation.

"Apparently, I haven't been clear enough," I said coldly, drawing another dagger. "You'll never learn my secrets, and you'll never surpass my reputation. I am faster than you, smarter than you"—I glanced at the body on the floor—"and deadlier than you. Board my ship again and I'll hang you from the mast."

Benny stood. "This is why I like you, Louie. You are my match in every way." There was something close to admiration in his tone and I almost believed him. "Next time we meet, let's have a drink instead. No daggers, no hostages."

"Sounds like a complete waste of my time."

When he reached the threshold, he dipped his head in farewell.

"Until next time, gorgeous."

When he was gone, I exhaled and rubbed my temples for a moment. I wasn't expecting conflict this early into the hunt, but the unpredictability of this work was one of the things I loved about it.

It was never boring. During the commotion, he'd slipped the maps into his pant leg. I'd noticed, of course, pleasantly surprised that he'd taken the bait.

How predictable.

I yanked my knife from the eye of the dead man and wiped it on his shirt. I would instruct Nelson, our assistant bosun, to remove the body, then check on Finny.

"Why is everyone underestimating me lately?" I grumbled to myself. Once Benny was gone, I climbed the stairs to the deck. I eyed the discreet hidden compartment doors, grateful that I had larger ones installed.

"I'm the greatest pirate ever!" I called out. The doors creaked open and my wary crew climbed out. My seamen Corey and Ushar reached into the hole to lift Lyonel out.

"My nerves can't take this, Louie!" he exclaimed.

I nodded sympathetically. "You did great, though! I won't let you get hurt on my ship. I promise."

It was a false promise and Lyonel knew it, but he nodded and shuffled back to his sleeping quarters, mumbling something about retirement. I'd set up a bed for him in the carpenter's room away from the others, since he was the loudest snorer I'd ever heard. I started to follow when the lilt of gentle sobs drew me down the stairs to the infirmary.

I approached the open door. Kendra was sitting beside Finny on one of the beds, rocking him gently while he sobbed into her shoulder. My heart leaped, and I pressed a hand against my chest. The gentleness of the moment seemed out of place on my ship. It was hard to reconcile the Kendra I knew, infuriating and nosy, with the person sitting before me.

I couldn't bring myself to interrupt, but also couldn't move my legs to walk away. I stood there for a few moments, watching Kendra comfort the boy, giving him something I could never offer. That sort of softness was carved out of me long ago.

I tore my gaze from the scene and returned to my quarters.

If Benny followed the false maps, he'd find himself far away from Port Roche. There was a chance he'd call my bluff. We'd have to be extra vigilant moving forward.

During a brief nap, I dreamed of the volcano on the island where I first met him. I stood on the edge of its destructive mouth when a hand rose from the raging lava. The skin was charred and fell off in chunks. Two round eyes pleaded from within the flames.

I reached for the hand, but when I touched it, the figure fell apart into a fine black dust. I gasped and leaned forward to catch the soot. The ground came apart underneath me and I plunged into the lava, sinking deeper and deeper into a sea of liquid fire.

Chapter Ten

Port Roche was a filthy town with filthier residents. Not that I was judging. They were no better or worse than me. If it weren't for Mother, I could've ended up in a town like this, spreading my legs for coin.

It was known as a place where outcasts could find a community. The local economy was primarily supported by the Undesirables who fled here and took up sex work, drawing numerous male clientele. There were more brothels than homes. It was common for merchants and knights to make a stop here during a long voyage.

Our contact was a frequent patron of these brothels. He was described as a middle-aged man named Vincent with a long beard, round belly, and a few missing teeth.

The plan was simple. Kendra and I would find the man, discreetly meet with him, offer payment, get the information, and be on our way. We made great time with Finny's batwing sails, but I had no intention of staying here longer than we had to. With Benny on our tail and the pressure of other pirates learning about the Sands, I felt the persistent inconvenience of time weighing on my shoulders.

Normally, I would love the tension and relish the pressure, but this hunt was different. If it existed, the Sands of Time would be the most powerful enchanted artifact in recorded history. It was hard to fathom what someone could do with that kind of ability.

As I prepared to leave the ship, a small voice whispered in the back of my mind.

I could go back to before.

I promptly shoved the thought away. Using enchanted items such as healing tinctures was one thing. Messing with time was another. I wasn't interested in that sort of responsibility. Whoever ended up with the artifact could do whatever they wanted for all I cared.

Once we were sure Benny wasn't following us, we docked and gathered on the deck to review the plan. My instructions were simple: stay on the ship and do not partake in the local attractions.

I noticed some of the crew glancing behind me. I turned and halted my speech. Kendra stood there in her disguise, and my mouth fell open.

She was playing the part of a prostitute and decorated herself accordingly in one of the many costumes she brought with her. The ruby red velvet dress fell off her shoulders, accentuating her elegant neck and collarbone. The neckline plummeted, exposing a generous glimpse of her cleavage. She wore lace gloves, which had recently come into fashion. The hem fell to the ground, and the skirt was full. Her hair, which she left its natural brown, was twisted into a low elegant bun. She'd applied a dark pink lipstick and dusted blush across her cheeks.

I sobered when my eyes landed on the fake brand on her chest. Kendra was born into this life. She didn't face the inquisition. She didn't watch the glowing branding iron approach. Her beautiful skin never melted underneath its cruel tip. The thought that she was spared the horror of having her body marked and violated gave me some peace. Seeing the fake one made me shiver.

She could live a normal life if she wanted to. She could pass for a normal woman, get married, or take up a safer profession. Mother would eventually let her go. But she chose to stay.

She clocked my stare and smirked.

"Like what you see?" she asked in a voice silkier than her own.

She unfolded a fan and wafted it toward her face. I forced myself to turn back to the group. Their lingering gazes sent a spike of frustration through my chest.

"All right, shows over. Stay sharp in case we need a quick exit. Once we ship off, we can break open that barrel of rum." I clapped, and they reluctantly dispersed. I turned to Kendra.

"Isn't this a bit much?" I asked.

"How so?" A few loose strands of her hair fluttered from the fan's breeze.

"You're going to draw too much attention. I highly doubt the workers here look like . . . *this*. We're trying to fit in, remember?"

She snapped the fan shut and frowned.

"Are you trying to tell me how to do my job?"

"This is my job if you recall. One you pushed your way into."

"*Our* job," she corrected. "I'm doing my part. I don't tell you how to sail."

"That's not the same thing."

"That's what it sounds like you're saying."

"Don't put words in my mouth."

"Then what are you saying?"

"We're trying to blend in! The last thing we need is men drooling over you while we're trying to work our contact!" I replied, louder than I meant to. She gripped the fan harder.

"Why can't you just say I look pretty?! Or is it really that hard for you to say something nice?" she blurted. My reply caught in my throat. She snapped her mouth shut, and her ears tinted pink. I became painfully aware of the glances from some crew members who stood near us. She shook her head and briskly walked toward the gangway.

"Let's get this over with. The less time we spend together,

the better," she threw over her shoulder.

"Couldn't agree more," I mumbled and followed her to the dock.

The town was what I expected. A century ago, Port Roche was a wealthy trading town. When pirate activity picked up in the area, most residents opted to move further inland, leaving remnants of the town's former glory behind. Large shop windows with elegant lettering were filthy and smashed. The paint had worn away from the façade of most buildings.

The streets were bustling with late-night partygoers. We made our way through the cobbled stone streets, dodging drunken sailors with their arms slung over giggling women. Some men were huddled in dark corners, enjoying the pleasures of both male and female prostitutes. One group of men passed us, then did a double take at Kendra. I scanned their faces, but none matched the description of our contact.

"Beautiful," one of the men slurred. His friends turned. I slowed my pace to walk behind Kendra, guarding her back.

"Hold up, sweetheart," one of them called and staggered toward us. Kendra kept moving, but I could tell from the tension in her shoulders that she was aware.

I'd given her a small, thin knife to hide in her sleeve, which rested against her palm for quick access. She had another disguised as an ornate pin woven into the twist of her hair. She's trained, but it was my responsibility to make sure we made it out of Port Roche as quickly and quietly as possible.

"Hold on!" the man called. He'd caught up with us and stumbled past me, reaching for Kendra.

I snatched his wrist, but before I could pin it to his back and force him to the ground, Kendra turned and smiled.

"Hi, handsome."

The man squinted at my hand through an ale-induced haze. He gave me a lazy smile and pulled his wrist from my grip. I let him go and clenched my jaw against the urge to shove him into the mysterious brown puddle behind him.

"You"—he waggled a finger at me—"would be perfect for my friend. He likes tough women, you know?" He leaned closer, and I flinched at the breeze of his stale breath. "He likes being told what to do. Maybe a smack here and there. Isn't that right, Bor?" he called to the shortest man in their group. His hair was thinning, unfortunate for his age, and he nodded eagerly.

"Tell me what to do, Mistress," he slurred. "I'll worship you."

The other men laughed, and he smiled, lazily looking me up and down. My disgust was boiling into something violent. I opened my mouth to tell them as much, but Kendra put her hand on my shoulder.

"We'd love to spend time with all of you. Maybe all at once," she purred. I could practically see the men melting. "But we're expected by someone. We're a little lost. Do you think you could help us?" She flicked her fan open and waved it gently. "I'd really appreciate it." She lowered her lashes and the men gazed at her, desperate and starving. I grimaced.

"We might be able to help. For a price," said the first man. He staggered closer to her. "Nothing's free in Port Roche."

Kendra sighed. "Nothing, indeed." She snapped the fan shut and turned on her heels. The man's face fell, and he grabbed her hand. I tensed. She flicked her eyes at me and gave me a small shake of her head. I stilled myself and clenched my jaw again.

"Wait. I didn't mean to offend you. I can help. Maybe if you're feeling generous, you can meet us for a drink when you're done," he tried again. Kendra smiled.

"I would love that."

The man's face lit up, and he released her. "What do you need?"

"We're looking for a man named Vincent," she said. "Long beard, a bit of a belly, maybe a few missing teeth?"

The man scoffed. "Darling, you can do much better than him."

"I know, but it's a favor to a friend. I offered to have a drink with him, but nothing more. Do you know where I can find him?"

The man wrinkled his brow. "Vinny's usually with Cassandra. I'm surprised he'd spend time with anyone else."

Kendra's face brightened. "You know her? We've been friends for a long time." She leaned closer to the man. "Between you and me, I think he's been a bit lonely lately. She thought some extra attention might cheer him up."

I held my breath. We had no idea how close this man was to Vincent. I watched the hazy expression on his face, waiting to see if he'd call her bluff, but he chuckled instead.

"Sounds like Vinny. He's an odd one."

"I don't judge. But, silly me, I forgot the name of the place. It's been a long time since I've been here. Can you point me in the right direction?"

His dreamy expression made me nauseous. This guy was already in love with her.

"Of course, sweetheart. If you follow this road six more blocks, then turn left, you'll find it on the right side. Look for the wooden sign with a painted flower."

"Thank you so much! You saved me a lot of time wandering around," she giggled. "I'll be sure to come find you all when I'm finished." She winked and turned to resume our walk. I followed and glanced over my shoulder at the men. They were frozen, watching Kendra walk away as though she was the most beautiful thing they'd ever seen. Which she probably was.

We walked another block in silence with her a few paces ahead of me. When we reached the next block, she spun and grabbed my arm, dragging me into a tight alley on our left.

"Hey!" I jerked my arm from her grasp.

"This isn't going to work if you act like that."

"Like what?"

"You know what I'm talking about. If you act possessive, you're going to scare our contact and the hunt will end here."

"Possessive?" I rolled my eyes. "Hardly. You can do what you want. I'm not going to interfere with your work."

"Then what was that?"

"Those men could've been dangerous!"

She scoffed and crossed her arms. "Oh please, I've handled way worse."

"What does that mean?"

She looked at me as though I was a complete idiot. "What do you think I do on a job?"

It was a valid question. I'd never paid that close attention. We never talked about work unless it was to brag or one-up each other.

"You let men touch you like that?"

"No, that's my point! No man has been able to put his hands on me, no matter the situation. Don't insult me like that again. I'm perfectly capable of protecting myself."

We stood in silence for a moment, glaring at one another. She was the first to look away.

"We need to split up. He's not going to talk to me if you're there."

"I'm not leaving you alone."

"Fine. Then pretend you and I aren't together. You can watch from a distance. I'll give you a signal when it's time." She stalked from the alley, then spun back around, pointing a finger at me. "I'm serious. Don't interfere or you could blow this whole thing. Got it?"

Reluctantly, I nodded. She was right. I was being unprofessional and foolish. My actions could give us away and put all of us in danger.

Focus.

We found the brothel, and I stopped her before she could

enter through the open door.

"I'll go first and scope it out. Wait a minute before you come in. If something's off, I'll signal you."

She nodded.

The room was packed. A long bar stretched along the wall straight ahead and tables flanked each side. The booths in each corner overflowed with rowdy patrons.

A set of stairs on the left side of the room led to a dim upper level. A large guard stood at the bottom, shooing away an older man. A moment later, a couple swayed toward the stairs and the guard stepped aside, offering the woman a polite smile.

I skimmed the crowd and found our man slouched over the bar, whispering something in a woman's ear, who I assumed was Cassandra.

She laughed, flashing bright teeth. Her skin was sea foam white, and her hair tumbled in dark waves down her exposed back. Her dress was simpler than Kendra's and left nothing to the imagination.

I approached the couple and leaned between them, ordering an ale. Vincent shot me a glare. I ignored him and turned to Cassandra.

"Pardon me, I didn't mean to interrupt." I smiled at her. The barkeep returned with my beer, and I retrieved the fat velvet pouch from my belt loop, handing him payment with a generous tip. Her eyebrows lifted, and I smiled to myself.

When I turned back to her, she was leaning toward me with her lashes lowered. I leaned my elbow against the bar, blocking Vincent out of the conversation.

"Care for a drink?" I asked.

"No thank you; I've had enough for one evening," she lied. I didn't smell alcohol on her and her eyes were clear. "But I always welcome good company. Care to join me?" She nodded toward the booth behind me in the far right corner of the room.

A booth wasn't ideal. It would be harder for me to reach

Kendra if she needed help. But I nodded and followed her lead right as Kendra entered. A few people, both men and women, noticed her entrance and paused in their conversations. Our eyes locked for a moment, and I gave her a small nod.

Vincent turned to stop us, but his gaze snagged on Kendra. She smiled shyly and approached the bar, filling the space where I stood a moment ago.

As we neared the booth, Cassandra flicked her head at the two couples occupying the bench. They promptly untangled themselves and slid out of the corner, leaving plenty of room for us. I motioned for Cassandra to sit first, giving me access to escape if needed. I angled myself to have a clear view of Kendra.

Cassandra scooted closer to me and I tensed.

Relax. Pretend that you like it.

"You're handsome for a woman." She rested her hand on my thigh, and I resisted the urge to push it off.

"High praise, coming from you." I leaned closer. "I think your friends are scared of you." I nodded to the workers who scurried away at her command.

"I'd like to think that it's out of respect."

"No doubt. I've been wandering around all night, checking out the pubs, and I didn't see a single soul that could rival your beauty." I glanced at her lips, then back to her deep brown eyes. "You must be popular."

"I'd like to think so." She brought her face closer to mine. "I've never seen you here before. You don't reek of fish and certainly aren't a knight. So my guess is . . . " She inched her hand further up my thigh. "Pirate?"

"That's a good guess, but tonight, I'm just a weary traveler seeking company." I nodded at Vincent. "I'd bet half of my coin that I can please you better than he can."

She gave me a sly smile and raised a brow. "I think that would be a safe bet." She leaned her mouth close to mine and lowered her voice. "Shall we find out?"

"Yes, let's. But," I nodded at Vincent again, "how about we go together? All four of us?"

Her smile faltered for a moment. She squinted at Kendra, likely despising the idea of sharing the coin with her, but fixed her smile once more.

"Okay, handsome. Let's go." She took my hand and led me from the booth. We weaved through the tables and approached Kendra. This was a deviation from the original plan, but too good of an opportunity to pass up.

"Hello, darling," Cassandra purred to Kendra. "We were just talking about how beautiful you are. Care to join us upstairs?"

Kendra's smile didn't falter. "I would love to, but I'm quite enjoying my time with . . . " She looked at Vincent.

"Vinny," he supplied. He hadn't taken his eyes off her.

"Why don't you join us?" I forced myself to wrap an arm around Cassandra's waist and pulled her closer.

"That sounds like a good time. Vinny?" Cassandra ran her hand up his forearm. Red splotches bloomed on his puffy cheeks, and he nodded eagerly.

"Great. Lead the way," I said to Cassandra.

The three of us followed her to the stairs. The large man guarding it smiled sweetly at Kendra and stepped aside without a word. We climbed the creaky wooden stairs. The soft sounds of pleasure grew louder as we moved further from the commotion of the pub.

When we reached the top, we turned right down a long hallway with closed doors. We reached one that was open and filed inside. The interior was more elaborate than I was expecting. Soft red fabric was draped over the large four-poster bed. A soft lantern cast the room in a warm glow. Two chairs faced the bed, implying that we weren't the first group to use the space at the same time.

Cassandra closed the door behind us and moved toward the bed. Her dress fell from her shoulders, revealing her brand. It was lower than most, which meant she'd been completely stripped of her clothes when they did it. I clenched my fists to brace against a flare of rage.

Keep calm. Stay focused.

Vincent scurried into one of the chairs, eager to get started. Cassandra brushed her knuckles against Kendra's cheek and brought her lips close to hers. "How about we start with you and me?"

Chapter Eleven

"Actually," I interrupted, stepping forward. "I have a more important job for you, Cassandra." I smiled. She frowned in return, aware that she never told me her name. I fished a healthy pile of coins from my bag and spun one on the tip of my finger.

"For you? Anything," she said with a coy smile.

"I need you to stand outside this door and let us know if anyone approaches." I dropped the coins, one by one, into her outstretched palms. "You'll know if it's a person or group that's not supposed to be here."

She raised a brow and her smile faltered. She never took her eyes off the coins. "This sounds like trouble."

"Maybe. But I have a feeling that you're no stranger to trouble."

She jingled the coins in her palms, counting them quickly. She nodded, then spilled them into the pocket of her dress. When she reached the door, she looked at us over her shoulder.

"Have fun." She winked, then left us alone with Vincent. He was tense in the chair and watched us warily.

"I don't know who sent you, but my debts have all been paid. Ask anyone," he said in a shaky voice, eyeing the closed door behind me. I grabbed the other chair and turned it toward him. Kendra perched on the edge of the bed.

I sat and said, "We're not here to hurt you. We don't want your coin."

"I have nothing else to give you."

I tossed the satchel of coins at his feet. He glanced at it. I smiled and leaned back in the chair.

"I think you do. You have information that I need, and I'm not leaving until you give it to me." He swallowed and sweat started to glisten on his brow. I nodded to the bag on the floor. "Hopefully, this exchange will be painless."

He snatched it up from the floor as though I might change my mind. Hugging the bag, he relented.

"Tell me what you want."

"You know something about the Sands of Time, and I need to know what that is."

The red splotches on his face returned. "I don't know what you're talking about."

My dagger was out of my belt and whizzing past his head before he could blink. It lodged itself into the wall behind him with a *thunk*.

He nodded nervously. "Oh, yes, now I remember. I think I did hear something about that."

"Do tell."

"A friend of mine returned from a deep sea voyage. His ship was wrecked. He was the only survivor." He fidgeted with the bag. I observed his body and studied his voice for any sign of a lie, but found none. "He claims that his ship was destroyed by a sea serpent."

"Impossible."

"Nothing's impossible. The ocean is vast and unexplored. You should know that better than most."

I frowned. "What's that supposed to mean?"

"The Ghost of the Sea. The only pirate to sail the deep without failure. The pirate who owns the dark." He nodded to my brand, which was partially exposed. "You're not a prostitute, so you must be a criminal. You sailed here at night, and you're searching for enchanted artifacts." His scrutinizing gaze flicked over me. "There aren't many women pirates."

He was smarter than I gave him credit for.

"If you know who I am, then you must be aware that I'm not known for my patience." I leaned forward and rested my elbows on my knees. "Now finish your story."

"I used to work in the king's archives. There's a scroll, maybe a thousand years old or so, that says that sea serpents act as guardians to the Sands of Time."

Sea serpents, or 'serpens marinus' in the olde language, were rumored to have become extinct centuries ago. If what he said was true, they must have migrated further from the coast where explorers and hunters couldn't sail.

"Where is this serpent?"

Vincent opened his mouth to respond when a thunder of heavy boots stopped him. My skin prickled with warning. Kendra and I shared a look. The tightness on her face told me she felt the same. Whoever was coming, it was for us.

The steps grew louder. Doors crashed open in the hall. The inhabitants shouted.

I whipped back to Vincent.

"Tell me now. Where is the serpent?"

His face had gone pale. The footsteps and crashing of doors grew louder.

"Vincent! Answer me!"

His voice trembled, and his eyes watered. "Somewhere northeast, about a two-day journey—"

Cassandra's hushed voice broke through the chaos. "Incoming!" she hissed through the door.

"You'll know when you're close. A storm unlike any other will appear from nowhere!" Vinny rushed.

"Hello, officers," Cassandra said in a tense voice.

Shit.

Nathaniel.

"Go out the window, now!" I hissed. I shoved the window open and lifted Vincent from his chair.

"I'll break my legs!"

"Better that than dead!"

"Step aside, or we will make you move by force." The deep timbre of Nathaniel's voice came from the other side of the door. I spun back to Vincent, who was working up the courage to make the drop.

"Shave your beard. Tell no one what you know. They won't be generous like me." I shoved him, and he fell.

"I don't appreciate you coming into our—" Cassandra's words were cut off by the sound of steel connecting with soft flesh. There was a heavy thump, and the door burst open. I grabbed the dagger that was lodged in the wall and pointed it at the men.

Nathaniel's presence made the room feel much smaller. His wild eyes met mine. Blood coated his blade and fell in thick droplets. Cassandra's body twitched on the ground behind him before going still. He slid his gaze toward Kendra, and a sick smile spread across his face.

I lunged toward her, but he was closer. She tried to back away, but his arm snaked around her, pinning her arms against her body. She winced, and he pressed the bloody sword against her throat. I froze.

"Evading arrest is a crime punishable by death, Lou-Ann."

"So is murder. But you already know that, don't you?"

"Interfering with an arrest is also punishable by death. As commander, I'm authorized to use lethal force if necessary."

"You call that necessary?" I gestured to Cassandra's body.

"I've never murdered anyone," his glare deepened, "Unlike you."

I scoffed and shook my head slowly. "You really just said

that.”

Something flashed across his face but disappeared before I could read it. Kendra was tense against his body.

His arms around her. His face near hers. His body pressed against hers. The sight sent waves of rage through me. My vision blurred at its edges.

“Get your hands off her before I cut them off.”

“You’re going to come with me willingly, or this woman dies.” He pressed the blade harder against her skin. The knights stood behind him with their swords drawn. He must not have learned his lesson. Brute strength means nothing to a pirate.

Or a master of disguise.

Kendra let the knife in her sleeve drop into her palm and gripped it firmly. She tilted her hip slightly, separating her body from his, and plunged the dagger into his groin.

He screamed and fell to his knees. Blood soaked his pants. He tried to instruct his knights, but his screams prevented him from forming words. The knights cringed. Kendra rushed to me and I folded my arm around her waist, backing away toward the open window.

“So close again, Nathaniel. Maybe one of these days you’ll manage to lock me in that stupid iron cage.”

His eyes flared with pain and rage. He reached a bloody hand toward me as I lifted Kendra and myself onto the window sill. I lowered my voice for her.

“This is going to hurt.”

She nodded and wrapped her arms around my neck, holding on tight. I took a step backward. My stomach flipped, and I positioned my body beneath hers.

We plunged into freefall.

Chapter Twelve

I was granted a few blissful seconds before pain exploded in my head and shoulder. I'd managed to protect Kendra's head from hitting the stone street, but I was not spared from the impact. The world wavered around me.

"Louie!" Kendra crawled out of my arms and cradled my head. I tried to reply, but could only manage a few groans.

Kendra swore and glanced toward the pub door. She slapped my cheeks. "Focus! Stay awake!"

Shouts and pounding steps grew louder from inside the pub. I squinted and struggled to focus.

"Help me up," I moaned. She pulled hard on both of my wrists and pain splintered through my right shoulder. I gritted my teeth and forced myself to stand. The momentum was too quick, and I slumped over her. She stumbled under my weight.

"Stand up!" She pushed me away from her and wrapped my arm around her shoulder. "Run!"

We stumbled at first, then found the right rhythm to run while she took most of my weight. The dizziness eased with each step. As soon as we reached the end of the block, the knights spilled out of the pub. We rounded the corner onto the main street and gasped in unison.

Nathaniel's ships dominated the docks.

Completely consumed by brilliant flames.

"Holy shit," I breathed.

Footsteps rumbled in the alley behind us, and we picked up our pace. Then the steps halted, and we could hear the exclamations from the knights.

"Fuck!" Kendra swore. Her dress was slowing us down.

The street was busy, but not enough to lose the knights in the crowd. There wasn't a single person moving. All eyes were on the fires.

The footsteps resumed. The pounding of their boots against the stones spiked my pulse. My heart threw itself against my ribs. I pushed myself forward and Kendra let me go, falling a few steps behind. She chanced losing a few seconds to hike her dress up and toss her heels.

The footsteps neared.

My ship was nowhere in sight.

We burst onto the dock. It ran the length of the town in both directions. I let instinct decide and jerked my body to the right. The smoke was thick and my eyes burned. We could only see about ten feet ahead of us before the world was lost. The heat from the flames was unbearable. Ash scorched my face and lungs. It coated my throat, and I lifted my shirt to cover my mouth and nose.

Screams from those still on board gave me a chill, despite the heat. Loud splashes erupted in the water to my left. People were jumping from the forty-foot-high deck.

I didn't hesitate. I pushed through the pain and ran as fast as I could. I heard Kendra close behind me. It sounded as though the knights' footsteps had grown quieter, but I wasn't about to check.

The shadow of a ship came into view through the smoke. My heart skipped.

Please be mine, please be mine!

The cloud thinned, revealing the blue-gray vessel.

Relief flooded me. We were almost there.

A whistling sound rushed toward me from behind. Kendra gasped, then stumbled and collapsed on the ground. I halted and spun around.

She was lying on her stomach. A long arrow rose from her back.

The men's shadowed shapes took form.

I whipped toward my ship and screamed, "I AM NOT THE GREATEST PIRATE EVER!"

I didn't come up with a code phrase to signal if I needed help. Hopefully, they would get the message. If we survived, I'd have to find a phrase that was a little less obnoxious.

I turned to the group of knights that descended on us. They reached Kendra first. Two knights ripped her from the ground and forced her upright. She winced, and they tried to drag her away.

Three knights came at me. There was no hesitancy in their movements. They were fighting to kill.

I lunged backward and dodged their blades. One of the knights slashed at my legs while the other swung horizontally at my neck. I ducked down below one blade, but the other sliced into my shins. If it weren't for the leather leg guards, he would've hit bone. Footsteps thundered down the gangway behind me.

My crew rushed to join the battle. Velo and one of my seaman, Indigo, threw themselves at the men. She speared one of the knights in the stomach. When she wrenched her blade from his body, blood splattered across her dark skin and clothes.

"Go, Captain!" she shouted. A bony hand grabbed my shoulder.

"Come!" Lyonel ordered while pulling me.

"They have Kendra!"

He nodded behind me. She was engaged in hand-to-hand combat with the knight who shot her with the arrow, and she was winning. Lyonel yanked my arm.

I stumbled after him and rushed up the ramp. The smoke

was getting thicker. I followed Lyonel's lead. The torturous pain in my head reared into raw agony.

A fog pressed in on me. The sounds and smells drifted away, replaced by a warm humming. We reached the deck, and my legs gave out.

Almost as though my ship wished to spare me from the pain, my head cracked against the hard floor and I was thrust into darkness.

Chapter Thirteen

By the time I awoke, it was nearly ten o'clock in the morning. I forced my crusty eyes open and was met by a few concerned faces. Kendra was there, getting stitched up by Mora, our healer.

She simply said, "Glad you're not dead."

Once Mora applied another coat of healing tincture to my wounds and confirmed I could walk, Velo and I made our way to my quarters.

"Nathaniel lost three ships, and we estimate forty knights," he said when we settled into the chairs at my desk.

"Good work."

This was a huge loss for Nathaniel. It would be a while before he could sail again. Especially with that injury. But his arrival was concerning.

That's a lot of ships to capture one person.

The king must've learned about the Sands. I knew that would happen at some point, but he was too close for comfort. Every hour counted.

"Did you get what you needed?" he asked.

I nodded, then winced. Even with the healing tincture, my head felt as though it was being struck repeatedly with a sharp hammer. Opening my eyes was a struggle.

"The contact told us to search for a sea serpent. We need to head northeast. Two-day journey. He said to look for a storm unlike any other that will come out of nowhere."

His eyebrows lifted. "You believe that sea serpents still exist?"

"We're about to find out."

Velo nodded, then leaned forward. "It would be helpful if I knew what we were hunting. You've been unusually protective of this information."

"Isn't it more exciting this way?"

"Knowing you, it's either because you think people will back out if they knew, or would do anything to have it. My guess is the latter."

Shit.

I'd always been honest with Velo. If I kept evading his questions, I would eventually lose his trust.

"Correct," I said.

"Even me?"

"Especially you."

Velo would do anything to save his daughter. He'd cut me down in a second if it meant he could possess the Sands.

He sighed and stood. "I'll update Lorelai."

When he reached the door, I said, "Wake me when the stars come out."

As I drifted to sleep, I thought of Victoria. What if I could save her? What if I prevented her death? I imagined finding her on her final morning and pulling her off that ship. I could also warn Velo about his crew and save his helmsman in the process.

I carried the fantasy into my dreams.

Sleep came in painful waves. There were a few blissful moments when my body was numb as sleep unfolded into consciousness. Then the pain would rush in and I'd fight the urge to cry, gulp a sleeping tincture, and do it over again. Mora came to check on me every few hours to reapply the ointments and make sure I hadn't died in my sleep.

When darkness fell, Velo helped me upstairs and left me with Lorelai at the helm. Most of the crew lounged on the deck. Some were eating while others downed rum. They sat in groups and spoke in low, lazy tones.

The sky was clear. A glorious cloud of deep blue, brilliant violet, and icy peach stretched across the darkness. Dense clusters of stars, varying in brilliance and size, blinked from their temporary positions. I tilted my head back and relaxed in the presence of the familiar landscape.

Despite being tied in a low ponytail, Lorelai's wild curls whipped around her face. She attempted to brush them down and gave me a kind smile. She was the calmest person I'd ever met. She had two daughters who lived with her mother. She visited them as often as she could without getting caught. She joined the crew not only for the coin but because she couldn't afford to have another child. Prostitution wasn't a viable or appealing option. If there was anyone who didn't belong in the world of Undesirables, it was her.

"How are you feeling?" she asked.

"Pretty shitty."

"We were worried about you there for a while. I'm glad you're awake."

"Thanks, me too."

There had been a sky shift. My constellations Ira, Era, and the goose were clear and bright. Sky shift number 4. Ira to the southeast, Era to the north, and the goose to the northeast.

Ira and Era were named after twins who were in my classes for most of elementary school. They were also my best friends until I was imprisoned. The constellations reminded me of their tight ringlet curls.

The top star in the goose constellation, which I saw as its beak, would take us a few degrees south of the northeast. Following that star would account for the currents that waited ahead, eventually pushing us northeast.

I relayed the instructions to Lorelai and pointed. "Follow that star."

"It always amazes me how you can do that."

"I'm not telling if that's where you're going with this."

She shook her head. "No. People have no business knowing what nature wants to keep secret. Plus, I'd rather not have a target on my head."

Velo stood by the railing on the deck and waved me down.

"Lyonel left the ship at Port Roche," he said when I reached him. He offered his cup of rum, but I waved it away.

"When?"

"Right after you did. I didn't want to risk sending someone to follow him."

The stabbing pain in my head worsened.

"He probably needed a quick . . . *stress reliever*. If anyone needs it, it's him," he said.

I shivered. "That's disgusting."

"Come on, he's just a man, after all."

"Please, I'm in enough pain as it is!" I covered my ears. Velo laughed and patted my back.

I turned at the sound of Kendra clearing her throat. Her hair was wet from bathing, and her arm was in a sling.

"You should be resting," I said.

"I was, but I got bored."

Velo smiled at Kendra, then dismissed himself, leaving us alone. I turned back toward the water. Kendra joined me and we watched the silver feathers of waves rock us.

"I should thank you. Stabbing Nathaniel in the groin was one of my life goals. I'm glad someone finally did it."

"I don't think procreation is in his future."

"You did the world a favor," I said, harsher than I meant to.

"What happened between you two? How do you know him?"

I was hoping she wouldn't ask, but I guess it was inevitable.

The dark horizon blurred. Memories threatened to pull me under, growing more vivid with each passing moment.

Nathaniel's finger landing in the hay.

The weight of the body.

Blood in my eyes and mouth.

"We grew up together." It was the simplest answer.

"Why does he hate you so much?"

Because I'm a constant reminder of how weak he is. It's easier to blame someone else for our mistakes than to take responsibility for them.

"I don't know. I guess he really hates pirates."

Kendra snorted. "I can't say I blame him. You're pretty obnoxious most of the time."

"Most of the time? I think I have a pretty even obnoxious-to-endearing ratio."

She laughed. "I'll give that to you since you were kind of cool back there."

"Kind of? Were you even watching? 'Get your hands off her or I'll cut them off.'" I imitated my tone from before. "Jumping out of a second-story window? I was a freaking hero."

"Only because I didn't want to upstage you."

"Oh? Was that when you were held hostage? You certainly took your sweet time stabbing him."

"It was clearly a villain reunion moment. It would've been rude to interrupt." Kendra's smile faded. "It's a shame about Cassandra, though."

"It happened quickly."

"I don't even want to think about how much coin we lost."

"We'll have to tap into your stash."

She spun to me with her jaw dropped. "No fucking way. Touch my stash and I'll toss your mattress overboard."

"Ah, so you *did* bring your stash."

Her jaw snapped shut and her face bunched. "Fuck you."

I laughed, and she marched toward the sleeping quarters.

"Thanks for worrying about me! So sweet!" I called after her. She flicked her middle finger in the air over her shoulder.

When she was gone, I continued tracing the constellations in my mind. My imagination conjured shimmering silver threads that connected the stars.

Why would Kendra bring all of her coin?

The question left a metallic taste in my mouth. She wouldn't risk someone stealing it. Despite the other girls' possible hunt through her room, it was riskier to bring it with her. Which meant that she was planning on being away longer than a few weeks.

Or she wasn't planning on returning.

To risk Mother's ire by running away would be too dangerous. I'd always suspected that she considered Mother as an actual parent, which made betrayal unlikely. She might have lied about Mother's instructions to join this trip. Or maybe Mother released her permanently. Maybe she was finally going to build a life for herself away from all of this.

A subtle heaviness settled on my shoulders at the thought of her leaving. Things would be so boring if she wasn't around.

Chapter Fourteen

Two days later, Velo, Lorelai, and I gathered at the helm. Velo stood behind me with a hand hovering over his eyes to block out the morning sun. Lorelai pointed her spyglass at the horizon, scanning the water for any signs of a sea serpent.

She lowered it and shook her head. "Nothing."

I sighed. "Maybe we aren't out far enough. Move further east." I instructed, but before I could walk away, Velo stopped me.

"Captain." He nodded behind us.

A sooty smudge of a cloud drifted in the distance. We watched in silence as it grew, steadily devouring the powder blue sky.

Lorelai turned to me. "Captain?"

"How long do we have?"

"Fifteen minutes at most."

"Then let's prepare. The serpent must be near."

Velo and Lorelai nodded, then dispersed.

"Hoist the sails!" My voice boomed across the deck.

My heart thumped harder. We'd successfully weathered many storms, but never one caused by an enchanted creature. Shadowed streaks of rain fell from the swelling clouds. Violent webs of lightning flashed from within.

Fifteen minutes later, we were swallowed whole.

Relentless sheets of rain pelted my ship and crew. I squinted and licked the salt from my lips. The deck was a chaotic frenzy of people hanging on for their lives. Some were still trying to tie themselves down, myself included.

Waves crashed onto the deck. I couldn't spot Kendra, Lyonel, or Finny. Hopefully, they made it somewhere safe. If anyone was thrust into the ocean, there was nothing I could do to save them. It would be a cold, cruel death.

The ship jerked to the right and everyone stumbled. A figure flipped over the side, but the thick rain and spray made it difficult to see clearly. I could barely make out the flailing of arms and legs as the person disappeared into the waves.

We jerked back in the other direction. I fumbled with my ties. My hands slipped over the rope. The ship jolted again, as though something had rammed into the hull.

Lorelai struggled to grip the wheel. She turned to shout something to me before the stern pitched. My body lifted from the deck, and one of my hands slipped off the slick rope. I held on by my fingertips, nearly losing my hold. The ship crashed back down, and I was airborne.

The rope slipped through my fingers and I flailed my arms to grab onto something, *anything*.

My body crashed into the hard deck. Pain exploded in my shoulder and head. The railing had stopped me from falling into the water. I wrapped my arms and legs around the posts.

Rain and seawater filled my mouth and burned my lungs. I choked and coughed. When I opened my eyes, the place where Lorelai stood was empty. The wheel spun out of control.

We tumbled over another large wave and spun out. The left side skimmed the water before the ship righted itself, then tilted dangerously far in the other direction.

I watched the waves and timed my move. As soon as we lifted on one side, I sprinted toward the wheel and forced it to stop with the full weight of my body. Squatting to maintain my balance, I pushed the wheel into a steady position, steering it to ride with the wave rather than parallel to it.

Screams pierced through the shrieking winds. I couldn't risk checking to see who it was. People were going to die, and there was nothing I could do except keep the ship upright.

We jerked to the side again and the wheel slipped from my grip. I stumbled and threw myself to the ground to keep from falling. I slid across the wet wood and dug my nails in, trying to claw my way back. When I looked up, my heart dropped into my stomach. A massive wave rose ahead of us, nearly twice the size of the others, blocking out the violent sky. The ship turned sideways and pitched. The wave pulled us upward, and I hung on as tightly as I could. My body lifted from the deck.

I shouldn't have challenged the sea. Now we were all going to die for a treasure that might not even exist.

A blinding flash of lightning cracked through the dark sky.

Something inside the rising wave caught my eye. A flash of brilliant blue.

I squinted through the sharp rain.

A shape three times the length of my ship slithered through the thickness of the wave. Brilliant turquoise scales glinted along its powerful body. A silver eye opened and locked onto mine for a brief moment before it disappeared into the dark water.

"Hold on!" I screamed to the crew as though they could hear me. As though it would do any good.

There was no escape. No skill or improvements to the ship could've saved us. My celestial maps were useless to me now. I tilted my head back and watched the full force of the violent sea drag us higher.

There were no moments after impact. No chaos, no snapping wood, or violent thrusts. No broken bones or crushed lungs. Only darkness.

Chapter Fifteen

"Human."

A deep growl cut through the fog. My eyelids were as heavy as sandbags. I didn't have the strength to complete the monumental task of opening them.

The growl rumbled with more force, and it spoke again.

"Awaken."

I wanted to shove the voice away, but its command didn't sound optional. I forced my eyes open, blinking as the unfamiliar surroundings came into focus.

The sea serpent's iridescent eyes bore into me. Brilliant turquoise scales covered the creature's long, snake-like body. In shadow, they darkened to a deep, rich blue, then brightened to an icy shade in the gentle beams of filtered sunlight. Its face was angular with a long, wide nose similar to sketches I've seen of dragons.

I jolted and tried to scramble away with no success. My back hit a soft wall. I was in a bubble, swaying deep beneath the ocean's surface. I could breathe, and there was no crushing pressure from the weight of the water. Fish lazily drifted past, unbothered by the enchanted creature's presence.

"Focus, human."

I turned back to the serpent. Its wide mouth remained closed as it spoke.

"My ship . . . "

I was alive, but where was my crew? Finny, Lyonel, Velo. Kendra.

"Your ship is safe. I have protected it, just as I am with you now. Though I could not save those already lost."

Its words brought forth a mixture of relief and sorrow.

"You created the storm?" I asked.

"I did. Though I do not have time to answer your questions. You must listen carefully."

As the serpent spoke, its body swished back and forth. Its left side curled into view, revealing deep, jagged gashes. The scales around the wounds seemed to be rotting and fell off in large pieces. Thick black liquid oozed from the openings and its mouth.

"Are you hurt?"

It growled. *"I have you humans to thank for this."* It curved to give me a better view of the wounds, which might have been caused by hunting spears and hooks. *"I have spared your life and ship because you have a very important task to complete."*

The serpent flipped to reveal its belly where a dozen translucent blue blobs clung to its body. *"You must take these eggs to Sapphire Island. There is a cove on the northeastern side where the magnapistris breed. You must bury these eggs in those waters as close to shore as possible. Bury them deep."*

My stomach flipped. There was no way I was going anywhere near a magnapistris. The eighty-foot-long sharks were rumored to be powerful enough to wipe out an entire fleet of ships with ease. I also wasn't about to argue with a sea serpent.

"Won't they eat the eggs?"

It made a sound similar to a scoff. *"Divinum do not hunt each other. The magnapistris will protect and raise my children as though they were its own."*

My mind stumbled to process the serpent's request. Humans had inflicted its wounds, yet it was trusting one with its unborn children. Sea serpent eggs would be the most valuable treasure ever retrieved, second only to the Sands.

"Why trust me?"

"Because I see you, and because I have no other options." The serpent tossed its head, and more liquid oozed from its mouth. *"I will not make the journey."*

Its voice softened at that. An unexpected, overwhelming pang of grief gripped my chest. I grimaced and pressed my hand to it. Waves of sorrow flooded me, and I steadied myself against the squishy wall of the bubble.

I sensed another meaning behind it *seeing* me, but before I could ask, it bent its head and ripped a few scales from its skin with its sharp teeth. It brought them toward me and pressed them into my bubble. Seeing the creature up close was simultaneously terrifying and amazing. The scales fell at my feet and I picked them up, careful not to touch the blood.

"You may find these useful. Fix them to yourself and you can swim at any depth without air. But it will not last forever. I have also healed your wounds." Its iridescent eyes flashed. *"Never forget that a divinum granted you mercy."*

The serpent's body seized, and more black liquid gushed from its wounds. *"Go!"*

"Wait! I need to know where the Sands of Time are!"

"Find the totem on the Isle of Night."

Its tail swung and smashed into the bubble. I crashed to the floor, and the sea rushed past me. I squinted and tensed against the rush. When I reached the water's surface, the bubble popped. I kicked my legs and flailed my arms. The water stung my eyes and rushed up my nose.

"Holy mother of fuck!" I sputtered and coughed. I kicked hard and tilted my face up while I stuffed the scales into my shirt to free my hands.

A shape bubbled up beside me and I lurched away from it, ready to fight if it was another creature that would gladly eat me. Instead, a round jelly-like egg bobbed on the surface. It was a little smaller than my head. There was a coiled shape inside, suspended in a brilliant blue liquid. Another appeared, then another, until all twelve eggs floated around me.

I scooped them closer and when I scanned the water, my eyes landed on my ship, which appeared gloriously intact. It was far enough that they wouldn't hear me, but close enough that they could see me. I kicked hard and shouted as loud as I could while waving my arms in the air. Some of the eggs drifted further and I swore. There were too many for me to keep close.

"Hey! Over here! Hey!" I screamed.

The ship remained still. Nobody appeared.

I pulled one of the scales from my shirt and held it above the water. Angling it toward the sun, I moved it side to side to reflect the light. I paused every few moments to scoop the eggs back toward me. My pulse spiked. Maybe it was my imagination, but the ship seemed to be getting smaller.

I kept moving the scale.

"Come on, come on!"

A few figures appeared at the edge of the deck. I couldn't make out who it was, but given their sudden urgency, it was a safe bet that they'd seen me.

Giving my legs a break for a moment, I relaxed to tread using my arms. Four of the eggs had drifted beyond my reach. I stretched for them, but two more eggs ducked under my arm and drifted in the other direction.

My heart thundered. The undulating waves were carrying the eggs out of reach.

When I glanced back at the ship, it was turning in my direction. I held the scale up again to offer another reflection so they wouldn't lose me behind the waves, but doing so cost me a few more eggs. Only three remained near me.

My arms weren't long enough to hold them all, or even half of them. I'd need a net of some kind. Or longer limbs.

An idea struck me. I pulled the scales from my shirt and stuffed them into my pants, cringing at the sliminess. I struggled to pull my shirt over my head, then tore the fabric completely on one side, then most of the way down the seam on the other, leaving the two halves connected.

This was a weak plan at best, but I had to try.

I circled the fabric around the eggs nearest to me and it clung to the sticky membranes. Kicking hard, I swam to each of the eggs, scooping them into the circle of fabric that I'd made. They were sticking to each other.

A larger wave rolled over me and my momentum faltered. I gasped, inhaling more salty water, which sent me into a violent coughing fit. The waves were growing larger and more frequent as the ship approached.

Salt stung my eyes, but I persisted. By the time the ship's shadow fell over me, I'd retrieved each egg.

"Louie!" a deep voice called from above.

A rope ladder splashed into the water beside me and I reached for it.

"I need a net or crate!" I tried to scream, but the sound barely made it through my burning throat. I tried again, forcing the words to carry upward.

A few moments passed. When I was about to shout again, a fishing net tethered to a long rope splashed into the water beside me. I dipped the net below the floating pile of unborn sea serpents and secured it tight. Someone pulled on the rope from above, and the net lifted into the air.

By the time I reached the deck, my body was trembling. I crawled from the ladder and collapsed onto my back, not caring who saw my bare chest.

My crew, or what was left of them, huddled around me. Someone helped me sit upright and draped a wool blanket over my shoulders, which I hugged gratefully. An endless stream of questions poured my way, but I couldn't hear anything over the chattering of my teeth.

"All right everyone, step back. Let the captain breathe," Velo said. They did as they were told, and he sat beside me.

When I tried to speak, my stomach clenched. A rush of salt and bile tumbled from my mouth onto the deck. I heaved, purging the saltwater from my stomach and lungs. Someone patted my back, and I cringed away from their tender touch.

By the time I was empty, awareness crept in. The crew was watching silently, waiting for me to finish. They all shared the same pinched expression.

My body continued to shiver as the rush from my experiences crashed. A rogue wave. A sea serpent. A dozen eggs worth more than I could imagine.

I hung my head and closed my eyes. There was so much I needed to process before sharing anything with the crew.

We could go to the Isle of Night. I could find the totem and continue with the hunt for the Sands. Even if I failed, I could sell the eggs for enough coin to buy my own island, furnish it with a castle, and purchase a few other islands as vacation homes. The king would be particularly interested.

Maybe I could bargain for my freedom. The king could clear me of all my crimes. There were even rumors that there were ways to remove the Undesirable brand.

As I considered my options, large bubbles rose to the surface ahead of us. The water grew violent and thrust upward.

A roar boomed, and we slammed our hands over our ears. The serpent's body crested. It thrashed, sending large waves in every direction. We watched as its body liquefied. Streaks of white-hot turquoise whipped upward. It arched and flicked into the air, rising higher and higher. I squinted against the brilliance.

The wailing eventually quieted, and the water stilled. A pool of vibrant blue settled on the surface for a moment before fading completely.

A heavy silence followed.

I'd taken many lives before. Normally, I felt nothing. It was an unfortunate necessity. But this was different. My chest clenched, and I gripped the blanket. A cry built inside me, but I swallowed it before it could pass my lips.

I would never be able to properly describe the power and beauty of the sea serpent. The creatures we hunted were so much grander than us.

We humans had seriously overestimated ourselves.

I tore my eyes from where the serpent had been. When the strange ache faded from my chest, I stood and addressed my crew. Every jaw was dropped. They turned to me slowly, and I forced a smile.

"Next stop: Sapphire Island."

Chapter Sixteen

"You can't be serious."

Kendra leaned on my desk next to me despite my repeated protests for her to move.

"I have a chair there for a reason." I motioned to the other side of the desk.

She leaned closer, and I leaned away. "You met a sea serpent, talked to it, and it trusted you with its eggs?"

"That's what I said." A headache pounded my skull.

"Unbelievable."

"Believe it. And get off my desk."

I shoved her harder this time, and she finally obeyed, moving around the desk to sit in the other chair. She slowly shook her head in disbelief.

"To think, it trusted a heartless pirate with such an important task."

"I'm going to do as it asked."

She jolted up from the chair as soon as she sat in it and slammed her palms on the desk.

"What?! Are you out of your mind? Do you know what we could get by selling just one of those eggs? Let alone the whole lot? This entire crew could retire and support their next three generations on what those are worth!"

She swung her hand toward the pile of eggs hidden inside a seawater-filled barrel tucked safely beside my bed.

"Do you know what a divinum is?" I asked.

She huffed and slumped back into the chair. "No, but it sounds like the olde language. Why?"

"That's what the serpent called itself. It referred to the magnapistris that way as well."

"Please do not tell me we're going to run into a magnapistris." I nodded, and Kendra groaned, throwing her head back. "Louie! For fuck's sake, let's just drop the eggs in the water and be on our way. Do they need to be in magnapistris-infested waters?"

"The serpent was clear. It's a three-day journey. I'll come up with a plan before then."

"Did it tell you anything about the Sands?"

"It said to search for a totem on the Isle of Night once we finish burying the eggs."

"Fantastic. First, face off with monster sharks, then an island of creepy night creatures." She groaned and rubbed her forehead. "I shouldn't have come."

"Finally, we agree on something."

I told the crew as much as I felt comfortable sharing. I lied and said that we'd find a clue to the treasure's whereabouts on Sapphire Island, but that we would have to complete the serpent's request to do so. I still hadn't shared what we were hunting, but they trusted me enough to know it was worth the effort.

We had enough rations and supplies to make it there. I wasn't worried about someone sneaking off with the eggs. However, I would need to keep them under constant watch for the rest of the trip, just in case. I also made it clear to the crew that anyone who touched the eggs would meet a swift and painful death.

While I'd explained that the serpent saved us from the storm, I chose not to mention that it had created it. There were rumors of enchanted artifacts with great power, such as the Sands of Time, but none had ever been confirmed. Revealing the truth about the serpent's power would only put the eggs, and similar creatures, at greater risk.

We lost nine people in the storm. Lorelai, our bosun Krawchek, Noala, Bun, Corey, Nicole, Jorn, Vira, and our carpenter Eve. It was more casualties than we've ever had on a hunt. We could sail with eleven of us as long as everyone pitched in to fill the empty roles. In return, I would offer them higher pay from the cuts that were reserved for the deceased.

Nelson, our seventeen-year-old assistant bosun and Krawchek's son, hadn't come up from the sleeping quarters since the storm. Kendra mentioned that I should check on him, but I was awful at comforting people. Despite my best efforts, I would likely blurt out something that would make him feel worse. Plus, he was afraid of me. Kendra was better at that sort of thing.

I didn't want to risk leaving the eggs unattended, so I came up with an alarm to alert me if anyone entered my room. I tied a thin string across the bottom of the threshold and discreetly secured it to the wall leading up the stairs. When nobody was looking, I'd tied it to the warning bell that hung beside the door on the deck. If anyone tried to enter my room, the whole ship would know.

That night, the crew celebrated surviving the storm with a large meal and plenty of rum. There was an unmistakable heaviness, but it was tradition to celebrate the life of a lost crewmate. I drank with them, enjoying their stories about our fallen crewmates. I'd have to send word to their families the next time we docked. My heart hurt for Lorelai's children, but it couldn't be helped.

Before I got too drunk, I brought a plate of food to Nelson and left it on the floor while he slept. I watched him for a moment. He'd grown so much since he joined the crew with his father five years ago. Now he could barely fit in his hammock. He'd always been a quiet kid, and his father, despite being an infamously aggressive drunkard, had loved him dearly. I gently closed the door and sighed.

When my head started to spin, I grabbed a blanket and stumbled to the upper deck.

There was another sky shift that night. The only constellation present was of a woman lounging on a chaise holding an empty bowl, positioned northwest. The shape was inspired by a painting I'd seen on the wall of a small abandoned temple hidden in the dense woods near my hometown.

When we were fourteen, Nathaniel and I decided to skip school and explore the dilapidated building to search for ghosts. And by that I mean I decided and dragged him along. He tried to put on a brave face, but it was obvious that he was terrified.

An ache squeezed my heart every time I saw that constellation. That once-fond memory had been tainted. Those gentle, golden years would forever be cast in shadow.

I shook my head and immediately regretted the quick movement. The world tilted, and I lowered myself onto the floor to stop the spinning.

"Having fun?" Kendra appeared beside me and took a seat.

"Absolutely. I think everyone needed this, though we're all going to pay for it tomorrow."

"Sounds like a problem for later."

I nodded and turned my attention back to the sky, unsure of what to say next.

"What are you looking at?" she asked.

"The sky, obviously."

"But what? What do you see that you want to keep a secret so badly?"

"None of your business."

"It's not healthy to keep things bottled up."

"That's strange; I don't remember asking for your sage wisdom," I said with a half-smile.

She replied with an exaggerated sigh. "Fine. I give up."

"You really thought I'd tell you?"

"Nope. I know you too well to expect that."

"Yeah, right," I scoffed. "You know me as well as I know you. Which is not at all."

"I know you're egotistical, vain, violent, clever, and talented. I know there's nobody in your life that you trust. I know we could continue on this hunt without burying the eggs, but you've chosen to risk everything by doing it anyway."

My earlier tension returned.

"I think you're overthinking it."

"I'm not."

"Well, I can't say any of that for you."

"I think you can. I think you know me better than you would like to admit."

I squirmed. The rum churned in my stomach.

"I don't know what to tell you," I said. My words slurred together.

"Tell me what you know about me."

A familiar flare of annoyance forced me to face her.

"Okay, fine. I know you were born into this life, yet you choose to live in our world, even though you could easily blend into society." I poked her chest where the brand would be. "I know you care about Mother. You care about people in a way I never have and never will. I know you're talented, smart, and frustrating all at once." She bit her lip, and I continued. "I know that you brought all of your coin on this trip. What I don't know is why."

Her face fell, and she turned away.

"Answer the question."

"None of your business." She threw my words back at me.

"It is my business."

"Why?"

"I should know if you're going to leave. You're part of my crew."

"And if I leave after we've found the Sands?"

I opened my mouth, then closed it. Once we completed the job, I had no valid reason, or right, to know where she was going.

"Whatever. Do what you want," I said.

"Oh, I see." She leaned closer. "You're going to miss me."

"Not at all."

"You care about me."

"I don't. I feel the same way about you as I do with anyone on this ship. I'll do my best to keep you safe, but betray me and I wouldn't hesitate."

"Hesitate to do what?"

I rubbed my face. A headache was beginning to press against my temples. "Let's not ruin the mood."

"Tell me."

"You know what the punishment is for betrayal."

"Say it. What would you do to me?"

I clenched my jaw, then said, "Spill your blood. I'd slit your throat in front of everyone, and make Nelson clean up the mess."

I forced as much truth into my words as possible, but they didn't carry the confidence I'd intended. Her lips parted. I closed my eyes and reached for some kind of mental clarity. Instead, the spinning worsened and I cringed. Two cool hands cupped my cheeks to ground me.

"That's the rum talking."

My chest ached at the nearly imperceptible tremble in her voice. Our faces were closer now. Her warm breath mixed with mine. I should pull away. Normally, my skin would crawl at someone else's touch. It wasn't safe.

But I didn't move. She searched my face. A warmth spread in my stomach, and I pressed a hand against it as though I could make it stop.

"Louie, I—" Her words were silenced by a loud clanging sound that echoed across the ship.

The warning bell was ringing.

Chapter Seventeen

"Shit!" I launched from the floor and clumsily stumbled down the stairs to the lower deck. Nobody stood near the bell.

I flung the door open and barreled down the stairs. The door to my quarters was closed. I kicked it open, snapping the hidden string. The bell clamored loudly.

My jaw dropped when I saw the figure standing beside my bed.

Holding an egg in his shaky hands.

Lyonel spun around to face me. His magnified eyes grew even larger, and his face paled. His shoulders bunched and the slick egg slipped from his palms.

I lunged forward to catch it.

The egg fell to the floor and burst open. Vibrant blue liquid splattered across our shoes and onto my bed frame. I dropped to my knees and cupped the small snake.

"No, no, no!" I scooped the liquid and what remained of the membrane, trying to piece it back together, but it was too late. The small creature wriggled and chirped a few times before going still.

An unfamiliar pang of sorrow stabbed my chest, and unbidden tears welled in my eyes. The serpent's grief had fused to my bones. The small creature was already growing cold in my hands.

When I lifted my dark gaze to Lyonel, he was huddled in the corner of the room as far away from me as possible.

I stood and gently returned the body to the open barrel. A quick count of the eggs confirmed that eleven remained. I turned slowly to face Lyonel.

"You." My voice rumbled dangerously, and he flinched. Footsteps bound down the stairs behind me and stopped at the doorway.

I stepped over the mess and grabbed Lyonel by the throat, slamming him against the wall. His head smashed against the wood, and he yelped. I brought my face close to his. The edges of my vision blurred and I slammed him again, harder this time.

"There are less painful ways to die than betraying me, Lyonel," I said, my voice laced with violence. Heavy tears tumbled down his wrinkled cheeks, but his fear did not reach me. No amount of begging or pleading could satiate my rage.

"I'm sorry Louie, I just . . . I just . . . " he stammered. I slammed him again.

"Just what? Hm? Have I not been good to you? Was the fortune I promised you not enough? You needed more?" I tightened my grip on his throat and his face turned from pale to red to purple.

"Stop!" a voice cracked. Hesitant steps approached, and I spun around. Finny was behind me, reaching out with a shaky hand.

"Step away from me or you'll join him."

His face was ghostly white and his eyes were glassy. Velo put a hand on his shoulder and gently pulled him back.

Lyonel was choking and sputtering. I released my grip slightly and he gasped air through his shredded throat.

"I swear I was just looking!"

"You're going to lie to me now?" I dropped him and he crumpled to the floor, wheezing and rubbing his neck. I snatched a dagger that was resting on top of my desk and pointed it at him.

"Do. Not. Move."

He nodded. I directed my attention to the barrel. The

outside appeared normal, and the water was swaying gently inside from the rolling waves. I leaned closer and spotted what I was looking for.

A sharp sliver of wood protruded from the inside. It was about three inches long. Long enough to be responsible for tearing an egg open. Ordinary enough that it could be dismissed as damage from the storm.

I ripped the shard from the inside wall of the barrel and held it up to him. He crawled away from me and pressed himself into the corner of the room, shrinking under my cruel glare.

"Drain the liquid from the egg and blame this. Clever." I tossed it at him. "I'm disappointed in you. Maybe I've been too kind," I said, towering over him. He tried to stammer another apology, but I silenced him with a kick to the side of his head. He fell and his glasses skittered across the floor. Blood oozed from his split lip, and he sobbed.

"Stop!" Finny cried. I spun to face him, and he shrank back against Velo.

"This man believes he can defy me. Do you share that belief?"

Finny whimpered and cast his eyes to the floor.

"Bring him upstairs before I paint the walls of this room with his blood," I nodded to Lyonel. Velo released Finny, who watched helplessly as his mentor curled into a ball and sobbed on the floor.

Several crew members, including Kendra, were standing near the door. When I turned toward them, they scrambled up the stairs. I followed and gripped the railing to steady myself. The effect of the rum was wearing off, but I was still a long way from sobriety.

I needed a moment to rebalance and process.

The rocking of the ship, which should have been comforting, made the rum slosh in my stomach. My skin flushed, and I swallowed the rising urge to vomit.

All eyes were on me.

Lyonel would have to die. I knew that. I'm the one who made that rule. If a pirate captain showed weakness, it was only a matter of time before there would be a mutiny. We weren't searching for gold or jewels. No treasure could compare to what we hunted. My crew appeared friendly, but greed and violence lurked behind every smile. I wouldn't be the only victim. Finny, Velo, and Kendra would likely be killed too.

I wiped my damp palms on my pants and stood to the side while Velo dragged Lyonel to the mast. Finny took a tentative step toward me, but my glare stopped him.

"Please, Captain," Finny pleaded. "I know what he did, and I know what you said will happen, but please consider sparing him. Mercy is an admirable trait—"

I slapped him hard. He froze with a hand hovering over his red cheek.

I stepped closer and lowered my voice for him. "You know the consequences for defying me. There are no exceptions. You joined a pirate crew. I realize this may not be what you were expecting. Not everyone is cut out for this life. You're welcome to leave as soon as we reach the next port. I won't stop you, and I won't be angry. But for now, this is how it will be."

Finny bit his quivering lip. "Please."

I turned to Kendra. "Take him to his bed."

She was startled, as though surprised that I had addressed her. She nodded and gently led Finny below deck. He protested softly but went willingly.

Velo tied Lyonel's hands behind his back and had him on his knees. His expression was resolved. None of this was new to Velo. He would've done the same thing. He *had* done the same thing. When he was captain, he was known for his short temper and brutality. Time had softened his countenance, but not his heart. Betrayal wasn't rare for a pirate. He knew that better than anyone.

"Louie, let me explain," Lyonel begged through his tears.

"Please do," I said. He swallowed.

"There's no guarantee that we'll find the treasure. I overheard you talking. I know what you're seeking. The Sands of Time, right?"

I clenched my jaw and glanced at the crew. Their eyes widened, and some gasped.

"Liquid from an egg would provide enough coin to feed me and my family for a long time. My daughter is sick, you see. I wanted to help her. I just . . . " Lyonel's words dissolved into sobs. Fresh sickness churned my stomach. It nauseated me to see how easy it was for him to lie.

What Lyonel didn't know was that I'd done a full background check before hiring him. I knew all about the family he abandoned when his daughter was two years old.

This man didn't give a shit about his family.

I *tsked*. "Lying to me again." I crouched in front of him. "What a loyal father. So loyal that you didn't lift a finger when your wife got sick and died, leaving your daughter alone. I also know that your daughter was murdered while working as a prostitute in Port Roche and that you didn't even go to collect her body. Her employer rolled it right into the water." I leaned closer to him and lowered my voice. "She died alone without a coin to her name."

Though she died years ago, when Velo mentioned that Lyonel left the ship, I thought it might have something to do with that. What other business could he have in Port Roche?

A missing piece of information that had been nagging me since that night resurfaced.

"Did you inform Commander Bartholomew of my whereabouts at Port Roche?"

Lyonel clenched his jaw and swallowed.

I scoffed and slowly shook my head. "Unbelievable." I leaned closer. "You've underestimated me. Which is a shame since these jobs have funded that sad little life you lead as a paranoid shut-in."

There was a violent meanness pouring from me that I couldn't stop. Callous hate rolled off me in waves. I could practically taste it.

"I wanted to retire. You promised that," he said.

"I did. Then you let your fear get the better of you. You grew impatient and greedy. A bad combination." I stood and directed my attention to the crew. I stressed each word to sound more clear-headed than I felt.

"Lyonel Gendy has defied my order to leave the eggs untouched. He betrayed us and conspired with our enemy. This man put us all in danger. The punishment for these crimes is death. Does anyone deny this?"

The group was silent.

I turned to Lyonel.

"I sentence you to death; the manner of which is still to be determined." A sob broke from him. "You will remain in the brig without food or water until it is time." I nodded to Velo. "Take him away."

"Wait! I've been good to you, haven't I?! I built the ship you wanted! I've served you well for years! Nobody knows this ship like I do!" Lyonel thrashed against Velo's grip, but his frail body was no match for Velo's size and strength. "Please reconsider!"

His panicked pleas faded as he was dragged below deck. I turned my attention to the crew and raised my voice.

"Lyonel was correct about the treasure. We are hunting the Sands of Time. The artifact will provide us all with more coin than we could dream of. But I want to be extremely clear. If someone decides to take the treasure for themselves," I locked eyes with each person, "I will tear them apart and send the pieces to their family."

It was a gruesome threat. The worst part was that I meant it. Violence had burrowed into my core, devouring every ounce of mercy and compassion.

I let the words settle in the heavy silence before continuing.

"I'm loyal to every one of you. I will protect you with my life, and I expect the same loyalty in return."

Some nodded, while others remained still. Nelson stood among the crowd with red, tired eyes. When I reached him, he flinched.

"Clean my office," I ordered. He nodded and rushed off to gather supplies. I turned away from the gaping crew to retrieve the deceased serpent from my quarters. I descended below deck and gently fished the body from the barrel, carrying it upstairs.

The crew whispered to each other, then silenced when I emerged. Some sported appraising expressions, while others averted their gaze. I ignored them and climbed to the upper deck, where I'd sat with Kendra not long ago. The sounds of shuffling feet faded behind me as the crew descended to their sleeping quarters, leaving me alone.

Pressure built inside me, threatening to rise to the surface and spill over. I clamped it down and took a slow, shaky breath. The small snake was curled into a spiral in my cupped palms. It was an ugly thing, but I couldn't find it in me to be disgusted.

I stretched my hands over the stern and released it. The shape tumbled down, and the creature disappeared in our wake.

Lyonel was right. He had served me well for years. But mercy would put a target on my back that I'd never be rid of. I had no choice.

That's what I told myself again and again. I stood there until the stars dipped beneath the horizon, replaced by the glow of dawn.

I have no choice, I thought, desperate to believe it.

Chapter Eighteen

Lyonel's betrayal came at a convenient time.

He remained in the brig for two days. I'd allowed Finny to visit him but made it clear that if he brought him food or water, he would die with him. It wasn't a serious threat. If he did, I'd turn the other cheek.

I busied myself with gathering as much information as I could on the mechanics of the ship. When Finny was ready, I'd review the schematics with him to double-check that I hadn't missed anything. I'd have to win him over before then. I didn't want him to rebel against me. He'd come around.

Or so I told myself.

He stayed in his bunk and refused to talk or eat. He also declined his combat training with Kendra, which had been going surprisingly well. I let him be. He was behaving the way any normal, well-adjusted person would. Watching the darkness burrow inside him—the same darkness that took me when I was two years older than he was now—prevented me from commanding him.

A part of me knew this would happen. When I saw his young face light up at the promise of adventure, I chose to keep the harsh reality from him. Convincing Finny was an easier way to get Lyonel to join the crew. It was selfish, but I didn't have time for regrets.

The eggs would be buried, and the Sands would be mine.

On our final day of travel, the water lightened to a crystal-clear blue, similar to the sea serpent's pearlescent scales. The five scales that the creature had given me were safely tucked away beneath one of the floorboards in my room.

The midday sun was unforgiving. The breeze did little to assuage the heat of the scorching rays. I'd noticed Kendra's tan turning red and ordered her to stay as covered up as possible despite the heat, to which she replied, "Mind your own business."

As Sapphire Island appeared to the southwest, I gathered the crew and explained the plan. Everyone stood around the deck except for Finny. I'd considered dragging him from his bed, but he wasn't needed for this task. Velo had brought Lyonel up from the brig and tied him to the foremast. He appeared gaunt, and he squinted against the brightness.

"Magnapistris live in these waters," I said once I had everyone's attention. "I will bury the serpent's eggs in a cove on the northeast side of the island. Alone."

"That's suicide," Falrey, a thick-bearded redhead, said while crossing his muscled arms.

"Possibly, but we don't have a choice. I doubt we could defeat even one magnapistris. If there's a whole school of them, we won't stand a chance. Stealth is the only way. The fewer people that go, the better. Our greatest chance of success will be to lure them away from the cove," I gestured to Lyonel, "With blood."

He hung his head. There was no begging anymore. He had resigned to his fate, which I was thankful for. It was embarrassing to admit, but his primal desperation to survive made me waver in my decision to end his life.

His blood and body wouldn't be much to one magnapistris, let alone a whole school. I had to hope that their senses were as keen as they were rumored to be and that they were hungry.

"You'll drop me off at the northern tip of the island. I'll make the rest of the journey on foot." I turned to Simon, who had replaced

Lorelai as helmsman, and said, "You'll surveil the waters and determine the exact location of the creatures. Once you find them, get as close as you can and dump his body. Move further from the cove and spill his blood, then use the side sails to retreat as swiftly as possible. Hopefully, they'll follow the trail."

I turned to Velo and lowered my voice. "Can you take care of him? I can't do both." I glanced at Lyonel, and he nodded.

I always made sure I was the one to execute the punishments or to be present during someone's death if it was under my orders. I should bear the weight of my decisions. But I wouldn't be able to reach the cove in time if I were the one to kill him.

"Coward," Lyonel rasped. He lifted his head, and his tired eyes bore a hatred I'd never seen in him. "You won't even kill me yourself."

"Believe me, I would if I could."

"You were wrong before. I never underestimated you. I overestimated your humanity."

I couldn't argue. Each execution was poison to my soul, if there was such a thing. I ignored him and dismissed the group. Kendra pulled me aside.

"I'm coming with you," she said.

"You're not," I replied.

"I am."

"I don't have the energy to fight with you right now."

"We're not fighting. We're calmly disagreeing."

I rolled my eyes. "I need you to stay here and make sure this crew doesn't strand me on that island."

"Velo can take care of that. I'm more useful by your side. Plus, the eggs are heavy. Are you planning to carry them by yourself?"

I scoffed and flexed my sleeveless arm, pointing at the toned curves and lines. "You see this? I could carry two dozen eggs with one hand."

It was her turn to roll her eyes. "Yes, sure, we're all very impressed. But can you carry the eggs and defend yourself from the wild animals on the island? Or maybe the, I don't know, massive ship-destroying sharks?"

"I'll be fine."

"You will because I'm coming."

I groaned. "Fine, I won't stop you." I squinted at her. "I guess you do know me. You know how to annoy me until I finally give in, just to make you stop talking."

She beamed. "Thank you."

We secured the eggs in two sacks. We wouldn't be able to transport them in water. I hoped they would survive the trip.

Thirty minutes later, Kendra and I were lowered into the water in a jolly boat with the sacks of eggs resting at our feet. We would row the rest of the way to land and hope that the magnapistris wouldn't find us before we reached the shore.

Kendra and I rowed in silence. When we reached the sand and dragged the boat onto the beach, I removed the scales from my shirt and handed her three. I was lucky that the crew was too distracted by the sea serpent's death to ask me about the reflective object I'd used to get their attention.

"Where did you get these?" She turned the scales over in her hands and marveled at the shifting colors.

"The serpent. It said that these would allow us to swim deep and breathe underwater. But it will only work for a limited amount of time, so we'll have to be quick." I retrieved two long wraps and handed her one.

"Oh darn, I was hoping to take a leisurely swim . . . "

Her sarcasm trailed off when I pulled my shirt over my head. Her ears flared red, and she turned away. I pressed the scales to my chest and circled the wrap around my torso to secure them in place.

Kendra fidgeted with hers and looked everywhere except at me.

"Are you shy now?"

Pink bloomed on her tanned cheeks. "I was just surprised."

I smirked. "Do you need help with yours?"

"No!" she exclaimed. "I've got it."

I smiled and busied myself with unloading the eggs. When she was finished, we each took a sack and hauled them up the beach into a thick forest. Though it would take longer, we decided to stay close to the shoreline to avoid getting lost.

Kendra was right. There was no way I would've been able to carry all the eggs by myself. Halfway through our hike, my muscles burned. There wasn't an inch of me that wasn't sweating. Kendra walked ahead of me, and judging by the shine on her skin and her ragged breathing, she was also struggling.

"I can't," she gasped, gently lowering the sack onto the ground. Red splotches covered her skin and her hair clung to her face. I followed suit, silently grateful that she made the first move to take a rest. It took a few moments for us both to catch our breath.

"It didn't feel this heavy at first, but damn," she said.

"You've been training with Finny every day. You should have better stamina."

"Not all of us have lumpy arms like you."

Just as I opened my mouth to argue, my eyes snagged on something shifting in the brush beneath her feet. I snatched the dagger from my belt and sent it flying into the dirt. It lodged into something fleshy. Kendra jumped to the side.

"What the hell! I was joking!"

I kneeled and spread the brush to reveal a snake. Its scales were brown with yellow-white diamond-shaped stripes along its body. The knife was lodged in its head. An instant kill.

Even though the snake was completely different from the serpent that died at my feet, I couldn't help but compare the two. I shivered and a wave of nausea rolled through me.

Kendra kneeled beside the dead snake and surveyed it. "I don't know much about snakes, but judging by this pattern, I'm pretty sure it's poisonous." She eyed me warily. "You saved my life."

"Again." I yanked the knife from its body and wiped it on the ground before returning it to my belt. I turned away to give myself a moment to reset my expression and lifted the sack over my shoulder.

"We need to hurry." I resumed the hike, and she jogged to catch up.

I wondered how it was possible that I was still experiencing the serpent's despair. The grief couldn't possibly be mine. The creature died days ago, yet the sadness that permeated our brief mental connection hadn't faded. It would be nice to have someone I could talk to about it, but Kendra didn't seem to know any more about the enchanted creature than I did.

The cove was beautiful. The clear water was a brilliant blue, and the sand was fine and soft beneath my boots. If I didn't know what lurked below, I'd rest my aching muscles in the warm rocking waves and float for a while.

We rested the sacks on the sand and I shielded my eyes to search the horizon. I found our ship right as a small shape tumbled overboard and splashed into the water below.

Lyonel was dead.

I braced for some variation of sadness that might rise in me, but I felt nothing. The death of the serpent affected me more than the loss of a man I'd known for almost a decade.

"Now what?" Kendra pulled me from my rumination.

"We swim."

I slid my boots and pants off, leaving my underwear and shirt on to protect the wrap that secured the scales. Kendra did the same, and we dragged our sacks to the water's edge.

"How are we going to swim with these? We'll sink like anchors."

"Since we'll be able to breathe and go as deep as we need to, that might not be a bad thing. Hopefully, we'll be undetectable that deep."

The ship had drifted north. When a dark liquid spilled over the deck, we started our dive. The shallow water was warm, but as we descended beyond the sun's reach, a chill gripped my skin. To my amazement, the scales allowed us to see clearly. Colorful fish and other creatures swam around us, busy and unconcerned.

However, walking along the ocean floor was more difficult than I'd imagined. The sand was soft and my calves burned from the effort. The eggs were buoyant, which helped. I didn't check behind me to make sure Kendra was still following. I reminded myself that she was perfectly capable of taking care of herself.

I tilted my head back and marveled at our depth. I hadn't gotten to enjoy the few moments the serpent gave me to experience its world. Maybe I was meant to be a sea creature instead of a violent pirate.

The water became cloudy the deeper we went. I made a point to keep scanning our surroundings for any sign of the magnapistris. If the sea serpent wanted it to defend its eggs, then we needed to bury them in water deep enough to accommodate the large creature.

I took a step and a sharp pain sliced into my foot. I flinched and lifted it to find ringlets of blood spreading in the water. Sharp coral spotted the ground around us. I spread the sand away to see how large the sea stone was and gasped.

It wasn't coral. It was a large, sharp crystal that housed something small.

Magnapistris eggs.

I swore, but the words were garbled by the water. I turned back to Kendra to attempt to communicate my findings, but she was mouthing something and pointing frantically in front of me.

I turned, and my stomach dropped.

A massive magnapistris was charging with its razor teeth bared.

I dropped the sack and lunged behind me to pull Kendra into my arms. I forced us to the sea floor just in time to dodge the creature's deadly bite. Its enormous body blocked the light from the sun as it sailed over us. It was so close that if I stretched my arm upward, I could've touched its underbelly.

The force of the current it created tossed us into an uncontrollable spin. With one arm, I tried to grab onto any of the rocks or long sea grass to stop our violent tumble.

The magnapistris arched itself upward and turned to circle and try again. Its tail swung toward us and I kicked hard, pushing us backward to narrowly escape a collision.

The tail pushed another strong current at us, shoving us down into the sharp, jagged eggs. My back scraped the crystals, and I cried out. We tumbled over and over, shredding ourselves across the treacherous sea floor.

My shirt and wrap ripped and came apart like wet paper. Kendra's chest pressed against mine was the only thing holding the scales to my body. We spun again, and she was forced away from me.

The scales lifted from my skin. Water poured into my panicked lungs. My vision blurred, and the pressure from the weight of the water crushed in on every part of me.

There was pain everywhere.

It was blurry, but I could tell the creature was making its way back toward us.

I'm going to die.

This was it. I'd never make it to the surface in time to force air into my lungs.

My body jerked and seized. I clawed at my throat and chest. Blazing anguish shredded my lungs. I closed my eyes.

Make it stop! Make it stop! I silently begged. To whom, I didn't know.

Suddenly, the agony ceased just as quickly as it came. I opened my eyes. My vision was clear, and I gulped air into my waterlogged lungs. Kendra had one arm wrapped around my waist while the other tightly pressed one remaining scale against my chest. We had slowed down enough to find our footing. Her face was contorted into pure, unfiltered terror.

The magnapistris sailed toward us. Its small black eyes locked onto mine.

I remembered the serpent's words.

"Divinum do not hunt each other. The magnapistris will protect and raise my children as though they were its own."

The serpent's eggs were still in the tied sacks, floating twenty feet away. I held the scale to my chest and charged toward the sacks, swimming and running at the same time.

A rumble vibrated the water around us.

The magnapistris was growling.

It swished its tail, propelling itself toward me.

A desperate garbled shout called from behind me, but I didn't hesitate.

The creature's jaw opened wide. Bits of meaty flesh were tangled in the many rows of sharp teeth.

The eggs were close.

Its growl shook the earth.

Almost there!

I lunged and gripped the sack, yanking the string to untie it. I grabbed one serpent egg and held it out in front of me.

The magnapistris faltered and snapped its jaw shut. It tilted its head upward but couldn't stop in time.

Its enormous shape slammed into me.

My body shattered.

Chapter Nineteen

Somehow, I survived. There was no doubt that I had more broken bones than not. Even with the scale, the shock to my diaphragm made it impossible to take a breath. When I tried to move, my body didn't cooperate. The only thing I could move were my eyes. From what I could see, my ribs caved in a few spots and a sharp white bone protruded from my hip.

There was no pain. No feeling at all.

The magnapistris made another wide turn to face me. As impressive as the sea serpent had been, the sheer mass of the magnapistris was terrifying. It growled again but didn't charge.

"Explain yourself, human, before I swallow you and your companion whole," its deep voice rumbled in my mind.

Tendrils of anger and hunger rose within me. Its voice and emotions were invading my mind the same way the serpent's had. I tried to form the words to answer it, but my mouth didn't move.

"I can hear you this way. Speak now," it ordered.

"I was sent by a dying sea serpent to bury its eggs here. It said you would protect them," I thought.

It watched me for a moment, swishing its tail. When I mentioned the serpent, a brief spark of concern and sadness flashed through our connection so quickly that I wondered if I might have imagined it.

"I see." It tilted its head to see the eggs that were still weighed down by the sack in the sand below.

"I don't mean any harm to you or your unborn."

The creature's anger faded into something closer to disdain.

"I am aware of your intentions. You cannot hide that from a divinum."

I wondered again what divinum meant. It must've heard me, because it said, *"We are divine beings. That is all you need to know."*

If I could move, I would've nodded. I'd suspected as much.

"My companion means you no harm either. She was helping me."

I couldn't turn my head, but I could see Kendra's arms and legs treading water out of the corner of my eye.

"Complete your task. We will protect the eggs," it said.

"Happy to help if I could move. Which I can't."

"Be grateful you cannot feel your broken body."

The water around us was tinted red. I was losing too much blood.

"If this other human buries the eggs, I will fix you," it offered.

I was about to ask how when I felt its presence slip from my mind. Kendra had moved into view and positioned herself in front of me to shield me from the divinum. From what I could see, she was holding a scale to my arm. When the magnapistris' black eyes flicked to her, she tensed.

They stared at each other, and after a moment, she nodded and turned to face me. Her brow was creased, and her jaw was locked tight. Her eyes scanned my shattered body.

Careful not to let the scale lift from my skin, she slowly slid it up my arm, across my chest, and down my stomach to tuck it inside the band of my underwear. She flinched every time the scale passed over a broken bone. I couldn't ease her concern by telling her that I couldn't feel anything.

She didn't seem to acknowledge her wounds. Bloody gashes slashed across her smooth skin. The blood that leaked from the cuts swirled around us and mixed with my own.

She got to work clawing deep holes in the sand below,

burying each egg with care. The creature watched her in silence. I closed my eyes while she worked. I didn't want to catch any more glimpses of my body.

When she was finished, she kicked off the ground and rose to face the creature once more. They stared at each other for several moments. Finally, she nodded and swiftly swam down to snatch a sharp rock from the seabed. She rose next to the magnapistris' body and ripped the stone across its flesh.

My pulse quickened, but the magnapistris didn't attack. Black blood leaked from the cut and dissolved in the water. Kendra pressed her mouth against its skin and drank. When she finished, she hurried back to me. She drew herself close and cupped my face.

She tilted my head back and pressed her lips against mine. Black liquid spilled into my mouth. I could partially see her hand massaging my exposed throat, working the enchanted blood down.

My eyes fluttered closed.

After a few moments, she pulled back while keeping my face in her hands. Her wide eyes flicked over my face, searching for something. She pulled further back and scanned my body. She didn't seem to notice what was happening to hers.

Her wounds were closing. The torn skin fused back together until it was smooth once more.

A tingling started in my fingers and toes, then moved up my limbs. I glanced down and watched the pelvic bone that had punctured my skin sink back into place. The collapsed rib bones rose to their rightful positions. A few moments later, my body was back to normal.

Kendra smiled and her shoulders sagged. I lifted my hand to hold one of hers that still cupped my face. Her smile fell, and the predictable blush crept up her neck to her ears. She jerked away from me and averted her eyes.

"Your work here is done. Leave and do not return," the divinum's voice growled in my mind.

Kendra and I nodded at the same time, confirming that he'd spoken to both of us. He turned and swam away.

"Thanks!" I called out to him, only to receive a grumpy *hmph* in return.

We crawled back onto the beach and collapsed on our backs. The warmth from the sand soaked into my skin.

I almost died.

Despite the heat, I shivered. When I opened my eyes, Kendra was watching me.

"We almost died," she said. I nodded.

"Correct."

"We almost died," she repeated numbly. I sat up.

"But we didn't, of course. Because we're—"

"The greatest pirates ever?" she supplied. I smiled and nodded.

She sat up and retrieved our sandy clothes. My mind was still processing what happened, but I already knew that I wasn't the same person that I had been when we arrived. *We* weren't the same. Whether that was a good thing or not was a question for another time.

We dressed. Since she still had the wrap around her chest, she offered her shirt to me which I accepted with a grateful nod. We tucked the remaining scales into our pants and made the journey back to our small boat in silence.

Anger, hunger, resolution, and annoyance churned inside me. The echo of the magnapistris' emotions and sensations drowned out my own. The more I learned about the forces around us, the more questions I had. I pondered this as Kendra and I rowed back to the ship.

"What are you thinking about?" she asked. I shook my head, too deep in my thoughts.

The crew lifted our small boat. When we stepped on board, Velo grabbed my shoulders.

"Are you hurt?" he asked while scanning my body for

injuries. I shook my head, and he released a sigh. Realizing he was touching me, he dropped his hands and took a step back.

"Come," I said. Velo and I walked past the curious crew to my quarters.

"The magnapistris only followed for a moment before heading toward you. What happened?" he asked once the door was closed.

I opened my mouth to fill him in.

"Do not tell him."

The force and urgency of the thought slammed into me, and I snapped my mouth shut. I couldn't tell where it had come from or why, but every part of me screamed to stay silent. It wasn't a threat, but a warning. Velo's eyebrows lifted while he waited for a response. Instead, I sighed.

"I'm tired. I'll brief you later." I started removing my boots. "Wake me when the sun sets."

Chapter Twenty

There were no stars that evening. By the time I emerged from my quarters, the sun had long been set. The sky was cloudy and moonless. We drifted in total darkness.

Despite my few hours of sleep, I was completely drained. I didn't even admonish Velo for letting me sleep in. My body was heavy, and a fog had settled in my mind. The crew lounged on the deck and spoke quietly to each other while sipping rum, completely uninterested in me.

I tightened the blanket around my shoulders and tiptoed up the stairs to the upper deck. I wasn't ready to talk to anyone about what happened with the magnapistris. I would need to be selective about what information I could share. The urge to keep the details of our encounter to myself had faded into a gentle pressure. I wondered if this was caused by the divinum's blood, along with the exhaustion.

Footsteps tapped up the stairs behind me and I turned away from the water to see Kendra approach with a handful of food.

"Figured you'd be hungry." She handed me some dried meat, bread, and a cup of water.

"Thanks."

We sat with our backs against the railing and ate in silence while watching the crew.

"Do you feel the way I do?" she asked.

"What do you mean?"

"Exhausted."

"I think it's from the blood."

She nodded, and silence settled between us.

Maybe it was the intimacy of the darkness or the reminder of the conversation we'd had a few nights ago in the same spot. She might've made fun of me for bringing it back up again, but I was too tired to care. I had to know.

"Where will you go once this is over?" I asked.

She ripped a piece of meat with her teeth and chewed it for a while. Finally, she said, "I don't know."

I waited for her to say more. A few more moments of silence passed, and I watched her profile. She glanced at me and lowered her head.

"I want to find my birth mom," she said.

I hadn't considered that would be something she'd want to do. My own family cut me off when I was sentenced as an Undesirable. To be fair, it was illegal for them to contact me, but nobody was keeping tabs on them.

When I settled into Mother's care, I wrote to let them know where I was and that I was okay, but I never received a response. It hurt at first, but we weren't an affectionate family. They parented me the same way they ran the farm. It was a job, and they would dutifully meet my needs. We never hugged each other or said anything close to 'I love you.' Fifteen years had passed, and I rarely thought of them.

"Do you know where she is?" I asked.

"I have a lead that she might be in Templan."

I straightened. "Templan?! Are you crazy?"

"I can blend in there much better than you could. Nobody would even know who I am."

"But is it worth the risk? You'll be right at the king's front gate! The city is crawling with knights."

"I'll be fine."

"You'll be in constant danger, for what? A woman who sold her child for a few coins?"

Her face hardened, and I immediately regretted my words.

"Maybe she had a good reason!" she snapped.

"I'm telling you, it's a bad idea."

"The worst thing that could happen is that she's an awful person and I leave."

"Or she turns you in."

"She wouldn't."

I threw my hands up. "You can't possibly be this stupid."

"You can't possibly be this much of a jerk!" she shot back. "What do you care? You don't even want me here!"

I opened my mouth, then closed it. She watched and waited for me to argue. When I didn't, her shoulders sagged. She nodded to herself numbly, stood, then silently descended below deck.

I groaned and lowered my forehead against my folded knees.

"You really are an asshole."

Chapter Twenty-One

When a dense cluster of lights came into view along the coast, we moved in to find a port where the crew could rest. I could see the exhaustion weighing on each of them. I didn't know what we'd have to face on the Isle of Night. Those who traveled there never returned. Plus, there wasn't much I could do on a cloudy night. It was safer to leave during the day.

As we approached the coast, I recognized a port. Lincoln Harbor, a half-day's journey to the Isle of Night. We'd leave in the morning and make it there by early afternoon.

Tension was building in my chest and shoulders. Though we hadn't seen any signs of Benny or Nathaniel's fleet, I feared they lurked nearby. Benny always had a way of finding me. He had contacts in almost every port and city.

We docked around midnight and found a few nearby inns that could accommodate our group. Most of the crew decided to venture into the local pubs and brothels. Once I'd given the letters informing the families of those we lost to the innkeeper for the postman, I went to my room.

While my body was exhausted, my mind was wired. The urgency of continuing our journey made it difficult to sit still. My tension worsened at the thought of someone from the crew mentioning the Sands. They all swore they wouldn't, but that didn't mean much.

Kendra hadn't spoken to me since our fight. I owed her an apology. That was something I never thought I'd need to do with her, but I needed to take responsibility for my words. They had been true, but that didn't make what I said, and didn't say, okay.

"'What I said was true, but I'm sorry I said it,'" I practiced while I paced back and forth from my closed door to my bed. "No, that's shitty. 'I'm sorry I made you feel bad. I'm an asshole.' That's not it." I groaned and rubbed my face roughly.

Just do it already. Keep it simple. Don't make it weird, I thought.

I took a deep breath, then left to find her room. My fist hovered in front of her door, but a quiet voice from inside stopped me from knocking.

"It's okay, you can talk to me," Kendra said softly. There was a moment of silence before another voice spoke.

"It's just hard, you know?" Finny replied. I lowered my hand.

I should walk away. This wasn't my business.

Instead, I pressed my ear against the wood. There was a shuffle of fabric.

"Oh," Kendra said. "I see. That must have been painful."

"It was. I was scared, but I didn't cry once."

"That's impressive. Do you want to tell me what happened?"

Finny was quiet for a moment. "It was my sister. Not my birth sister, but my parents took her in when she was four. She was my best friend." His voice hitched, and he cleared his throat. "We think she was half siren, but I was never sure. Someone must have reported her after seeing her black blood because the knights came for her one night. They weren't dressed like knights, though. They wore dark clothes and didn't speak a word. Their boots woke us up, and before I could even say anything, they dragged her from her bed. I tried to run after them, but they hit me until I couldn't get up. She was gone."

His words settled in the silence. My heart hurt for him.

Imagining him beaten and helpless while chasing after his sister was too much to bear. My rage ignited on his behalf.

"And the brand?"

I froze.

"I followed their tracks and found out where they were keeping her. I begged the knights to let her go, but they turned me in and accused me of attacking them. As if I could hurt a knight." He let out a quiet, wry laugh.

I swallowed my rising fury. I could kill those men. I bet Mother could find them. I could make it look like an accident. A fire, maybe.

"There was one inquisitor who was kind to me," he continued. "I could tell he didn't belong in that job. He came to my cell one night and said that he was worried about me going into the king's service. He thought that I would be a target as a trans man. I agreed, declared my gender female, and was sentenced as an Undesirable. He connected me with Lyonel, so I wouldn't have to . . . well, you know."

More silence followed.

"I'm sorry. I didn't mean to upset you. Please don't cry," Finny said gently. Kendra sniffled.

Her words were muffled. "I'm sorry that happened to you and your sister."

"Thanks." His voice wavered.

Finny was such a gentle soul. Lyonel was all he had keeping him from the darker professions available to an Undesirable, and I killed him. It was no wonder that he hated me.

"Are you going to stay with us?" she asked.

"I don't know."

"I understand. This must feel overwhelming. What happened with Lyonel was awful, but I hope you know that Louie has her reasons for doing what she did."

"There was no reason to kill him like that. She used him as

bait. She's a monster." His voice rose, and each word struck me like a well-deserved slap.

"She may seem like a monster sometimes, but things are different with pirates. If she was kind and merciful, the crew might decide to take advantage of that. It could backfire and put us all at risk. It happens more than you'd think. She may have been harsh with you, but she acts like that to protect you. Plus, most of it is tough talk. She's got a big heart, believe it or not."

"I don't believe it."

"Fair. Harsh as she may be, she's the most loyal person you'll ever meet. She'll protect you with her life. Trust her, Finny. And if you can't, then trust me. Deal?"

For a moment, I wondered if I had misheard who they were talking about. I never imagined Kendra would describe me as loyal and bighearted, especially after how I treated her.

Their conversation quieted, and I returned to my room.

As I lay in my bed that night, I thought of all the ways I could help Finny. If he stayed with me, he'd witness more bloodshed. I didn't have enough coin to give him so he wouldn't have to work. But if he stayed by my side, Kendra and I could protect him. We would make sure nobody hurt him like those knights ever again.

Ultimately, the choice would be his.

When an hour passed and I still couldn't calm my mind, I downed a sleeping tincture, which thrust me into a cruel nightmare.

Finny's feet were sealed in hot tar. He tried to scream, but no sound escaped his lips. He fell to his knees, further sealing himself to the ground. I tried to grab him, but my own feet were stuck. He fell forward. Tears tumbled down his red cheeks. The harder he struggled, the more trapped he became. Tar crept up his body, encasing him in a shiny black goo. I desperately tore at the tar to release my own feet, but it was no use.

He was gone.

Chapter Twenty-Two

A hard knock startled me awake.

"Wake up, duckling, before we leave without you," Velo called from the other side of the door. I glared at the empty tincture bottle on the bedside table. Not a single part of me was rested.

A laundress had washed my clothes and left them in a neat pile outside my door. I gratefully changed, then left the inn. I flinched at the bright morning light and scanned the street for my crew. No familiar faces wandered through the crowd.

The warm breeze carried a gloriously savory scent and I followed it to a small restaurant. I bought enough food for the entire crew and paid two boys to help me carry it. When I approached the ship, the crew erupted in applause. They swiped their plates so quickly that someone might've thought I'd been starving them.

I decided to offer Finny the chance to leave before we shipped off to the Isle of Night. He had information I didn't want him to share, but most people would doubt the word of a fifteen-year-old boy. Especially one as sweet and awkward as him.

The door to the sleeping quarters was open, and I found him curled on his hammock facing the wall. I knocked on the door frame, but he didn't stir.

"I brought you something."

His body tensed, but he didn't reply. I sat in the hammock across from him and lifted the cloth that covered the breakfast. Eggs, potatoes, sausage, and toast with butter.

"Mmm, smell that? Fresh food." I leaned forward and subtly wafted the smell in his direction. "A million times better than plain bread and dried meat." I didn't need to mention Nelson's cooking. Plain bread was a luxury compared to the stew he usually made that we all pretended to like, then discreetly spilled overboard.

Finny remained silent. I couldn't blame him for wanting nothing to do with me. Forcing him to talk to me would only make things worse. I thought of what Kendra might say and cleared my throat.

"I know you're sad. Or mad. Or both. I understand that. My first time on a voyage like this was really hard. I saw things I wish I hadn't. We've been in this life for a long time. We're used to things getting bloody. But I know this is all new to you and that you weren't expecting it."

His head tilted, and I knew he was listening.

"I'm not going to force you to continue with us. I hope you do, of course, because we could really use your engineering expertise. But I can't keep you here. We're going to ship off in about an hour. You can come with us, or you can get off here and I'll give you coin to get home." I stood and gently placed the food on the floor. "I'm going to leave this here. Make your decision and let me know. I'll respect it either way."

I closed the door on my way out and when I reached the deck, I ran into Kendra on her way to the quarters. When she saw me, she turned on her heel, and I placed a hand on her arm to stop her.

"Hey, can we talk?"

Someone cleared their throat behind me. I turned and Velo stood there, eyeing us both. "We're shipping off soon. I thought we could go over the plan for today," he said.

"Yes, let's do that." I turned back to Kendra. "I'm sorry for what I said and how I reacted before. You were right. I'm a jerk, and I'm sorry. And . . . about that last thing you said"—I glanced at Velo—"you're wrong."

Her eyebrows raised, but her jaw remained clenched. When she didn't reply, I sighed and followed Velo below deck. I was grateful for the few moments of silence during the short walk to my quarters. I was disappointed, but it wasn't fair to expect her to accept my apology right away. I shook it off and fixed my attention on the impending expedition.

We sat at my desk and I spread out one of the updated maps between us. I pointed to the Isle of Night, south of our current location.

"Here's our next stop. It should take us half a day if the weather cooperates."

"You know the stories, right?"

"Other than it's always night there, no."

"It's crawling with enchanted creatures that thrive in darkness. It'll be extremely dangerous. We'll have to be hypervigilant. And no, you can't go alone this time."

"I won't argue with that."

"Do you know where we'll land?"

"Not yet, but I know we're looking for a totem. Let's get there first and I'll work on a plan in the meantime. Can you tell Simon?"

Velo grunted and stood. "Flying by the seat of your pants, eh, Captain?"

I smiled widely. "You love it."

He chuckled and shook his head. When he reached the door, he turned back to me.

"I'm concerned about the girl," he said. I straightened.

"I have it under control."

"She's a weakness, duckling. You're letting her in too much. Even the crew has noticed."

My stomach flipped. "I'll handle it."

He nodded, but his furrowed brow told me he wasn't convinced.

When he opened the door to leave, Finny stood on the other side. He startled and pressed himself against the door frame to let Velo pass. When he was gone, Finny took a small step forward but didn't cross the threshold.

"Have you decided?" I asked.

He nodded. "I want to stay."

"What changed your mind? Was it the food? I knew the food would do the trick." I gave him a warm smile to ease his tension, but he bit his lip and dropped his gaze to the floor.

"No, it's not that. I don't have anywhere else to go. Mr. Gendy was the only friend I had." He paused and chewed the inside of his cheek. "I don't want to be alone."

I motioned to the chair on the other side of my desk. He hesitated, then took a seat. His shoulders were hunched, and his eyes were locked on the desk.

"Finny, look at me," I said gently. When he did, I gave him a soft smile. "I'm sorry I slapped you. That was wrong of me, and I won't do it again. As long as you're part of this crew, you are under my protection. You're safe. Relax a little, all right?"

He nodded and forced his shoulders down.

"To be clear, you are aware that things are going to get more dangerous and what happened to Lyonel might happen again, correct?"

He nodded, and his face hardened. "I'm fully aware of the risks, and I'm choosing to stay. I think I can be of more use to you than sitting around waiting for things to break."

"You're aware of what we're hunting?" He nodded. "I know it might be tempting to want to use something as powerful as the Sands to go back in time and stop bad things from happening. But you can't do that, no matter how noble your reasons may be. Do you understand?" He nodded again.

I mentally scoffed.

Hypocrite.

A knock tapped on the door, and Simon poked his head in. "We're ready to ship off. All clear?"

I stood. "Yes, proceed. And you," I directed at Finny, "are coming with me."

I found Kendra on the deck, helping drop the sails. When she saw me, she climbed down.

"Hey," I said. She crossed her arms. "I need you to increase your training sessions. Velo will teach him how to sail."

She turned to Finny with raised eyebrows. "You're staying?"

"Yes. I think I'll be helpful if you can teach me," he said.

"Not think, you know. From here on out, there are no uncertainties. There may be a time when you need to defend yourself. You don't want to face an enemy 'kind of' sure that you know how to fight. Your knowledge of this ship is your greatest strength so far. Velo will teach you how to sail when he has time." I patted him on the shoulder. "Congratulations. You've been promoted to bosun."

Kendra's jaw dropped. "Bosun?! Are you crazy?"

"In case you haven't noticed, we lost Krawchek in the storm. Velo has been doing both jobs, and Nelson is," I searched for a nice way to say incompetent, "better at other things. Finny is perfectly capable of making sure the ship is stocked and everything is working as it should. He knows this ship inside and out. Fight training first." I turned back to Finny. "If I have no doubts about this, neither should you."

He swallowed and nodded, looking paler than he had a moment ago.

When I told Velo of my decision to promote Finny, he barely concealed his disapproval. He was starting to doubt me. It had been a long time since I was his mentee, but the idea of him doubting my decisions made me waver. I projected calm authority when he expressed his concerns, despite my insecurities.

There was no time to start Finny's sailing lessons. By the time he finished his three-hour training session with Kendra, we were approaching the Isle of Night.

The island was contained in a shroud of darkness. I wondered if the eternal night was caused by the same thing that created the sky shifts. I made a mental note to keep an eye on the stars while we searched for the totem.

The sky behind us darkened as we neared the island. A storm was approaching with unnatural speed. Lightning flashed within the swelling gray clouds, eerily similar to the last storm we weathered.

We were already too close to the island, which meant we faced a high risk of the storm crashing us into the rocky shore. The ship wouldn't survive the collision. Our best chance was to try and outrun it.

"If this is the same type of storm as before, we won't make it," Simon said. Velo and I stood with him at the helm, considering our options. I called to Finny, who was shining with sweat from his session with Kendra. He joined us, and I pointed to the batwing sails.

"We need to get to shore, and fast. The wind is in our favor. Unfurl your sails." He nodded. "All hands!" I bellowed over the deck.

I helped with the main sail, then went below deck to make sure our supplies were secured. Kendra was hunched over one of the rum barrels, grumbling to herself about the poorly tied knots.

"Hey," I said. She startled and smacked her head against the shelf above her.

"Fuck!" she hissed and rubbed the spot where a bump would eventually be. I bit my lip to keep from laughing, and she frowned.

"If this is unrelated to the massive storm heading our way, then I don't want to hear it."

"I'm trying to apologize."

"It's fine, just drop it." She tried to step around me, but I moved to block her.

"I'm sorry, okay? I got upset, and I said some stupid things."

The beams of sunlight filtering in from the open door illuminated the edges of her brown hair like a golden crown. I took a step closer. "What part was more upsetting to you? What I said about your mother? Or what I didn't say?"

"What you said hurt. But what hurts more is that you refuse to communicate. I know why you pretend—"

Her words cut off when the ship jolted forward, and we were both thrown to the floor. I flinched in anticipation of my head slamming against the wood, but I landed on something softer instead. When I opened my eyes, Kendra was on top of me with her hand cradling the back of my head to soften the blow. She lifted her head from my chest and pulled her hand out from under me.

"Ouch." She gave me a half-smile and flexed her fingers.

She propped herself up on her elbows, but most of her body remained flush against mine. Her steady heartbeat thumped against my chest through our clothes. Her hair fell around my face, blocking out the light. The exclamations from the crew upstairs faded.

I held my breath. Her face was close to mine. I brought my hand to her waist to push her off, but her shirt had lifted. Once my fingers met the warmth of her sun-soaked skin, I couldn't pull away.

Her eyelids lowered and her lips parted. I bit mine, trying to brace against the heat spreading through me.

"*She's a weakness.*"

Velo was right.

She was my weakness.

She lowered her face to mine. I could have stopped her, but I didn't. I didn't want to.

Her lips hovered. A heated desperation flushed through me, but I couldn't move. She was completely in control, and there wasn't a thing I could do about it.

An explosion of thunder crashed from above. We both startled and stared at each other for a brief moment before rising from the floor in unison and bounding up the stairs.

Sharp rain blasted me in the face. The sun that shone only moments ago had been swallowed by night. Charcoal clouds masked the stars.

We'd reached the Isle of Night.

Chapter Twenty-Three

Finny and Mora struggled to close the left batwing sail, while Velo and Nelson worked on the right. We were slicing through the water with incredible speed, but the storm was faster. There was no way a natural storm could've caught up with us that quickly.

The wind had shifted, forcing us west.

Directly into the coast.

The deck was absolute chaos. My crew was struggling. Ushar and Falrey were dangling from the ropes at the top of the foremast. Jerma and Indigo were attempting to tie themselves down. Kendra rushed to help Finny with the batwing sail. I gripped the railing and charged up the slippery stairs of the upper deck to Simon. He was fighting to turn us east into the waves with little success.

"What's happening?!" I shouted over the howling wind.

"I don't know! It won't budge either way!"

I squinted through the rain to see if anything was restricting the rudder, but there was nothing. There wasn't a sign of another sea serpent either. Only the massive rolling waves that tossed us from side to side. Water crashed onto the deck and rushed past my calves. Fortunately, everyone remained on board, and those on the mast were almost back onto the deck.

I locked eyes with Velo, and the panic on his face made my

stomach drop. Even in these winds, we should be able to curve to the left. The wheel should be moving.

The sharp rocks drew closer by the second.

"What do we do?!" Simon shouted. I rushed forward and gripped the slick wheel with him. We both pushed with everything we had, but it didn't move.

A brilliant flash of lightning slashed the sky, followed by a deafening crack of thunder.

Another wave rolled us and more water splashed onto the deck.

The crew was barely holding on.

We lurched forward, picking up speed.

I pressed my eyes closed and braced for impact.

A massive wave rose on our right, pushing against the current and winds. Everyone who was still standing was thrown to the ground. The ship tipped horizontally, and we climbed higher and higher along the wave's curve.

Simon and I slid across the soaked deck. We crashed into the railing, and I managed to grab Simon's arm before he spun overboard. I braced my feet against the railing and used my whole body to pull him back onto the deck. He tumbled to the floor beside me, and we wrapped our arms and legs around the railing.

The wave was pushing us away from the rocks.

The splintering sound of wood cut through the roar of the storm, and we lurched again from the impact.

My ship groaned.

The storm raged.

My crew screamed.

The wave pushed us to the left, guiding us around the rocky shore. I squinted through the darkness. We were riding parallel to a sandy beach.

Then, as though by enchantment, the storm silenced.

The wind stilled, and the massive rolling waves eased into a gentle swaying. The clouds evaporated, revealing a clear, starless sky. The only light came from the bleached full moon perched high above.

Simon and I shared a look of astonishment. The wheel rocked gently from side to side, free of its invisible hold. Unable to trust my shaking legs, I crawled on my knees to the edge of the stairs.

The soaked crew was scattered across the deck, sporting the same dumbfounded expressions. I did a quick headcount and confirmed that we hadn't lost anyone. The relief came in a cold, nauseous rush. I rested my cheek on the wet wooden deck for a moment to collect myself.

Velo was the first to rise. Once I felt able, I did the same and locked hands with Simon to help him stand. I carefully descended the stairs, and the crew rose one by one.

I joined Kendra in untying Finny from the mast. Once he was free and relatively calm, I ordered him to lead the hunt for where the tear was and assess the damage. When I prepared to address the group, the ship came to an abrupt halt, tossing us back to the floor. I shoved myself upward and scrambled to the railing. The rocking waves had gently pushed the ship into shallow waters, wedging us into the soft sand below.

I cleared my throat and hoped that I sounded steadier than I felt. "Is anyone hurt?" I called out. Everyone shook their heads numbly. "Good. I think it's safe to say that was the strangest storm any of us have encountered. We survived, but I don't think we're safe. Take a moment to prepare yourselves for whatever waits for us."

They nodded and turned to each other, speaking in low tones.

"Are you okay?" I asked Velo.

"Yeah, you?"

I nodded. "Have you ever seen anything like that?"

"No. It must have something to do with whatever keeps this island in darkness. Whatever it is, it's powerful and dangerous." His eyes searched the shore.

The sea serpent might not be the only divinum capable of creating a storm like that. Something forced us to land here.

"I agree, but we don't have a choice. There's a totem on this island that will lead us to the Sands. Once we find it—"

"No," he interrupted. Velo hadn't disobeyed a single order under my command, until now.

"If we don't, we'll lose the Sands," I tried again.

"No. It's too dangerous."

"Since when has that stopped us?"

"There's danger, then there's stupidity, Louie. It's important to know the difference."

I straightened. "You can stay here if you want, but I'm going."

"You're not going anywhere."

"You're giving me orders now?"

"I'm strongly advising you."

"You aren't my mentor anymore."

He gripped my shoulders. "You almost died! We almost died! I've watched you run headfirst into danger over and over again, and somehow you always make it through." His face was creased and his fingers dug into my arms as though I'd disappear if he let go. "Fighting men is one thing, but you can't win against a divinum no matter how tough you think you are!"

I froze.

I'd never heard anyone refer to the divinum by name, especially not Velo. He'd told me on more than one occasion that he knew nothing about 'enchanted creatures.'

"How did you know that?" I asked quietly. His eyes widened, and his mouth snapped shut.

My heart sank. The answer vibrated in me, loud and clear.

He's hiding something.

Chapter Twenty-Four

Velo's fear was genuine. It was clear that he was concerned about me. So why lie?

The answer was in the persistent pressure on the back of my neck. A warning I shouldn't ignore. But the authenticity of his fear for my safety made me hesitate.

The conversations around us had quieted. We had an audience. The crew had noticed my conflict with Kendra, and now my quartermaster was questioning my authority as captain. Velo's words from twelve years ago whispered in my mind.

"The worst thing you can do as captain is show weakness. If the crew decides to mutiny, they'll kill you and those closest to you, and there won't be a thing you can do about it except watch."

I stepped backward out of his grasp.

"We are going on land to get the totem. You are welcome to stay here, but I'm going."

His face fell. I turned to the crew and snapped, "Why are you all still standing here? Dry yourselves off and check the ship for damage. Jerma, Indigo, and Ushar are coming with me. Equip yourselves. We leave in ten minutes."

Some people frowned, but everyone followed my orders.

After I regrouped with Simon, I found Finny below deck and he briefed me on the damage. The rocks had ripped a hole in the hull about seven feet long, but it was higher than the water level. Falrey and Mora were covering it with extra sail canvas. Nelson cut and prepped wood in the carpenter's workroom under Finny's instruction. A fraction of my tension eased. It seemed that Finny had settled into his new role, which allowed me to focus on our impending expedition.

My hands trembled as I changed into dry clothes. Despite the wet heat, I'd opted for my protective leather vest and stuffed my belt with as many daggers as I could fit.

There was a soft knock at the door and Kendra called from the other side, "Can I come in?"

I took a few deep breaths, finished lacing my dry boots, and opened the door. She'd changed as well and equipped herself with several daggers. I looked her over and shook my head.

"You're not coming."

She smirked. "It's funny that you think I'd listen to you."

The pressure on my neck worsened. Velo's words repeated in my mind, louder than before.

She's a weakness. A weakness. Weakness.

My face softened, and I put my hands on her shoulders without thinking. There were only a select few people in my life that I would accept touching, and she'd become one of them.

Her body relaxed, and she took a small step toward me.

"You can't possibly still doubt my ability to protect myself," she said.

I sighed and released her. "Fine. Let's go."

She followed me up the stairs. We filed into a smaller boat along with Jerma, Indigo, Ushar, and Velo.

Velo hadn't looked at me since our fight, which was for the best. My stomach was already in knots. I couldn't afford any distractions.

We dragged the boat onto shore, and I led the group into the dark forest. The warm light from the lanterns we brought did little to help us navigate. The thick trees captured the moonlight. A heavy curtain of unnatural darkness hung around us, creating a wall of shadow that swallowed our lantern light beyond five feet in any direction.

But the oppressive darkness was nowhere near as discomforting as the silence. There were no signs of life. No buzzing of insects or chirping of critters. No rustling leaves or creaking branches. Everything was dry, as though it hadn't rained. Even the air was silent and still.

An hour into our hike, Ushar sighed behind me and asked, "Are we getting close?" His dark hair was damp, and his golden skin was starting to glisten with sweat. I was fairly certain his muscles were just for show. Meanwhile, his twin sister, Jerma, seemed completely unfazed by the exercise.

The enchanted tracking crystal I held out in front of me was supposed to glow in the presence of enchanted items. It illuminated the moment we reached the beach, but the light hadn't dimmed or intensified. The totem itself might not be enchanted, but I hoped that the crystal would alert us to any nearby divinum.

As much as I'd hoped to have a solid plan by now, the island was massive. It would take us months to search every area for the totem. I thought if we could reach high ground, we might see something in the distance that could be a clue. But that would be impossible considering the density of the island's darkness.

Just as I considered ordering the group to turn back to regroup with the others, a loud crack from somewhere in front of us split through the silence. Everyone halted. I held my breath and searched the blackness, straining to hear any rustle of movement.

A rush of cold spread across my skin as though we'd stepped across a threshold into winter. Goosebumps rose on my arms. An intense pressure of warning squeezed my shoulders and the back of my neck.

I drew a dagger and held it out in front of me, ready to strike at the first sign of movement. The crew readied their weapons and crouched into fighting stances. The crystal vibrated in my hand and the blue light flared.

Every part of me screamed to run. I turned to instruct the crew to fall back, but it was too late.

Tall, dark figures lunged from the shadows. Ice-cold arms wrapped around me, trapping my arms against my body. I twisted and struggled against the restraints. Startled shouts from my crew rang out from behind me.

"Welcome, human," a voice that sounded like a choir of many chuckled in my ear. Before I could see its face, darkness crashed over me like a rogue wave, shoving me into a silent nothingness.

Chapter Twenty-Five

"Beautiful ghost," a deep voice called to me. Gradually, my senses awakened. Soft fabric beneath me. The heaviness of my body. Warm light laced over my closed eyes. The distant hush of waves licking the shore.

"Wake up, sleepyhead." There was a creak, and I felt a shift of weight beside me.

I forced my heavy eyelids open and squinted at my surroundings. Wooden beams decorated the stucco ceiling above me. Light from a lantern flickered across its surface. I was lying on a bed in a small room.

"Finally! I was getting worried," the voice said. A voice I knew too well. I turned to face him, confirming my fear.

Benny sat on the edge of the bed, waving a paper fan at me. His handsome face was soft in the dim light. His cotton shirt was loose and dipped low in the front, revealing part of his strong chest. He smiled at me affectionately and stopped fanning.

"What the hell," I croaked.

"I imagine you're confused and disoriented. Rest assured, you're safe and unharmed. I made sure of that," he said proudly.

I scanned the room. It was small and simple, with cream-colored stone walls and dark wood accents. To my left, there was a nightstand with a lantern beside Benny. A wardrobe sat in the right corner of the room next to a closed window. It was too dark to see outside, but it sounded as though we were close to the sea.

I remembered my weapons and reached for where my belt should be. Instead, I felt the gauzy fabric of a thin white night dress. I scowled at Benny.

"Explain now before I punch your teeth out."

He released a contented sigh. "If you have the energy to flirt with me, you must be feeling better."

I gritted my teeth, and he laughed. "Okay, okay, calm down. You're at the home of Viscount Delois. His guards saw what happened to your ship and went to see if you needed help. It seems they got a little carried away. They are a bit terrifying, even to me."

"My crew?"

"They are also resting."

I propped myself up on my elbow and assessed my body for injuries. Besides the grogginess, I felt fine. I glared at him again.

"Did you change me?" I sniffed. "And bathe me?"

He smirked. "If I said yes?"

"I'd kill you here and now."

"You have no weapons. What would you do, strangle me?" He leaned closer. "Because I think I'd be into it."

"Ugh, gross. Move." I tried to swing my legs over the edge of the bed to stand, but they wouldn't cooperate. He put his hands on them and gently pushed me back down. I tried to jerk away from his touch but didn't have the strength.

"You shouldn't move yet. The sedation will wear off in a few minutes," he said. "I don't touch unconscious women. A maid tended to you."

I relaxed onto my back again. "Who is this viscount?"

"A very old, extravagant enchanted creature. He owns the island. Though he doesn't belong to any sort of nobility. I'm not sure why he calls himself a viscount. He might as well consider himself a king."

"What kind of creature?"

He grimaced. "The bloody kind." I tensed, and he added, "Don't worry, he's not going to hurt you. They live off blood from willing humans in exchange for sharing their own, which can extend a person's life. It's a mutually beneficial arrangement. People travel here to offer themselves to him in exchange for a long, comfortable life of luxury."

"How have I never heard of this before?"

"Those who come never leave. They present themselves to the viscount and if they are chosen, they get to stay. It's competitive, so unless they told someone where they were going and why, who would know?"

"If they aren't chosen?"

"I didn't ask. Frankly, I'd rather not know."

I eyed him warily. "Why are you here?"

He gave me a playful smile. "That will be revealed shortly." He stood and walked to the door. "There's a change of clothes in the wardrobe. Dinner is in twenty minutes."

"My daggers?" I asked, already knowing the answer.

He *tsked*. "It's rude to bring weapons to the dinner table." He opened the door but paused and added, "I wouldn't escape if I were you. He has information that you're going to want to hear."

When the door closed and his footsteps retreated, I sat up and wiggled my toes. I was already feeling stronger than I had a moment ago.

The wooden wardrobe was filled with simple dresses that were approximately my size. I guessed they belonged to the human inhabitants. I cringed at the lace and velvet. Matching heels lined the bottom. A dress and heels would make it difficult to fight, which I suspected was intentional.

I chose a black velvet dress that was tight around my chest but offered sufficient movement around my legs. The deep slit would be beneficial in case I needed to tie it up. Each dress had an unfortunately low neckline, and I decided that the viscount was a creep. It skimmed the top of my breasts and my scar was completely exposed. The shoes I chose didn't match but had the shortest heel. I changed quickly, then searched the room for anything I could use as a weapon.

The lantern was glass. I could break it and use the shards, but concealing and using it without slicing my skin would be difficult.

I lowered myself to the floor and checked under the bed. The wooden frame was old, and a piece was chipped. I wiggled my nail into the seam and forced it apart. The crack split further, and when I gave it a firm tug, a sharp piece about six inches long broke off in my hand.

Tearing off a strip of thin fabric from the nightdress, I wrapped it around the base of the wooden shard as a handle, then tied the makeshift stake to my upper thigh. It was far enough above the slit to not be seen, but low enough that I could quickly grab it.

There were no guards outside my door. The small room I'd slept in was a closet compared to the rest of the house. The wide stone hallways were spotted with sconces and draped in deep red velvet fabric. My heels tapped against the marble floors, and I focused on keeping my balance. The last time I wore anything other than boots was almost a decade ago.

The hum of conversation and clinking dinnerware drifted up a grand staircase as I descended. My mouth watered at the savory smells that accompanied the sounds. I followed it to a large open doorway.

The walls of the massive dining room were painted that same deep red color. A crystal chandelier dangled above a long wooden dining table that had enough seats for thirty people. Human servers dressed in crisp white shirts and black pants were lighting the tall candle sticks and draping the table with meats, cheeses, fruits, and bread.

Tall pale gray creatures stood with their backs against the wall. Their thin arms hung to their knees. Their thin faces, which barely resembled a human's, had large eyes with lids that closed vertically and wide mouths that flashed razor-sharp teeth. Their terrifying features made the elegant clothing they wore seem ridiculous.

Another decorated divinum, maybe the viscount, sat in a large ornate chair at the head of the table. Velo, Benny, and Jerma were seated on the left side, while Indigo sat on the right. Jerma and Indigo wore dresses similar to mine. Velo and Benny sported ridiculous flowy shirts and vests in the same fashion nobles wore.

Benny lounged in his chair and sipped amber liquid from a short glass. There was no water to be found. The only drink option was wine, which possibly meant that the bottles were spiked with something.

Everyone turned to me when I entered. My gaze flicked over my people. Their faces were tense, but they appeared unharmed. Kendra was missing, and I swallowed a rush of panic.

The viscount beamed and stood, spreading out his long arms. It was hard to tell if divinum had a gender, but if it did, I'd guess they were male.

"Louie Aurum." His voice was similar to the one I heard when we were captured. A chorus of high and low tones all at once. "The infamous and allusive Ghost of the Sea graces my island. Please, come sit."

He waved me over and a server pulled out the chair next to Indigo, whose fists were clenched and shaking beneath the table. Benny sat directly across from me. Once we were settled, the viscount addressed me with an eerie smile.

"Benny has told me so much about you. I'm delighted to have you as my guest. We were quite worried when we saw your ship in that storm. The weather is so unpredictable here."

There was nothing natural about that storm. I didn't have enough information about divinum to know if they could share the same ability, and I doubted a sea serpent would serve a viscount. We were on our way to the island; there was no need to force us here. My lack of understanding about divinum and how enchantment worked put us at a disadvantage.

Despite his manners, predatory danger radiated from the viscount in thick waves. Preparing myself for anything, I returned his smile and forced my shoulders to relax.

"Unpredictable, indeed. We were lucky nobody was harmed. Thank you for your hospitality. It's been a long journey."

"You look stunning in that dress," Benny said from across the table, swirling his drink and taking his time trailing his gaze over me. He was taking advantage of the opportunity to test me knowing I couldn't tell him to go fuck himself.

"How kind of you to say. I'm not used to wearing such fine clothes."

"I agree, it suits you," the viscount added, then turned his attention to the door. I followed his gaze and my stomach flipped.

Kendra stood in the doorway, fidgeting with the skirt of her thin floor-length dress. Her freckled, tanned skin stood out against the pale blue gauzy fabric. The low neckline and flowy fabric told me that she probably didn't have the same variety of options as I did. The dress would be even harder to fight in than mine.

Her eyes met mine. When she moved to sit beside me, the viscount patted the empty corner seat next to him across the table from me.

"Actually, dear, your seat is here beside me."

She forced a small smile and circled the table to sit next to him. I clenched my fists but maintained a polite expression. Ushar filed in next and glanced around the room warily before sitting in the empty seat to my left. Once he was settled, the viscount gestured to the food.

"Please, help yourselves. You must be starving," he said. We all glanced at each other. When nobody moved to fill their plates, he lowered his tone and locked eyes with me. "Eat." He was still smiling, but the threat was clear. It wasn't a request.

I filled my plate with the smallest foods available. Grapes, strawberries, cheese, and crackers. Maybe I could mitigate the effect of whatever might be in the food if I only ate a small amount.

The viscount wasn't satisfied. He roughly tore the leg from the roasted chicken and dropped it onto my plate. I forced a smile. The others followed my lead and tentatively filled their plates.

The viscount retrieved a chilled bottle of white wine from an ice bucket and poured Kendra a glass. I gripped my fork to keep myself from launching across the table to smack it from his hand. She nodded gratefully and took a dainty sip. When he turned his attention back to me, she patted her lips with the cloth napkin and spilled the wine from her mouth into the linen.

"Tell me, Captain. What brings you all the way south to my small oasis?" he asked.

"We're on our way home from an unsuccessful mission. It's embarrassing to admit, but we lost our way and turned around to find a port where we could rest and get our bearings."

I glanced at Benny and assessed his reaction to my explanation. He downed the rest of his drink, apparently uninterested in joining the conversation. He had been unrelenting in his obsession with learning my navigation secrets. Me getting lost would've been a huge deal to him. But his lack of interest and presence here on the island confirmed my suspicions.

He knows about the Sands and the totem.

"There's no need to be embarrassed. It happens to the best of sailors. Yet another reason why I like to keep my feet firmly planted on land," the viscount said, taking a sip of red liquid from his glass, which appeared to be blood.

"I completely understand. Sailing is not for everyone."

"Indeed. What was the job that brought you here? Searching for anything interesting?"

"Not at all, I'm afraid. We were tasked with retrieving a collection of enchanted stones, but it turned out to be a false lead."

"That's unfortunate, though it works to my benefit. I'm lucky I get to dine with a pirate such as yourself."

I smiled. "That's generous of you to say. How do you both know each other?" I asked, nodding to Benny.

The viscount leaned back in his chair and tapped his glass with a sharp nail. "We met recently. He appeared here only a few days ago."

"What a coincidence," I feigned awe. "I suppose your crew didn't want to join us?" I asked Benny.

"My ship suffered some damage, so they're fixing it. Viscount Delois was generous enough to let us stay until the repairs are complete and provide the materials we need," he replied.

Liar.

"How kind of him."

"It's no trouble at all. I'm thankful I get to share my table with travelers such as yourselves. I'm sure you have many interesting stories to tell," the viscount said.

The rest of the group picked at their food in silence, taking only small bites and subtly disposing of the chewed food into their napkins. The viscount's eyes flicked to my untouched food.

"Our lifestyle certainly isn't boring," I replied.

"No, I'd think not. You must have learned so much during your travels."

"Nothing of importance."

"Don't be modest. Pirates have more knowledge of the world's secrets than any academic could hope to learn."

That familiar pressure of warning spread across my neck and shoulders. I could sense the transition. The wooden shard that was secured to my leg cut into my skin with every small movement. I let my hand fall into my lap, prepared to grab it from under my dress if needed.

"It's the truth. The secrets you speak of are of no interest to me."

The viscount watched me with rapt fascination. I suppressed

a shiver. He was by far the creepiest thing I'd ever seen.

"Would you all like fresh napkins?" he asked, and everyone froze. He let out a bark of laughter. "I can assure you, the food is not poisoned. We have no need for that."

Though it sounded like an off-handed thing to say, the message was clear. If they wanted to kill us, they would. Velo's eyes met mine from across the table. We had no choice. The viscount waited while each of us took a bite of food. I chewed the chicken for as long as I reasonably could, but when he wouldn't look away, I was forced to swallow it.

He refilled Kendra's cup and leaned closer to her. "Drink it."

Divinum or not, this *thing* must have a death wish. I clenched my jaw so tight that I could've broken a tooth.

"Since we're on the topic," the viscount continued, "I've been struggling with something and I'm hopeful you can help."

My hand inched closer to the makeshift dagger.

"I can certainly try."

He nodded to one of the guards, and they stepped through the door behind me that the servers had used. He returned a moment later and rolled a cart into the room.

On top sat a wooden totem about three feet tall. Intricate lines, dots, and curves decorated its smooth surface.

"I assume you know what this is?" the viscount asked.

"I don't, but I have a feeling you're going to tell me."

Benny leaned forward with a sly smile.

"Come now, Louie," he said. "We've known each other a long time. I know this pretense is killing you."

I mirrored him and leaned forward. My breasts swelled against the tight fabric and Benny's eyes flicked downward. "You're correct. Let's get to the point, shall we?" I faced the viscount. "How can I help you with a stump?"

"This *stump* has been in my collection for a century. I enjoyed it for its uniqueness and figured it was left by the ancient inhabitants of this island. It wasn't until Benny arrived that I learned of its purpose. I must say, I'm eager to learn more."

I didn't notice Kendra's hand clenching the steak knife until the viscount snatched her wrist and gripped it tight. She startled and tried to pull away, but his hold was too strong.

"That would be a very bad idea, my dear." His voice rumbled. She froze and my crew held their breath. My fingers twitched, ready to grab the wooden shard.

"You want the Sands of Time but can't decipher the totem." I interrupted. Reluctantly, he released Kendra and returned to the conversation.

"Benny was right—you aren't one for pretense."

"I'm sorry to disappoint, but I don't know any more than you. I wasn't even aware that anyone lived here, let alone someone who had the totem. If your guards hadn't found us wandering the woods, we would still be searching in the dark."

The viscount frowned. "That's not the answer I was hoping for."

Shit.

Honesty was the wrong move. I needed to give them a reason to keep us alive.

"Maybe I can help," Velo said. He stood and walked carefully to the statue behind me. The guards tensed.

Velo leaned toward the statue.

"That's close enough," the viscount warned.

"This looks like the olde language," he said, pointing to the markings that framed the dots in the middle. "I'm a bit rusty, but I can make out a few words."

He lowered himself to be level with the totem and translated, "'Flames in ice, the dead deep under, rise and fall of the red sea.' There are a few characters I'm not familiar with, but if you give us a little time, I can work on it."

This was a huge risk. The viscount could be old enough to

know the olde language. My pulse quickened, but I kept my body still.

If anyone could get us out of this situation, it was Velo.

He straightened and faced the viscount, addressing him with the same posture and tone he'd used when he was captain. He exuded an easy, yet powerful authority that the other person would obey without realizing that he was in control. No matter how much I practiced, I was nowhere near as smooth as him.

"We all have a shared goal," he continued. "We want the Sands, but we aren't the only ones. The king has joined the hunt. We encountered his commander on the way here. He has us outnumbered. We're better off working together to find the Sands before he does. However, I'm not so naïve to think you'd share the treasure. So here's what I propose," he said as he returned to his chair and leaned back. "Let's make a deal. We work together on finding the treasure, and the crew that makes it out alive keeps it."

Benny's eyes lit up. There wasn't a bet that he wouldn't accept, and Velo knew it.

"I like it. Viscount?"

Our host leaned back and took a leisurely sip of his drink. My crew held their breath. Finally, he smiled and set his glass down.

"Agreed."

My shoulders relaxed. There was no way the viscount planned on letting us leave the island alive, but Velo had bought us some time with his charade. If it even was a charade. He knew more about divinum than he'd previously let on. Maybe he really could read the olde language.

The viscount stood and said, "We need to move quickly if the king is searching as well. You have until tomorrow evening. Please finish your meal. I'm rather hungry myself, so please excuse me." He breezed from the room, passing behind me. I shivered, and when he was gone, the crew finally released a collective sigh.

I stood and the rest of the group followed. Without acknowledging Benny, I led them from the room. As we reached the door, one of the guards grabbed Kendra's wrist.

"You've been summoned to join the viscount and his other guests," he said with that same strange voice.

I stepped between them, but the divinum didn't let go.

"Take your hand off her," I said.

"Back down, human, or I'll tear out the throats of everyone in this room," he growled.

"All this tension for no reason." Benny stepped forward and put his hand on the divinum's arm. "I'm sure this beautiful woman will go willingly. Isn't that right?"

Kendra lowered her eyes but nodded. "Of course."

The divinum released her and threw me a glare. He led Kendra toward the door the viscount left through. Benny put his hands on my shoulders to turn me away, but right before Kendra crossed through the door's threshold, she glanced at me with the smallest of smiles. Turning her head, the pin that held her hair glinted in the candlelight.

The same hairpin dagger she wore at Port Roche.

She's playing meek. She knows what she's doing.

Playing different roles was Kendra's specialty. She could lie like silk. If anyone could survive with a group of bloodthirsty divinum, it was her. I told myself this over and over again as Benny led me back to my room.

She would survive. I knew that for certain. It was what she'd have to do to survive that made my clenched fists shake.

Each of us split up to return to our rooms. Velo and I shared a look. He clenched the hand by his side and flicked two fingers, then disappeared down another hallway.

He would find me in twenty minutes.

When Benny and I reached my room, I opened the door and turned to stop him from following me inside. The movement made the room spin, and I gripped the door frame to steady myself.

"Are you all right?" Benny asked.

"I'm fine. You can leave now."

I tried to shut the door, but he stopped it with his boot.

"Actually, there are a few things we still need to discuss."

My knees buckled and I slumped against him. He caught me and held me upright. I tried to push away, but my strength was fading.

He shook his head and scooped me into his arms. "Shouldn't have eaten the food."

I struggled in his arms. "Put me down, you creepy motherfucker."

"I love it when you talk dirty." He smirked and laid me on the bed. The ceiling spun, and my skin dampened with sweat.

"What was in it?" My words slurred together.

"Probably a sedative to keep you from running away. But you already knew that."

He propped a knee up onto the bed and swung himself on top of me. I twisted and bucked, but he pinned me with his weight. His hands snaked around my wrists. I struggled uselessly against his tight hold.

"Get off me right the fuck now," I warned, but the words lacked the force I intended.

"No, I don't think I will. Seeing you like this, completely vulnerable, is too good of an opportunity to pass up."

"I thought taking advantage of women was beneath you." Moving my mouth was getting harder. Panic fluttered in my chest.

"I'm hurt you would even suggest that, though I can see why you would be confused." He gave me his signature wicked smile. "You have information I want, and I'm not leaving until you give it to me."

Chapter Twenty-Six

My body was weak, but my mind was clear.

The wooden shard dug into my leg under Benny's weight. I wouldn't be able to grab it with him on top of me.

The crew ate the food, too. The others should be safe in their rooms, but Kendra was at the mercy of the viscount. The thought turned my blood to ice. She needed help, and there wasn't a damn thing I could do about it.

I was completely at Benny's mercy.

Holding both of my wrists in one hand, he pulled a thin rope from his pocket and tied them to the slats of the wooden headboard. When the knots were secure, he released me and leaned back.

Still straddling me, he pulled something from another pocket. It was an elegant ear wrap that was popular among the nobles. It was curved and made of silver wire, decorated with small red gemstones.

Benny hooked it around his ear.

"Let's get started, shall we?" His hand wrapped around my throat, holding it firmly, but not enough to choke me. "I'm going to ask you some questions, and you are going to answer them honestly." He tapped the ear wrap with a smirk.

Shit.

A truth wearable.

These enchanted items made it impossible for the person being questioned to get away with a lie. If they told a lie, the item would hum, but it didn't force the person to answer honestly unless skin-to-skin contact was made. With Benny's hand around my throat, I'd be forced to answer any questions he asked honestly. I only hoped that he didn't ask the right questions.

"Getting desperate, are we?" I mocked, but my heart slammed against my ribs. Kendra would be weaker than me by now. She'd be lucky if she could even talk. I had to find her. "How about we make a deal?"

He arched a brow. "What sort of deal?"

"A trade. I'll tell you whatever you want to know, if you save the girl the viscount took."

Proposing this was a huge risk. I'd revealed a weakness that Benny would try to exploit, but I didn't care.

"Why would I do that when I can get the information I want right now? Besides"—he lowered his face to mine—"I know better than to make deals with pirates."

I snapped my teeth, aiming for his nose. He lurched backward and laughed.

"Fine. You want information, but you also want the Sands, right? I'll give it to you." I tried to sound calm, but my voice pitched with desperation.

When the ear wrap didn't hum, his eyes widened. "Does that mean you know where it is?"

"No, but you know if anyone can find it, it's me. I'll give up the hunt. You can have it."

"I must admit, I'm a bit jealous you'd give up the Sands for a woman."

"Take it or leave it, Benny. This is the only time I'll make you an offer like this."

He took his time turning it over in his head, still holding my neck. My dread worsened with every second that passed. Giving

Benny the Sands could be disastrous, but I'd do it in a heartbeat if it meant I could save Kendra.

Finally, he said, "I decline your offer."

I thrashed against him again, but it was useless. "Get off me!" I slurred. I could barely talk, let alone wrestle him off me. My eyes burned, and I bit my lip.

"I'll get the Sands without you. I suggest you worry about yourself. Now, back to my questions." He tightened his grip. "Let's start with that girl since you've got me feeling jealous. You seem to care about her. What is she to you?"

"She's part of my crew."

"Do you have feelings for her?"

"Like I said, she's part of my crew. I need to keep her safe." At least I could tell half-truths.

"Do you love her?"

My lips formed the word no, but instead, I said, "Yes." I gasped and pressed my lips together. I tried to say no again, but the word wouldn't come.

Benny shook his head with an amused smirk. "The Ghost of the Sea has a beating heart."

"Did you buy this thing so you could ask me stupid questions?"

"Do you regret sleeping with me?"

I didn't need the truth wearable to answer this one. "Yep, absolutely."

"Did you enjoy sleeping with me?"

"No."

"Did it feel good?"

I pinched my lips tight to trap the truth. He asked again.

"Answer the question. Did having sex with me feel good?"

I frowned and rolled my eyes. "Yes, okay? Happy?"

He let out a loud laugh. "I knew it! You certainly seemed to be enjoying yourself when my head was between your gorgeous legs."

"Ask me if I think you're a creep. Please, ask me."

"If I'm such a creep, then why did you let me touch you?"

"Why do you care so much?" I asked. He squeezed tighter. "I wanted to feel good, and you were there. We got carried away."

"You used me for my body."

"You offered."

He chuckled again. "That's true. But I'm not naïve enough to think you'll let me do it again."

"Correct."

"Why did you kill the commander's father?"

I froze.

The question was a blow to my gut. The room, which hadn't stopped spinning, stilled for a moment. Air caught in my lungs.

The saw cutting bone, back and forth . . .

The body, so heavy . . .

Blood in my mouth, in my eyes . . .

"Don't ask me that question," I slurred weakly. The answer was already building. I clenched every muscle to stop the words from rising. He watched me closely.

Just as I parted my lips to reply, he said, "I rescind the question. Frankly, I don't care."

I released the breath I'd been holding, and the words evaporated before they could be spoken. He'd taken pity on me. A small act of kindness from a vain, heartless man.

We were silent for a few moments. My thundering heart slowed, and the rushing sound in my ears faded.

"Do you know what the totem says?" he asked.

"No."

"Was your quartermaster honest earlier about what it said?"

"I don't know."

Benny frowned.

"Were you lying when you said you don't know any more than me about the Sands' location?"

"No."

"Does anyone on your crew have more information about the Sands?"

"Not that I know of."

His frown deepened. "To be clear, there's nothing more you can tell me about the Sands?"

"You're driving me crazy. Yes, okay? I have no new information to give you about the Sands."

He removed his hand from my throat and leaned back. I glared at him while he stroked his chin. "I thought you would be more helpful."

"Sorry to disappoint."

His hand returned to my throat. "How do you navigate your ship?"

My heart skipped. I'd have to stay as close to the truth as possible.

"I have a helmsman."

"How does he navigate?"

"I assume the same way yours does."

Frustration creased his face and he squeezed harder, cutting off some air. "Do you use any enchanted items to help you navigate?"

"No."

"Maps?"

"Yes." I relaxed beneath him and gave him a lazy smile. I needed to steer him away from these questions before he got too specific. "Can't you accept that I'm just better than you?"

He squeezed tighter, sealing my throat. I choked and struggled. Pressure built in my face and pressed against my eyes until finally, he relaxed, opening my airways a fraction. I sucked air in through the tightness.

"Do you have a secret way that you navigate?"

A different kind of pressure built in my lungs, pushing my answer out against my will.

"Yes," I gasped.

A triumphant smile split his face.

"What is your secret to navigating at night?"

I lifted my head, pressing my throat into his grip to choke myself, trapping my response. He swore and pulled his hand away. I gasped and coughed.

He grabbed my jaw and forced me to look at him. His eyes were wild now. "What will it take to make you cooperate? Should I stop being a gentleman?" He dug his fingers into my skin. "I'm going to ask you again. What is your secret to navigating at night?"

I pressed my lips together, but the strength of the truth wearable was too strong. This was it. There was no hiding it now. With every minute that passed, Kendra was in danger. He'd keep questioning me until I gave him the truth, and this needed to end. My secret wasn't worth her life.

"The stars," I answered through clenched teeth.

"How?"

"I track them."

He leaned closer. "How?"

I jerked my chin out of his grip. He brought his free hand across my cheek with a loud clap. My head twisted to the side from the force of the slap and a sharp pain stung my cheek.

"How, Louie?!" he shouted.

I gave in to the pressure and released the truth.

"A map. I made a map in my head."

"You found a pattern." His face brightened. He didn't phrase it as a question, so I didn't have to answer, but it was already too late. He knew. "You're going to draw this map for me."

"Is that a question?"

"It's an offer. Draw the map for me and I'll save that girl."

Hope sparked for a brief moment before I stomped it out. There was no way he'd risk the viscount's ire to help her.

"I know better than to make deals with pirates," I threw his words back at him.

"I could bring her here when they're done with her. I could cut off her fingers one by one until you give in to me."

"She'd kill you before you got the chance."

He scoffed and released me. "In her state? I doubt she'll be doing much killing tonight." He rolled off me and stood. "I like you, Louie. That's why I've been nice to you. But my patience has worn thin, and our time is short. You're going to draw that map for me, or I'll tear that girl apart and make you watch."

Chapter Twenty-Seven

Benny didn't untie me. Velo never came. I knew nothing about what happened to Kendra.

Once I had my strength back, I tried to break the headboard, but it wouldn't budge. The rope was too tight and thin to wiggle out of. Benny was a sailor. He knew his knots.

I lay there for hours, imagining all the sick things that could be happening to Kendra. Horrible images circled in my mind. I couldn't make it stop. It had been fifteen years since I'd felt this helpless. The only thing I could do was distract myself.

Benny found out about the Sands and knew to come here to look for the totem. Someone was feeding him information. We'd only docked twice since we left, and while I didn't have eyes on my crew, I was fairly certain they'd distracted themselves with other things. I doubted they would risk our chances of reaching the treasure first by revealing the details of our hunt.

I stared at the ceiling and ran through the timeline of events.

I didn't share our first location until after we shipped off from Gallow Harbor, which meant nobody from my crew could've revealed where we were going. It's possible Nathaniel found out that we were headed to Port Roche from the king.

Lyonel told Nathaniel where we were headed at Port Roche,

but there was no way he could've overheard my conversation with Vincent.

Our next stop was Lincoln Harbor. Someone from my crew might have told someone about our experience with the sea serpent and our upcoming trip to the Isle of Night. It was an impressive tale.

One of Benny's contacts could've reported that information to him. If they found out shortly after we arrived at Lincoln Harbor, he would've had a whole day on us. Maybe less since he'd have to sail along the coast. It's unlikely he could've won over the viscount in that time. The fact that his crew was missing was also concerning.

The warning from before whispered in my mind.

"Do not tell him."

Velo knew more about divinum than I thought. He was clearly hiding something from me, but he hated Benny. Why would he feed him information when we were at an advantage? Especially with my star maps? What could he gain from that?

Unless he knew something I didn't.

I couldn't dismiss him as a suspect, but the possibility that Velo could've double-crossed me didn't ring true. Or maybe I was in denial.

Benny knew we were coming here. Someone caused that storm to force us on shore. I didn't have enough information about our host to know if he was capable of creating a storm like that. As far as I knew, the only creature that could was a sea serpent. Unless they were controlling one, which was highly unlikely given the serpent's power and size, they must have an item or artifact. One that might be enchanted with a serpent's blood.

I remembered the serpent's words when I asked about its wounds.

"I have you humans to thank for this."

Realization dawned, and I closed my eyes.

Benny wounded the sea serpent and took its blood.

That still didn't explain how Benny knew about the totem. It was hard to imagine Benny being in a position to demand information from the serpent. It was even harder to believe that he was able to inflict that sort of damage and that the divinum died from a few gouges. The serpent's power was unlike anything I'd ever witnessed and enchanted creatures were rumored to be extremely difficult to kill.

The serpent's grief that pulsed through the mental bond when it had to let its eggs go was devastating. It mourned not for itself, but also its children, knowing it would never see them again and terrified that they wouldn't survive.

All because of Benny.

I squeezed my eyes shut and focused on smothering the deep sorrow left behind by the mourning divinum. I let Benny live because he never proved to be a serious threat to me. He even said it the night we slept together. I only killed when necessary. I wasn't interested in eliminating every other pirate unless I needed to.

But he'd gone too far. By killing the serpent and trapping me here while Kendra suffered, he sealed his fate.

Benny would die by my hand.

The creak of the door startled me, and Velo slipped inside. He'd removed his vest but still wore the same clothes he had at dinner.

"Finally," I said.

"Damn, he got you good." He rushed to the bed and worked on undoing the knots.

"There's a dagger strapped to my right leg."

He lifted the dress, completely unfazed by my underwear, and untied the wooden shard. Slicing into the rope, he said, "I tried to come, but they drugged the food. It took a while for it to wear off."

"I know. It's okay."

The rope snapped and I sat up, rubbing my raw wrists. "We need to find Kendra." I swung my legs over the side to stand up, but he held up a hand to stop me.

"Not without a plan. I already scoped it out. There's about twelve of them, plus the guards."

"What are these divinum?" I asked, and he looked away. "Velo, I know you know. You need to be honest with me. What are they?"

He sighed. "Nox domini. Their blood is powerful enough to slow the aging process for a human. They can knock someone unconscious by touching them, which is how they brought us here."

"How do we kill them?"

"There's only two ways that I know of. Sunlight, or blood from another divinum. Their blood is poison to them. If blood from one enters the body of another, they'll rot from the inside out."

"Is that the case for all divinum?"

Velo hesitated. I gave him a flat look, and he said, "Yes."

"I think Benny killed the sea serpent and stole its blood. He's likely the one that caused the storm. If we can find the blood and some weapons, we can coat our blades with it."

Velo smiled and arched an eyebrow. "Always thinking on your feet. You've impressed me yet again."

"Don't be too impressed. We're going to have a conversation when this is over about what you've been keeping from me."

His smile fell, and he nodded.

"I need to find Kendra. Gather the crew. Tell them the plan, and find the blood and weapons. We'll join you as soon as we can."

He nodded. "Go through the door they brought the totem through. There's another door at the end of the hallway. I peeked through it, but I didn't see Kendra."

I swore and rubbed my face roughly. "I'll start there and see what I can find out." When I rushed toward the door, Velo grabbed my arm.

"You're not seriously going in there with a piece of wood."

"Maybe this can't kill them, but I bet a stake to the groin would slow them down."

"I suppose I can't convince you to wait for the crew."

"You know me so well."

He sighed. "Be careful."

We parted ways, agreeing to regroup here once we completed our tasks.

The halls were eerily quiet, which made me grateful that I'd opted to go barefoot rather than alert the guards with click-clacking heels. I made it to the stairs without seeing any guards. The viscount must have been confident that we wouldn't try to escape if he left us unguarded. He'd underestimated me, which was simultaneously fortuitous and insulting.

I tiptoed down the main staircase and followed the hallway to the dining room. I peered around the doorway, but it was empty. Muffled, faint chatter came through the same door that Velo mentioned.

I opened it carefully, revealing a dark, candlelit hallway that continued to my left. The voices were louder now. There were a few doors, but the one at the end of the hallway was larger and more ornate than the rest.

I approached it and turned the door knob carefully. It moved without a sound. Even if it had, I doubted anyone would've heard it over the raucous conversations and laughter. Through a small crack, I scanned the massive room on the other side.

Every surface was made of white marble. The walls stretched several floors high, and the domed glass ceiling revealed a dark, starless sky. The flickering light from the sconces and lanterns cast everything in a warm, sensual glow. Velvet furniture was scattered around the room, draped with vacant-eyed naked humans and lounging nox domini. Some were feasting on their humans, while others boisterously played cards at a table at the far end of the room. I scanned the faces of the humans, but Kendra was nowhere to be found.

Benny was predictably playing cards and swayed in his seat. The idiot got too drunk and distracted to make good on his threat.

The viscount sat next to him and was busy entertaining his guests with a loud story to notice much else.

Two divinum were sparring, striking and wrestling one another with impressive speed. I leaned over to get a better view of the left side of the room and nearly gasped. Sitting there on a pedestal was the totem, completely unguarded.

It wasn't clear if we needed to take the totem with us or if the carved message had the information we needed. I should've asked Velo if he really could read the olde language. I took a moment to try to memorize the inscription, but it was too far away to see the characters that framed the dots in the middle.

Just as I was about to give up, I saw it.

Some of the dots were bigger than others.

I traced the shapes in my mind again and confirmed my theory. There was no doubt about it.

They weren't dots. They were stars in the shape of my favorite goat, Bonny, turned on her side. The bigger dots were the brighter stars.

I had a map to the Sands of Time.

Chapter Twenty-Eight

It wasn't a direct map, but the angle of the constellation meant that we'd need to continue south. It wasn't everything, but it was a start. I smiled triumphantly and gently closed the door.

A small tap on my shoulder made me jump and I spun around, swinging my wooden dagger. Kendra ducked and grabbed my wrist.

"Shh!" she hissed, then released me.

My body sagged in relief. I folded her tightly in my arms and pressed my face into her hair.

She's alive. She's alive. She's alive.

She stiffened, then pushed me away. "We have to go!" she mouthed.

I nodded and blinked away tears. We lifted our skirts and rushed silently through the hallway, back through the dining room, and up to my room, where Velo and the crew were waiting. Everyone appeared unharmed.

"That was fast," I said as we approached.

Velo handed me my belt, which still held my daggers, and I strapped it to my waist. It looked ridiculous against the black velvet dress.

"I don't suppose you found our clothes?"

"No. But I did find these." He pulled three glass vials from his pocket. They were several inches tall and filled with a thick, black liquid. "He had them hidden under his mattress." Velo rolled his eyes.

Benny had something valuable and deadly to divinum, yet he hid it in such an obvious place. He was either extremely confident that they wouldn't find it or a lazy idiot. My guess was both.

"Have you seen any guards? Or Benny's crew?" I asked. Indigo shook her head.

"None. The windows are all locked, and the glass is unbreakable. We've tried everything, except the front door," she said. I frowned.

"Something's not right. The viscount might be cocky, but he's not stupid. He wouldn't leave us unguarded unless he was confident we wouldn't escape."

"Maybe the doors are secured with an alert lock item," Ushar said.

If that were true, once we touched the doorknob, it would release an ear-shattering scream. The nox domini would be on us in a minute, or less.

"You might be right. Let's finish this, then check. We should be able to see it from the stairs."

The crew nodded and worked on lathering the blood onto the weapons. I pulled Kendra aside, and she turned her head away from me.

"Are you hurt? What happened?" I asked.

"Nothing happened. They all got drunk on blood, and I slipped out without them noticing."

She wouldn't meet my eyes.

"Look at me," I said.

She tried to step around me. "We don't have time for this."

I moved to block her and when she tried again, I grabbed her face in my hands and forced her to look at me. She was pretending to be okay, but the tension in her jaw told me otherwise.

A red spot on the left side of her neck caught my eye. I tilted her head and saw what she was trying to hide. A curved row of puncture marks coated in dried blood. She stepped back and covered the mark with her hand.

I grabbed both of her wrists and turned them, confirming my fears. The same marks spotted the underside of her forearms, trailing along her veins.

My vision darkened at the edges, and my hands were trembling when she pulled away from me.

The fury was blinding. It felt as though I would combust and drown the manor in flames.

That vile creature drank her blood.

He touched her.

Put his lips on her.

He and his guests *fed on her*.

I was vibrating with cold, murderous rage.

"Louie," she said, but I couldn't hear her clearly through the rushing in my ears.

I spun and collected three daggers that were already coated in the serpent's blood. I snatched one of the vials from Velo's hands. He gave me a strange look while I coated my fists with the viscous liquid.

Just in case I got the chance to rip out his tongue.

Chapter Twenty-Nine

"Louie, don't!" Kendra shouted, but I was already halfway down the hall. She rushed to catch up, but her dress slowed her down.

I took the stairs two at a time, not bothering to be quiet. She kicked off her heels and stumbled after me. It only took me a few moments to reach the door to the viscount's lair.

"Don't!" she called again, but she was too late.

I kicked the door open, and it splintered against the marble wall on the other side. Every human and nox domini silenced and turned to me. Benny paled when he saw the coated daggers in my hands. A third one was hooked on my belt as a backup.

The viscount's eyes widened, then he fixed his face and stood.

"Louie, you're awake! Please join us."

I lunged at the nearest nox domini and slit his throat before the viscount could say another word.

Black blood sprayed the white marble wall and floor. His hand wrapped around the wound to stop the bleeding. He dropped to his knees and choked on his blood. I watched a black web of poison spread from the wound.

He twitched once, twice, then collapsed to the floor. Dead.

Everyone in the room was still and silent. The viscount's

smile froze on his face.

I pointed the blade at him.

His lips curled into a snarl, and he shouted, "Guards!"

Chaos erupted. Nox domini bared their teeth and charged at me. Rushed footsteps from my crew barreled into the room. The humans screamed and ran for a door on the far wall. The viscount's guards poured in from another door on the right side of the room.

The nearest nox domini lunged at me. I ducked and shoved my blade upward, slicing into his stomach. He screeched, and blood poured over my arms and face. I shoved the body off me and stood.

My crew launched into battle. I wiped the blood from my eyes and glanced behind me. Kendra was backed up against a wall with only her hairpin dagger. I pulled the extra dagger from my belt and slid it to her. A nox domini weaved through the crowd toward her. She dove to the side, rolled beneath him, and grabbed the dagger.

I returned to the chaos in front of me just in time to dodge a punch from one of the guards. Two more rushed toward me. I rolled backward and spun my leg underneath one of them, knocking him to the ground. The other two reached for me at the same time.

I tried to roll again, but the one on the ground gripped the skirt of my dress. Another grabbed my braids and yanked them upward. Pain sparked over my scalp. The third wrapped his cold hands around my throat.

Jerma appeared behind him and speared a long dagger through his stomach. Kendra slid behind the nox domini that held my hair and sliced his throat. He screeched and released me. Free from his grip, I dropped to the ground and buried my dagger into the back of the one that held my skirt.

Kendra helped me stand. Jerma was already wrestling with another. Across the room, the viscount was hiding behind one of the guards, making a run for one of the exits.

I charged, dodging a guard and slicing the chest of another.

The viscount was almost at the door. I arched my arm and flung the dagger at him. It sailed across the room and sank into his arm. He screamed and stumbled backward.

Another knife whizzed past me and lodged into the eye of the guard who was protecting him. Kendra rushed to my side, and we bound toward the injured viscount.

He fell to the ground and yanked the dagger out of his arm.

I reached him first and slammed my foot across his head. His face smashed against the hard marble floor. The blade flew from his hand and clattered to the ground. Pain shot through my ankle and up my leg. Ignoring it, I launched on top of him, pinning him to the floor.

The black veins of poison were already spreading up his neck. He growled at me, and I punched him with my blood-coated fist. More poison spread from the split skin on his cheek and he shrieked. I picked up the dagger and grabbed his straggly hair, tugging his head backward.

"You thought you could touch her and keep your life?" My voice was low and laced with murderous rage. "Not my crew." I plunged the blade into his chest. It scraped his ribs, and he released a demented scream. "Not her." I stabbed again, burying the dagger to the hilt.

The poisonous blood spread to the rest of his body. He thrashed and shrieked. When he finally went still, his skin loosened and his large eyes bulged. I stood and watched him melt at my feet.

Once I was certain he was dead, I turned away from the steaming pile of liquid flesh. Kendra was behind me, staring blankly at the body. Her blue dress was soaked in black. I wiped the blade on my skirt.

"Sorry. I should've let you kill him," I said.

The fight was settling around us. Velo pulled his knife from the back of a twitching nox domini. Most of the guards had come apart the same way the viscount had. The ones that remained were writhing on the floor.

Indigo spit on one, and Ushar stomped the head of another.

A soft light fell across the carnage from the glass ceiling. The darkness was fading, unveiling the pale blue glow of dawn. The viscount must've maintained the illusion of night. Now that he was dead, the island would need a new name.

Remembering the other man I'd sworn to slaughter, I searched for Benny but he was not among the bodies. He must've escaped during the fight. The totem was also missing from the pedestal.

Uncertain whether any nox domini remained in the manor, we sprinted from the bloody room toward the front door. An alert lock was wrapped around the handles, confirming Ushar's theory.

I slammed the back of my blade against the enchanted item and it shattered, releasing a shrill ear-piercing scream. I flinched and tossed the pieces off the doorknob, shoving it open.

We squinted in the morning light and took off into the woods without looking back. Without the enchantment, the island came to life. Birds chirped, and leaves rustled in the gentle breeze.

Mixed with the fresh sea air was the unmistakable smell of smoke.

A thick plume rose above the trees.

"No, no, no!" I picked up speed and weaved through the damp forest. My legs burned, and when I finally burst through the forest's edge, my ship was resting exactly where I left it.

Completely devoured by flames.

My crew. My ship.

But what concerned me more than the wreckage was the man walking toward us, and the three massive navy ships looming behind him.

Chapter Thirty

I spun around. "All of you hide!" When the crew didn't move, I shoved Velo into the trees. "Go!"

The rest followed, hesitant at first. They slipped into the forest's shadows and disappeared. Kendra wouldn't budge. I shoved her harder. "Go!" I hissed. She shook her head with a resolute expression. I pushed again, and she shoved me back.

"I'm not leaving you!" she said.

I turned back to my least favorite person. It was too late. He was here, and he'd seen her.

Nathaniel walked toward me in full uniform. Ten knights trailed behind him. Four had arrows locked on us, while six raised their swords. I stood tall and dug my heels into the sand. My heart thumped wildly against my ribs. The clenched fist that gripped my dagger was vibrating.

We could run, but he was too close. The archers would shoot us down before we made it to the trees. We were also landlocked without a ship. Nathaniel would tear this island apart to find us.

He stopped about ten feet away and pointed his sword at me.

"Drop it," he demanded.

I released the dagger, and it fell onto the sand with a muted *thump*. He stepped closer, and I resisted the intense urge to run. He sported a triumphant smile and pulled shackles from his belt. He stopped and towered over me. The breeze carried his scent. Salt and leather. I suppressed a wave of nausea.

Kendra stepped between us and faced Nathaniel.

"Back up," she warned.

He frowned and flicked his head at one of the men. They stepped forward with a pair of shackles. Kendra gripped her dagger tightly.

"Don't," I said to her. There was an unmistakable tremor in my voice. He could kill her right in front of me, and there was nothing I could do about it. It was a nightmare I'd never considered. One I knew I'd never recover from.

Nathaniel finally had me.

She glanced at me. I shook my head, and her face fell. She let the knight chain her and lead her toward the water.

"Turn around," Nathaniel ordered once she was gone. Every muscle in my body was tense. I turned and he grabbed my wrists. He was too close. My breath quickened, and my body flushed feverishly. I couldn't stop the shaking. He finished locking the shackles but held my wrists for a moment.

He lowered his voice so only I could hear. "You're trembling. Is it anger? Fear?" He brought his lips to my ear. "Both?"

I shivered. He finally backed away and shoved me toward his waiting knights.

He didn't bother searching for the rest of my crew. We were loaded into a jolly boat and rowed to the closest ship, which was almost double the size of mine, if not bigger. I sat with my back facing my charred ship. I couldn't bear the sight.

The brief trip was torturous. Once we were lifted and boarded, knights led us past a staring crew of men. Kendra was taken to another door, while I was dragged below deck.

Three knights led me down several sets of stairs to the ship's windowless underbelly. We walked through a small, lantern-lit brig. They opened one of the heavy steel doors and shoved me inside.

Two knights held me still while the third switched out the short shackles for longer ones that were connected to the floor. I'd be able to sit upright, but the chain wasn't long enough for me to stand. When they were finished, the knights walked out of the cell and locked the barred door behind them. They filed out of the brig, leaving me alone.

I sighed and sat cross-legged on the hard floor. I'd escaped one captor only to run straight into the shackles of another. This whole being captured thing was getting old. Nathaniel had no reason to hurt Kendra. At least, not yet. He couldn't make the excuse that she'd resisted arrest or interfered in any way.

Wherever Nathaniel was taking me, it would be a while before we got there. He'd come to talk to me at some point. I took the opportunity to shift my body to lie down. My hands were bound behind my back and the floor was hard, but I didn't care.

I closed my eyes.

Chapter Thirty-One

FIFTEEN YEARS AGO

When Nathaniel didn't return from confronting his father about the abuse, I decided to check on him. By the time I arrived, his father's farm was cast in a golden glow from the setting summer sun. It had been a boiling August day. I was slick with sweat from jogging most of the way.

I crept to the house and peered through a dirty window. Trash littered the living room, and nobody was in sight. I crouched and moved to the back of the house to peek into the kitchen window. Dishes were piled in the sink and a mountain of papers covered the table, but there was no sign of movement.

I hurried to the barn. It was quiet at first, but as I got closer, I could hear a faint whimpering sound. When I peered inside, my stomach dropped.

"Nathaniel!" I gasped and rushed to him.

He was lying on his side, cradling his left hand. Thick droplets of blood stained the hay on the floor beneath him. His body shook, and tears were steadily draining from his lifeless eyes. The whimpering came from his dry, parted lips.

I fell to the ground beside him, and my hands hovered.

Gently, I stroked his hair from his sweaty face.

"Are you hurt? What happened?" I whispered. There was nobody else in the barn, but his father could arrive at any moment.

Nathaniel didn't answer. He simply held his hand to his chest and moaned.

I tentatively touched his arm. "Can you show me?" I asked, but he didn't seem to hear me. I lowered my face to his, trying to meet his eyes. "Can you hear me?"

I stroked his cheek, and he leaned into my hand. Delicately wrapping my arms around him, I helped him sit upright. He winced and moaned louder.

Then I saw it.

The corpus imperium ring was welded to his ring finger.

I gasped and drew back. The skin around the ring was charred and leaking blood. "Your father did this?"

He didn't answer. He didn't need to. I could guess what happened. He must have told his father that he wasn't going to do those things for him anymore. This was his punishment.

I urged him to stand. "We need to go. You can't stay here."

"Go away," he groaned.

"I'm not leaving you! We need to go!" I hissed. He finally looked at me, completely broken.

"He'll make me kill you."

"No, he won't."

"He will! I know he will."

I gingerly lifted his hand. The ring was melted to the bone.

"We need to run. He can't command you if he can't find you."

"But someone else could," he sobbed.

He was right. For as long as he lived, he wouldn't be safe. He'd have to be on guard all the time. His father condemned him to a life of servitude, either by his hand or another's.

There was only one way to remove the ring.

"Nathaniel, listen to me." I put my hands on his shoulders

and forced him to meet my eyes. "We need to remove the ring."

"How?"

I cringed. The thought made me cold and nauseous. "Your finger. That's the only way."

His glassy eyes went round, and he released another sob that shook his shoulders and broke my heart. But there was no other way.

I scanned the barn and found tools hooked onto the wall beside the open door. Among them was a rusty saw. I swallowed and squeezed his shoulders.

"You need to decide right now. He'll come back soon. What do you want to do?"

He glanced at the saw. Heavy tears spilled down his cheeks. He nodded numbly. I rushed to the saw, which was heavier than I thought it would be.

We didn't slaughter animals at our farm. I'd never seen violence of any kind. Now I needed to cut Nathaniel's finger off. I had to hurt the person I loved most.

I retrieved a short stool that was next to a milk pail and set it in front of him. I pressed his knuckles against the edge of the stool and pulled the ring finger to rest on top so I didn't accidentally cut his other fingers. He was shaking harder now and hyperventilating. We were both damp with sweat. There was a dirty rag resting in the hay, and I grabbed it.

"Put this in your mouth," I instructed. He took it with his shaky right hand and stuffed it in, muffling his sobs.

I knew if I stopped to think about what was happening, I wouldn't be able to do it. It took two hands to lift the saw.

"Ready?" My voice was rough. He squeezed his eyes shut and nodded. I rested the teeth of the saw above his knuckle but below the ring. Squinting and biting my lip, I pushed.

Nathaniel's muffled screams tore my heart to pieces. Every part of me wanted to stop. As I pushed and pulled, I kept repeating variations of the same thing, both to comfort him and to mask the sounds. "It's almost over. It's okay, it's going to be okay."

When his finger finally separated from his hand, he fell over and curled into a ball once more. Blood spilled and his right hand hovered over the injury, unable to do anything to stop the pain.

The finger rolled off the stool and fell into the hay.

I turned to the side and vomited. Over and over, I heaved, emptying everything inside me.

"What the hell are you doing?" His father stormed into the barn, bringing the sharp stench of whiskey with him. He was shirtless, and he had the bony body of someone who preferred booze to food. I wiped my mouth and scrambled to stand between him and Nathaniel.

"I'm going to report you. The knights will come and take you away," my voice cracked.

He barked a laugh and staggered toward me. My legs shook, but I held my ground. When he got close enough to see Nathaniel's hand, red crept up his neck and bloomed on his cheeks. He turned to me slowly.

"You fucking bitch."

I took a step back. He charged at me clumsily. I grabbed the bloody saw with both hands and swung it. The blade tore into soft flesh and he screamed.

The gash on his chest was hardly deep enough to bleed. He swayed on his feet and brought a hand to the wound. When he looked at me again, his body shook with rage.

He came at me with a growl. Panic surged, and I tried to weave around him toward the door. Before I could reach it, two arms wrapped around my waist and lifted me into the air. I screamed, and he threw me to the ground. The saw knocked out of my hand and skittered across the floor.

I scrambled through the slippery hay, but he held me tight. I clawed and kicked. Screams ripped from my throat. He yanked my hips toward him and flipped me onto my back to straddle me. I hit and scratched at his arms and face.

He knocked his arm and smashed his fist across my face. Pain exploded from the impact. Another hit followed, then another and another. I tried to cover my head with my arms, but the punches came too quickly. Blood pooled in my mouth and I choked.

"You're not telling a fucking soul!" he cursed through clenched teeth.

I pressed my eyes shut. His boney hands wrapped around my neck and squeezed. I thrashed beneath him and clawed at his arms. He leaned away from me while crushing my throat so I couldn't reach his face. Blood obscured my vision. Shadows converged on me, and I saw sparks.

A loud crack exploded above me. Air rushed into my lungs, and the man's weight lifted. I gasped and wheezed. When I coughed, blood sprayed the ground.

His father was moaning and crawling away from me. Nathaniel towered over him, clutching a shovel in his right hand. His chest fluttered with short, ragged breaths. The fog in his eyes had cleared, replaced by something darker. I pushed his father's leg off me and scrambled away from them.

When Nathaniel lifted the shovel above his head, I squeezed my eyes shut and turned away. He let out a guttural scream. The sharp sound of bone cracking made me flinch. A moment later, another followed, wetter this time. I slammed my hands over my ears. It was muffled, but the sounds didn't stop. Nathaniel smashed the shovel into his father's head over and over again.

My chin trembled and I swallowed my sobs. I wanted to be as invisible as possible.

When the barn fell quiet, I didn't move. I couldn't. My body was locked in a tight ball. A gentle pressure on my shoulder made me jump. I kept my eyes shut tight and my hands over my ears.

"It's okay. It's over now." Nathaniel's muffled voice came from behind me. I cracked my eyes open. The sun was nearly set. Shadows pooled in every corner of the barn. I lowered my sore hands. He groaned, and I heard the hay shuffle behind me.

"I need help. It's bleeding too much; I can't feel it anymore." His teeth were chattering. I needed to help him, but my body refused to move.

He appeared to my right and hurried from the barn toward the house. I scrambled to my feet, not wanting to spend one second alone with the broken body behind me.

I slipped inside the dark house and followed the sound of running water. Nathaniel stood in the dim kitchen, running cold water over his left hand and resting his forehead on the counter. Red water stained the white sink and swirled down the gurgling drain.

"It hurts," he whimpered.

I grabbed a rag from the counter and handed it to him.

"Wrap it in this." My voice was gravelly. Each word burned my throat. He took it with a shaking hand and wrapped it gingerly around the wound.

"You need a healer," I said. He shook his head. Panic twisted his face. His voice rose, nearing hysteria.

"We can't! We just killed him!"

A distant part of me marked the 'we.'

"It's bleeding too much! You might die!"

Nathaniel sobbed and laid his forehead back on the counter.

"It was self-defense! We'll get the knights and tell them what happened," I said.

"His head is crushed! We'll have to tell them about the ring, and then they'll know about the things I did. They'll kill me."

"But those things weren't your fault! It'll be worse if we don't tell them."

Nathaniel straightened, turned off the faucet, and walked briskly to the living room. I followed close behind. Picking up a glass bottle with clear liquid, he knocked the cap off with his thumb and dumped the contents over the wound. He hissed and squeezed his eyes closed. The smell of liquor stung my nose.

When he was finished, he wrapped the hand again and took

a slow, shaky breath.

"We need to get rid of it."

It took a moment to process his words. "We can't."

"We can. I can't do it by myself; I need your help."

"Nathaniel—"

He cut me off and spoke carefully. "We don't have a choice. If the knights find out, they'll take us both. They'll kill us. I can't let that happen to you." He stepped closer, and fresh tears welled in his eyes. "Please, Lou-Ann. I need you," he pleaded.

I urgently wanted to run home and tell my parents. They were practical. They'd know what to do. But the desperation in his voice stopped me from bolting out the door. If the knights didn't believe us and he was punished for the crimes his father forced him to commit, he'd be sentenced to death.

I bit my lip and nodded. He ordered me to grab the comforter from his bed while he lit a lantern. We rushed to the barn, and I paused at the open door. His father's dark shape lay still on the other side.

Nathaniel draped the blanket over him, and I tentatively approached. My body hadn't stopped shaking. My stomach clenched, but there was nothing left to throw up. Nathaniel was trying to roll the body into the blanket with one hand.

"Help me!" he snapped. I moved to the other side and helped him wrap his father's body. I kept my eyes fixed on the blanket, avoiding the bloody mess. My shoulders shook with silent sobs.

"We need to take it to the cliffs," he said after we lifted the body into an old wooden cart. There was a cliff that overlooked the ocean, but it was an hour away on foot.

"That's too far," I said. My voice trembled so badly that I could hardly get the words out. "Please, let me tell my parents. They can help."

"We already moved it! The knights will know what we were trying to do and that you helped me. Your parents wouldn't have a choice but to report us."

A small sob bubbled out of me.

He hooked a lantern to the side of the cart. I pulled while he pushed. We hauled it through dirt roads and overgrown trails in silence. Maneuvering it over tree roots and stones was nearly impossible. Every time we stopped to rest, Nathaniel would urge us onward moments later. I cried silently, letting the tears fall freely since he couldn't see my face.

Every so often, I'd catch a glimpse of the stars through the trees, which I tracked to make sure we wouldn't get lost. By the time we reached the cliffs, two hours had passed. My arms and hands burned. Every part of me was in pain. The rag Nathaniel used to wrap his finger was saturated with blood.

The cliff's edge was sharp and dropped straight down to jagged rocks and ramming waves. The silver moonlight feathered on the water's surface. Its beauty was a stark contrast to my horrifying reality. I ached to dive into the silky waves and disappear.

"Don't just stand there! Help me!" Nathaniel ordered.

We tilted the cart, and his father's body tumbled onto the ground. The blanket came loose and a pale arm spilled out. We dragged the blanket to the cliff's edge. With a firm shove, the body rolled over the edge and disappeared. I cringed at the faint splash that followed.

Chapter Thirty-Two

We walked back to his house in silence. I stumbled the whole way, struggling to watch my footing through my swelling eyes. When we arrived, Nathaniel ordered me to give him my bloody clothes. He said he would take care of the barn. He gave me some of his clothes to change into and sent me away. I don't remember walking home or getting into bed.

My parents saw my swollen face and bruised neck and demanded an explanation. They didn't believe my excuse that I'd gotten into a fight with some kids in town. They believed Nathaniel had beaten me, and I begged them not to report him. My parents eventually agreed on the condition that I would never see him again.

Nightmares crept into my waking life. I saw his father's crazed eyes in every shadow. Every slammed door and creak of the floor made me startle. I stopped eating and only slept when my body forced me to. The fear ate away at my conscience.

When three days had passed and the nightmares wouldn't end, I snuck out and hurried to the farm. I found Nathaniel in the kitchen, attempting to treat his infected wound.

I told him I couldn't take it anymore and that I was going to report what happened to the knights. He dissolved into tears and fell to his knees, begging me not to. Eventually, my love for him outweighed the guilt. I left to return home, but my feet carried me to the barn. When I peeked inside, the hay had been swept and the blood was gone. The shovel and saw were washed and leaning against a wall behind other tools.

I don't know what made me search for the ring. At the time, I thought it was to protect him. Looking back, I think it was self-preservation. When I found it, I doubled over and gagged. I rolled it in the same dirty rag Nathaniel stuffed into his mouth to stifle his screams and put it in my pocket. When I returned home, I buried the finger at the base of a large oak tree behind my house.

A week later, the knights crowded our front porch to take me away. My parents watched silently while they shackled me and tossed me in a barred transpocart. I kicked and begged for them to help me. I screamed that it wasn't true; I hadn't hurt anyone. But they simply shook their heads and went back into the house before the transpocart door was closed. That was the last time I ever saw them.

Nathaniel reported the crime. Except in his version, I was the one who killed his father and convinced him to get rid of the body. He told them he helped me because he was scared. They followed his directions to the spot where he claimed I buried our clothes. My sacred stargazing spot. The same place where we first had sex.

According to him, his missing finger was due to an unrelated accident.

The knights transported me to Templan and locked me in the palace dungeon. I was starved and left in my own filth for weeks while awaiting my trial.

Every day and night, I waited for word from Nathaniel. There must've been a reason for his lie. Maybe he was scared and made a mistake. He loved me. He would make it right.

When he finally appeared at my cell door, I could barely move. He said everything I hoped he would.

"I'm so sorry. I was scared. I'll make it right, I promise."

I told him about the ring. We could give it to the inquisitors as proof that he was being abused. He begged me not to say anything. He said he would find a way to fix everything, and I should tell him where I hid the ring.

That was the moment I recognized that the pressure I felt was my instinct. For the first time, I listened to it. I told him I couldn't remember where I put the ring. Before he left, he said, "I love you, Lou. I won't let them hurt you."

When the inquisitors bound me to the chair for questioning, I still believed he would come. My questioning was brief. They didn't allow me to tell my side of the story. It was clear they didn't believe me.

Assisting a murder was a Class Three offense. The punishment for a Class Three crime was three years of imprisonment or joining the king's service. Men could serve as knights. Women could work in the palace.

I would've guarded his secret. He knew that. If he'd done the right thing, I would've had the chance to live a normal life after three years in the palace.

He sold me to protect himself. He used my love to ensure I wouldn't reveal the truth. He'd been questioned first and convinced the inquisitors that I had seduced him. I was a liar and a killer.

Even when the inquisitors pressed the glowing branding iron to my skin, I screamed for him. When they dragged me back to the dungeon, I begged for him. Laying on the dirty floor of my cell, I cried his name until my voice was gone and hunger pulled me into sleep.

He never came.

Three weeks later, Mother appeared at my cell door. She asked the guard what the price was for my contract, paid it, and brought me to the boarding house. When we arrived, she sat me down in the small kitchen and waited while I ate in silence. There were no questions or judgments. She gave me one day to sleep, then put me to work.

I didn't see Nathaniel again for three years. Mother sent me on a job to hunt down a woman who had staged her death as a robbery and ran off with another man. Her husband was blamed and imprisoned for her suspected murder. My orders were to bring the woman back alive to clear his name.

When I finally located her, she was posing as a maid at a naval base. I tracked her right to Nathaniel's bed. So many agonizing feelings thrashed through me. I ran back to the boarding house without the woman.

Mother sat at my bedside and said, "That man took your life. Whatever you're feeling, light it on fire. Stoke the rage and destroy him."

So I did.

A week later, I scaled the wall outside of his room and snuck in through the window. They were naked and sleeping soundly in his bed. My whole body trembled with fury. Not because he was with another woman, but because he was happy. His face was peaceful and relaxed. He had someone in his life who cared for him.

I'd never be able to trust someone enough to let them get that close. Even though I'd only been a mercenary for a few years, I could already think of a few people who would love to take my head. The list of enemies would only get longer. But he could have it all. He could live openly and do whatever he wished without worrying about being killed in his sleep.

I dragged the sleeping woman from his bed by her hair. She shrieked, and Nathaniel startled awake. When he saw me through the darkness, terror flashed across his face.

I was the apparition that invaded his nightmares.

I was the phantom that stalked from the shadows.

I was his divine inevitability. No gods or enchantments could save him from me. His fear was water in the desert of my soul.

I yanked her upright to stand. She screamed and thrashed against me. I put a hand over her mouth and forced her to face him.

The chill of my sharp blade on her neck sent goosebumps across her skin. Nathaniel put a trembling hand out to stop me.

"Louie, don't do this. Let's talk."

My new name on his lips fanned my rage.

"Do you love her?" I asked.

He swallowed. "You and I can work this out. She didn't do anything to you." His voice wavered, confirming his feelings for her. The sound made my heart ache as though it were clutched in a strong fist.

I gave him a cruel smile, then ripped the blade across the woman's throat.

My first kill.

The air vibrated with his screams. He lunged forward. I dropped her into his arms, and they collapsed on the floor. Torrents of red spilled through his fingers, which he pressed desperately against the wound.

I didn't stay to watch. The echoes of his broken cries followed me down the wall I'd climbed. My heart absorbed his pain and pumped it through my body.

I was alive again.

Chapter Thirty-Three

The loud clang of a lock sliding into place startled me awake. My neck and back screamed when I tried to see who had entered the brig. My body ached from sleeping on the wooden floor.

I groaned and grumbled, "I'm too old for this shit."

Boots clomped down the short hallway and stopped at my cell. I opened my eyes and glanced up at Nathaniel.

"Oh, great. You're still here." I pushed myself up. "I was worried you'd fallen overboard."

"Thanks for your concern, but I'm very much alive," he replied.

"Great," I mumbled and blinked the sleep from my eyes. "Congratulations on capturing me. You must be so proud."

He smirked. "I am. You didn't make it easy."

"I think you were just really bad at it." I tried to adjust the shackles into a more comfortable position. "I'm sure you've been waiting a long time for this moment. So let's hear it. The big speech you've been practicing all these years."

His eyebrow twitched. "What is there left to say?"

"I think I said my peace twelve years ago."

A scowl replaced his smile. "Yes, you made your feelings known, loud and clear."

"What happened after she bled out in your arms? I'm sure it

didn't look good. A wanted woman, dead in a commander's room."

He lunged at the bars of my cell door and gripped them until his knuckles turned white. "You're a fucking monster."

"No, I'm a murderer, remember?"

His face turned red, and his eyes were wild with barely contained rage. He pulled a black book from inside his uniform jacket and tossed it to the floor.

A large black leather book.

Mother's book.

There was only one way he could have this.

It couldn't be true.

"If it's any consolation, I killed her in her sleep. Based on her reputation, I expected more of a fight. I slipped right in, and she didn't even stir. I'm a little disappointed." He kicked it under the door. It slid across the wood and stopped in front of me. "Should I use a truth wearable? Or do you believe me?" he sneered.

Air swept from my lungs, and I doubled over. My empty stomach clenched. Imagining Mother dying that way was too much to bear. Defenseless at his hands. Her death was an insult to everything she was.

I squeezed my eyes shut and swallowed the pain. I shoved it into a deep, hidden part of myself. A place even I couldn't find. *Wouldn't* find.

I forced the storm inside me to calm. When I lifted my head to face him, he wore a sick smile. He was enjoying my pain.

"If you wanted to die a painful death, all you had to do was ask." I straightened my back as much as I could. "All that bravado. But I know the truth. I know about the nights you couldn't sleep, fearing I'd appear in your dreams. The nights when every creak made you jump and scan the shadows, searching for me. The unrelenting fear that I would come for you."

His smile faded. My words struck true. He could try to hurt me all he liked, but nothing compared to the power I had over him.

"I hardly thought of you," I continued. "When I did, I took great pleasure in thinking about you waiting for me. That's the real reason you've been hunting me, right? So you can finally sleep? So you can stop checking every shadow in every corner?"

His breath quickened, and beneath his glare simmered the deep fear he'd been wrestling with since I killed his lover. Maybe even before then.

"You're alive because I allowed it. You breathe because I let you. You will die by my hand. You know it," I leaned forward, "and it fucking terrifies you."

He slammed the bars.

I leaned back and yawned. "Anything else to add?"

His body trembled, and the muscles in his jaw clenched. If he were brave enough, he could've beaten me to death right there. He could finish what his father started back in that shadowed barn. Instead, he turned on his heels and shot to the door, slamming it shut behind him.

When he was gone, I lowered myself to the floor and curled into a ball on my side. I was fairly certain I'd lost my privilege to food and water. The dizziness I'd tried to stave off gave way. The room spun, and my shaking erupted into full tremors. My teeth chattered, and I folded my knees to my chest.

Nathaniel was afraid of me. What I said was true. But the real reason I hadn't killed him was one I could hardly face. Every time the truth tried to surface, I'd force it back into hiding.

I was afraid of him.

I always had been. While I was a hurricane to his winter rain, the destruction he'd caused had woven into my flesh and bones. He had the power to decimate my life and shred my heart in a way no one else could. His betrayal dissolved my innocence, my kindness, and my trust.

Even though fifteen years had passed, that night was a fresh stain at the core of who I was. I'd experienced, and caused, much bloodier crimes than what happened that night. But it would always be the sinister creature sneering at me from the darkness.

I loathed myself for it. There was nothing to be afraid of. I knew that. He was nothing.

Yet he was everything.

Chapter Thirty-Four

Since my hands were bound, I used my foot to kick the black book away from me. It slid back underneath the cell door, still in view. I closed my eyes to block it out.

Mother was dead. Half of my crew was dead, while the others were stranded on an island. Kendra was locked away somewhere. My ship was reduced to ash.

"Really? You can't give me a fucking break?" I grumbled to the gods that didn't exist, despite knowing the reality. I had no one to blame but myself. I was their captain, and I failed them. Spectacularly.

Hours passed, and I only grew weaker. Just as I was finally drifting to sleep, the lock on the brig's door clicked open. Heavy footsteps approached my cell, and I groaned.

"Back for more?" I asked.

"Sit up," a deep voice ordered. I forced myself upright, and when I scanned the man in front of me, my jaw dropped.

"Kendra?"

At first glance, she looked like a short man with broad shoulders, a strong jaw, thick brows, and dressed in an officer's uniform. It was her deep blue eyes that gave her away.

She twirled. "Impressed?" she said in her own voice. My despair evaporated. I laughed and shook my head.

"Very. How did you do that?"

She rubbed her chin. "Dirt, and some of my hair."

"How did you escape?"

"That's a long story. Actually, it's a pretty short story involving a handsy knight who can expect a large bump on his head when he wakes up."

She was holding a large bottle in one hand, boots in the other, and a bundle of clothes tucked under her arm. She set the bottle and boots down and pulled a large key from her pocket, sliding it into the lock of my cell door. It clicked, and she pulled it open. She unlocked my shackles next, and I rubbed my wrists, finally free.

"Change quickly; we've got about three minutes." She tossed the spare uniform and boots at my feet.

I slipped the filthy dress over my head and used it to wipe the crusted nox domini blood from my face and arms. As I buttoned the jacket, she grabbed my chin and lifted it.

"Where the fuck did this come from?"

I furrowed my brow and gently inspected the skin on my neck. There was a small ache under my prodding fingers. "Benny got a little carried away."

"Carried away? I can see where his fingers were! Did he do anything else?" she asked, clenching her fists, preparing for a fight.

I scoffed. "He wishes." I swatted her hand away and finished buttoning. "We'll take care of him once we get out of here." I laced the boots and followed her to the door. "What's the plan?"

"There are jolly boats at the stern. We'll cause a distraction, then steal one."

"You think we'll make it to shore in a row boat?"

"Do you have a better idea?"

I sighed and shook my head. "What kind of distraction?"

She smiled wide and wiggled the bottle at me. I smirked and snatched one of the lanterns that was hooked to the wall. When we reached the top of the steps, she peeked through the open door.

"Follow me," she whispered. We tiptoed onto the deck and crept behind a crowd of men. Nathaniel was speaking from the upper deck, facing us. If he wasn't so into himself, he could've easily seen us sneaking behind his crew.

We made it across the deck and crouched behind a pile of wooden crates. She twisted the cap off the bottle, which released the sharp odor of liquor.

"We're estimating ten ships in total, all bearing the queen's crest. While she hasn't entered our waters yet, we'll be ready when she does," Nathaniel bellowed. I put a hand on the bottle to still Kendra. "The king's orders to retrieve the artifact are still in effect. Once reinforcements arrive, we will resume the search."

So it was true. The king was also hunting the Sands, and there was a war brewing.

Kendra glanced at me, and I nodded. She tossed the open bottle, and its contents spilled onto the deck. It was too large to shatter, but the crowd turned quickly toward the sound. I threw the lantern into the wetness. The glass globe shattered, spilling oil and fire.

A tall flame erupted and snaked down the trail of liquor. Everyone jumped backward and covered their faces to protect themselves from the sudden heat. The bottle rolled, leading the flames toward the crew.

They jumped out of the way and watched the fire. Nathaniel shouted, "Don't just stand there, water! Get water!" The crew launched into action, crashing into one another in a wild frenzy.

"This would be a great play," I whispered, and Kendra smiled.

"A comedy for the masses," she replied. We hurried to the stern. I moved to let her get in the boat first, but she shoved me toward it.

"I'll lower you. Go!" she shouted over the chaos.

I swung myself into the boat and she worked the crank. It jostled, and I gripped the sides. "Hurry!" I shouted. She threw me a flat look, then whipped around to look behind her. She turned back to me, wide-eyed, then kicked the brake. The rope released, and the crank spun wildly.

My stomach jumped into my chest as the boat descended into freefall. Kendra threw herself over the railing and crashed onto it before it fell too far. My butt lifted into the air, and I tightened my grip on the sides. The slight resistance offered by the ropes slowed us down enough to keep us upright.

The boat smashed into the water. Both of us were tossed into the air for a moment, and one of the oars smacked me in the face. We landed with a heavy thud. The boat rocked dangerously, and water splashed inside. We grabbed the oars and began to row. I pushed as hard as my arms would allow, and she did the same.

Screams from behind us carried over the water. There were two other ships, one ahead and one behind. Kendra and I rowed perpendicular, straining to get out of the way before we were run over by the following ship.

We pushed and pulled with everything we had, but the ship was too fast. I'd hoped the rising flames on Nathaniel's ship would've drawn their attention away from us, but it was curving off course.

Heading straight for us.

"Shit!" I picked up speed. We were both wheezing from the effort.

"Turn back!" she ordered.

"Are you insane?!"

"We can squeeze between them!"

"The wake will flip us!"

"We either risk it or get run over! Decide, Captain."

My heart thundered.

The ship was approaching fast.

We had no choice.

I forced the oars into the water to brake, and she did the same. I gritted my teeth against the resistance. The boat slowed, and we rowed back in the direction we came.

The waves were rising from the push of the incoming ship.

It was too close.

"We're not going to make it," my voice broke.

"Keep going!"

My arms were shaking and giving way. We rocked violently from side to side. I squeezed my eyes shut, still rowing.

If this is how I die, I'm going to be pissed. I directed the thought at the gods.

"Look!" Kendra shouted, and I opened my eyes.

The following ship was continuing its curve around us. We were close now, and I could see small figures leaning over the deck. They were waving wildly at us. The large vessel slowed, and Nathaniel's burning ship sped past. I turned back and glanced at the deck.

My eyes met Nathaniel's. He was high above us, but I could see his face well enough to recognize the familiar mixture of frustration and failure that I saw every time I'd escaped.

I raised my arms and flipped him two middle fingers.

"Holy shit," Kendra said.

I turned back and followed her stare.

The other ship had slowed and seemed to be trying to stop. The faces that looked down on us were wonderfully familiar. Velo had a huge smile and was shouting something I couldn't hear. The surge of pride I felt toward my crew nearly made me cry.

We returned to rowing. Two rope ladders spilled over the railing and brushed the water. When we reached them, the ship had slowed enough for us to each grab one.

My tired arms shook, but I pushed through the ache and climbed the rope rungs. When Kendra and I reached the top, a few people pulled us onto the deck. I stumbled, and the entire ship erupted in applause.

Velo smacked me on the back. Others hooted and hollered. I smiled wide despite the exhaustion. Someone started singing, and the rest followed.

"Yo ho! Yo ho! Captain fooled a king! Yo ho! Yo Ho! A pirate king so clever! No scallywags can win against the greatest pirate ever!"

It was a terrible song, but one we loved all the same. They stomped to the beat and spun with their arms hooked. I clapped with them and the aches and pains faded, replaced by elation and laughter.

When I wiped the tears and salt from my eyes, I got a better look at the crowd. It wasn't just Velo and those I left on the island that celebrated before me.

My entire crew danced and sang. Finny, Nelson, Simon, Falrey, and Mora twirled and cheered in the warm summer sun. Kendra hooked her arm in mine, and we spun and clicked our heels. I sang horribly and loudly.

All of us survived.

Chapter Thirty-Five

When the crew settled and returned to their posts, winded and smiling, I pulled Velo aside.

"Lighting ships on fire must be our thing now."

"It's quick, destructive, and effective. Just like you," he replied with an approving smile.

I groaned and gripped my cramping stomach. "Food, water, bath, and rest. Then we talk. Head south until then."

He nodded and got to work instructing the crew. Nelson prepared two heaping plates of food for me and Kendra. Despite my despair about losing my ship, the enormous navy ship was luxurious in comparison. The barracks were nicer, the food was better, and the weapons were sharper. They also had drainage and two bathing rooms.

Once I ate and bathed, I met Mora in the infirmary. She was excitedly talking to herself while inspecting various supplies and tools. After a moment, she noticed me leaning in the doorway, watching with affectionate amusement. She startled and a blush bloomed on her olive cheeks.

"Find anything good?" I asked. She nodded.

"Definitely. I'd expect nothing less from the king. I haven't found any enchanted tinctures, which isn't a surprise. We'll work with what we have."

She clipped her black, silky chin-length hair out of her face and motioned to one of the chairs. I sat, and when she saw my throat, she frowned and shook her head.

"Say it," I said. She sighed while retrieving supplies.

"It would be nice to not treat you for a while."

"Are you worried? That's sweet."

"Worried about you? Never."

Mora joined my crew seven years ago. I'd spent a lot of time sitting in a chair while she tended to my injuries. Nothing made her queasy. She was easy to talk to and gorgeous. I'd grown out of my crush long ago, but her efficient yet gentle talent for healing was still comforting.

"There's not much I can do for bruising without a tincture. This ointment will cool and numb it. Use it until it heals on its own." She tilted my head and gently dabbed the ointment on my skin. "I hope you killed whoever did this."

"It's at the top of my to-do list."

Someone cleared their throat from the doorway. Kendra stood there with her arms crossed.

"My other favorite patient. Sit." Mora nodded to another chair, but Kendra walked to us and snatched the ointment bottle from Mora's hand.

"I'll do it. You can go."

Mora gave me a sly smile. "I'll be back in ten minutes to treat those." She gestured to the puncture marks on Kendra's arms. When she was gone, Kendra pulled a chair toward me and swiped a glob of ointment on her finger.

"You're a healer now?" I asked.

"I'm your healer."

I pressed my lips together to hide my smile. I lifted my chin, and she gingerly dabbed the ointment on the bruises. Her lips were pursed in concentration and I watched her focus.

We sat in silence. I should've told her about Mother. It wasn't fair to keep the news from her. It was selfish of me to not say anything, but knowing how painful it would be for her, I couldn't bring myself to do it. We finally had a moment of peace.

But if I were her, I'd want to know.

When she trailed the ointment over the spots she already covered, my hand gently wrapped around her wrist and I lowered my chin to face her. I prepared the words that would break her heart, but when her deep eyes met mine, I faltered.

Pink inched up her neck and warmed her ears.

"I'm lucky to have a thorough healer like you," I said with a soft smile. She frowned and tried to pull away.

"Don't joke. I'm mad at you."

"Why?"

She huffed, and I released her. "You charged into a room of enchanted creatures, barefoot and alone. It was dangerous and stupid."

"Dangerous for them, maybe."

"This isn't a joke! You let your anger get the best of you and almost got yourself killed!" Her voice pitched, and she tossed the ointment roughly onto the table beside us.

"Why are you so upset? I'm fine. Everyone is fine."

"You still shouldn't have done it."

I crossed my arms. "They deserved to die a painful death, and I wasn't leaving until that was accomplished."

"Losing you would've hurt a thousand times more than what they did! I can't, I *won't* let you do that again. Not for me."

"That's not up to you."

"Louie, enough!" Her voice rose to a shout. "Please listen to me. I should've said this a long time ago." She took my hands in hers. "I know we don't get along and that you don't like me. That's my fault. I wasn't there for you when you first moved in with us. It was clear how much pain you were in. You were so broken and hollow. But instead of being your friend, I made you my rival. I hated how much attention you got from Mother, and I took it out on you. I was terrified you would take my place and that she'd eventually kick me out." She swallowed and clenched her jaw before continuing.

"It's my fault our relationship became like this. I was immature and selfish. I regret it, but I'm here for you now. I care about you, and that's not going to change no matter how hard you try to push me away. So please, for fuck's sake, don't do something like that again. *Please*." Her chin quivered, and she did her best to keep the tears from spilling over.

I returned her admission with stunned silence. I desperately wished I didn't believe her, but the trembling in her voice and the desperation in her wide eyes made that impossible. There was no doubt now. She truly cared for me in a way nobody ever had, and I was terrified. Hope was a dangerous thing.

But she was worth the risk.

My hand laced through her hair and cradled the back of her head. The pink blush deepened and spread to her face. I brushed her warm cheek with my thumb, and she allowed the tears to fall.

"Promise me," she said.

"I can't promise that I won't fight for you. But I can promise that I'll keep myself safe. I'll consider your pain before I risk my life."

She leaned her forehead against mine and whispered, "Thank you."

I cupped her cheeks and moved my lips closer to hers, slow enough that she could stop me. If we crossed this line, there was no going back. She would be mine, and I would be hers.

"How do you care about me?" I asked. She pressed her lips together. "Kendra, you need to tell me before I do something that makes you uncomfortable." I hovered inches away, giving her the power to decide.

"I . . . like you. A lot."

Chapter Thirty-Six

Kendra's lips brushed mine, and heat flushed over me. The desire I'd been desperately trying to ignore was all-consuming. A kiss wasn't enough. I needed all of her. Her gorgeous body, brilliant mind, and kind soul. I was at her mercy, ready to give her anything. If she betrayed me, so be it.

I let her take the lead. She cupped my cheeks and deepened the kiss. Her quiet whimper vibrated against my lips. She pulled away and led me by the hand toward one of the beds, then carefully pushed me onto my back to straddle me. Her hair swept my cheek, and I brushed it behind her ear.

We were both breathing hard. Her eyes were dark, and her cheeks were flushed.

"I need . . . " she said, but bit her lip. I moved my hands to her waist.

"Tell me," I prompted gently.

"All of you. I need it all."

"Take it."

I pulled her down and kissed her again. The last thread of her control snapped. She moved against me desperately. Her hands greedily explored everywhere, and I let her. A soft moan escaped her lips, and a fresh wave of heat rushed over me. There was no sweeter sound. I wanted to hear it again, along with every other sound she could make.

Her pleasure was my purpose.

I flipped her underneath me and slowed our kiss.

"I'm going to give you what you want. No tricks, no jokes. Let me make you feel good. Let me give you everything. Okay?"

"Yes," she breathed and arched her body against mine. I pinned her hips to the bed.

"Let me lead, or this is going to be over too quickly."

She smirked and opened her mouth to tease me. I silenced her with a kiss, then pulled away. "Don't even think about it."

Her giggle dissolved into another moan as I trailed slow kisses along her collarbone. "Mora," she sighed, and I smiled against her skin.

"She's not coming back any time soon."

I took my time learning her body, studying every twitch, shiver, moan, and gasp. I memorized every touch and kiss the same way I learned my star maps. Her body was another secret for me, and me alone. The way she begged was nearly enough to make my pleasure spill over, but I held on. I didn't want it to end.

When she finally came apart beneath me, her cry of pure ecstasy stoked my need. She tensed and shook while gripping the thin bedsheet.

Once the waves calmed, her body went limp and she closed her eyes. I settled beside her and traced the shape of her in my mind, committing everything to memory. The way her eyes fluttered closed. The gentle rise and fall of her chest. The way her hair spilled around her, some pieces sticking to her face. Her flushed cheeks and soft curves.

Just when I thought she'd fallen asleep, her eyes slowly opened and she caught me staring. Her slack jaw tensed, and she moved a hand to cover herself. I stilled it with my own and propped myself up on my elbow.

"Don't do that. Let me look at you."

She relaxed and turned on her side to face me. "We just did that," she said with a giddy smile.

"We did."

"Can I make you feel good now?" Her hand tentatively touched my waist, and I held it there.

"You have, believe me."

She sighed. "I don't want to get up."

"Then don't. I don't need you right now." She frowned, and I laughed. "Okay, I need you, but not to meet with Velo."

"Don't go."

I gave in to the urge to stroke her hair. "Close your eyes."

She did, and sleep swiftly took her. After a few minutes, she was breathing deeply with a tiny snore. I laughed inwardly, not wanting to wake her, then stealthily slipped out of bed.

There was so much to think about. I had a map to the Sands, but that only told me which direction to sail. Then there was Benny and Nathaniel to deal with. Plus, the possibility of a double-crosser among my crew.

But as I adjusted my clothes and smoothed my braids, all I could think about was her. I had been denying the depth of my feelings so much that the revelation was dizzying. The inevitability of it felt right. A puzzle piece settling into its proper place. Now I couldn't imagine not being with her.

There was no denying it now.

I loved her.

I loved every part of her. The annoying parts, her competitiveness, her kindness and talent. I loved her deeply, and that terrified me. With love came pain. I'd learned that lesson.

But it was worth it. *She* was worth it. I would do anything to make sure she survived this journey; even if that meant giving up the Sands of Time.

Chapter Thirty-Seven

I found Velo rooting through a mess of papers in the captain's quarters. When I entered, he gave me a knowing smile.

I closed the door behind me. "Don't say a word."

He chuckled and shook his head. "I don't want to know anything."

"She's not a weakness," I said in anticipation of his lecture.

His face softened and he sighed, leaning back in the chair. "I know. I just . . . don't want you to go through what I did. But I shouldn't have doubted you or her. You can take care of yourselves. I'm glad you're happy."

I smiled, then cleared my throat.

"I'll be happy when Benny and Nathaniel are dead and the Sands of Time are mine. Ours," I corrected.

I still hadn't eliminated Velo as a suspect. He could be playing both sides, traveling with me while feeding Benny information. It wouldn't matter which one of us found it first. He'd get paid either way.

"What did you find?" I asked.

"I think this was Nathaniel's primary ship. He kept a lot of sensitive information here. I found a letter from King Francis. It seems like your benefactor is none other than Queen Lenora."

"That makes me want to find it even more."

Velo set the letter down. "I know you don't care what happens to the treasure after we sell it. But in the wrong hands, the Sands of Time could be catastrophic. We don't know the full extent of its power, but if it really can allow someone to control time, is it safe to hand it over to the queen?"

I chose not to mention my growing desire for the Sands. My confrontation with Nathaniel had brought old regrets to the surface. The temptation to undo the damage he wrought was overwhelming.

Even if Velo was still loyal to me, it was highly likely that he'd also considered what the Sands could do for him. I'd never know what it felt like to care for a child, but I'd bet anything that he'd considered using the artifact to prevent his daughter's death.

"I agree, but we can sort that out once we retrieve it. It would be worse if the king got his hands on it. Or Benny. I can't imagine what he would do with that much power."

"Yet another reason to kill him."

"He sealed his fate on the island. He's a dead man walking."

His expression creased with bitter displeasure.

"Why do you hate him so much?" I asked. "He's an easy person to despise, but it feels personal with you."

Velo looked at the desk with the unfocused gaze of someone lost in a memory. "He broke my daughter's heart. He told her he loved her and manipulated her into asking me for coin, which I gave, thinking it was for her. When she told him she didn't want to continue, he disappeared with the rest of the coin she'd been working hard for. She was devastated, and then . . . " His voice became rough, and he swallowed the rising grief.

"In that case, I grant you the honor of cutting off his head."

"I would love that more than anything, but I made a promise that I wouldn't." He blinked a few times and cleared his throat. "I found something I think you're going to like."

I followed him to a large chest. The lock was smashed and when he lifted the lid, I gasped. It was full of enchanted items. It took me a moment to recognize some objects.

I rifled through the pile. "He stole these from Mother," I said, picking up a chipped pink tracking crystal that I'd stolen from a countess years ago. One of Mother's rules was that we had to hand over all enchanted items to her. We could only use them with her permission. The crystal glowed brilliantly. More colors illuminated from within the pile.

This confirmed it. She was dead.

But if these items were Mother's . . .

My heart leaped. I dropped the crystal and fervently dug through the items. Tucked in the bottom, underneath a shadow blanket, was a small dark blue velvet pouch. I carefully retrieved it and carried it to the desk.

I untied the strings and carefully spilled the jewel into my open palm.

A ruby red stone.

A stone that was once set in a ring welded to a teenage boy's finger. The gods were on my side this time.

I beamed and held it out to Velo. He leaned closer but didn't take it from me.

"Do you know what this is?" I asked. He shook his head. "This is the weapon that will kill Commander Nathaniel Bartholomew."

"I don't suppose you'll explain."

"Nope. But I would recommend that you don't touch it." I returned it to the velvet bag and tucked it into the pocket of my shirt, which I'd found in the sleeping quarters.

Nathaniel sat in this room, completely oblivious that his worst nightmare was four feet from his desk.

After I was released into Mother's care, she let me visit my home one last time. My parents weren't there, but the finger and ring were exactly where I'd buried it. I had the stone removed. While I wasn't certain, I had a strong suspicion that Nathaniel had searched far and wide for it.

Now it would bring his demise. How poetic.

I sat in the chair on the opposite side of the desk and pushed the papers aside to read the unfurled map underneath, then paused for a moment.

"How did the crew escape the island?"

"Benny's crew ambushed them. Finny got everyone to safety using the compartments you had built. They slipped out through the crack in the hull. Which is ironic considering that he probably created the storm to damage our ship so that we couldn't leave the island."

I beamed with pride, then asked, "What did you do with this ship's crew?"

"You don't want to know. But I can say that most survived."

"Such a brute." I hesitated before asking the question that had been weighing on me. "Why did you pretend not to know anything about divinum?"

"Information is a weapon, duckling. You know that."

"Information I would use against you?"

"Maybe not you, but someone with a truth wearable might. The fewer humans know about divinum, the better."

"I wouldn't."

"You're forgetting what I taught you."

I rolled my eyes. "Trust no one. I remember. But right now, I could really use your secret knowledge."

He took a moment, then said, "Victoria's mother was a siren. She was taken shortly after Victoria's birth, and I never saw her again."

Velo's pain was written on his face, clear as a map. I didn't want to think about what would happen to a siren after being captured.

"The origins of enchantment stretch further back than we can imagine," he continued. "Many ancient civilizations worshipped the gods they believed were responsible for the power."

"You believe the gods exist?"

He shrugged. "I'm not qualified enough to have an opinion one way or another."

My attention returned to the map. Ancient people were rumored to have lived primarily on the southern islands. There were three below the southern tip of the continent, and only one was known to have temples.

My vision narrowed on the small, unassuming circular shape near the bottom of the faded parchment. Chills prickled my skin.

The Sands of Time were on Initium Island.

I had a location. I had a map.

The treasure would be mine.

Chapter Thirty-Eight

I tapped the map, and he leaned closer.

"Initium Island?"

I nodded eagerly. "This is where we'll find the Sands, and I know exactly how to get there."

I sprinted up the stairs to the deck before Velo could reply. Simon was at the helm, struggling to keep his eyes open. Drool was shining on his dark lips. I smothered my laugh and tapped him on the shoulder. He jolted and squinted at me.

"Captain! I was sailing south, as you instructed."

"Switch out with Falrey before you run us aground. Get some sleep. Let him know to keep going south, but move far from the coast. We might run into the queen's ships. Also, keep an eye out for Benny. We're heading to Initium Island. I'll give you more specific instructions in a few hours."

He raised a thick eyebrow and nodded.

We'd have to sail south, then curve inland once we were out of the king's waters. He wouldn't be able to arrest us without permission from the king of the southern empire.

I found Finny checking the gears below deck.

"I need to speak with you. Privately," I said.

I led him away from the others and pulled the satchel from my pocket.

"I need this forged to a dagger. You can't be around anyone while holding it. Protect it with your life. No matter what happens, do not give it to anyone other than me, and don't tell anyone. Understand?" He tensed and nodded. Despite my reservations, I gently placed it in his open palm.

When I returned to the captain's quarters, Velo was sorting through more paperwork. I went to the chest and pulled out any items that may be useful in our search. The island was small, but I had no idea where the temples were.

I grabbed two glowing tracking crystals that had fallen to the bottom. The bright light they emitted was nearly blinding. I squinted and set them on the desk.

Velo hissed and jolted out of the chair. He stumbled backward and grasped his chest. Ringlets of smoke rose from his necklace. He tore at it, struggling to get it over his head, then threw it to the floor. The skin where it touched was dark red. We stood there, silently gaping at it for a moment.

I picked up a glowing crystal and held it out in front of me. Its light surged, then dimmed when I pulled it away. The necklace continued to sizzle on the floor.

"What the hell was that?" Velo exclaimed, rubbing the burn mark.

I set the crystal back in the chest, and the smoking pendent calmed. Getting on my knees, I inspected it closer without touching it.

"Has this happened before?" I asked.

"No."

We used a crystal while searching the Isle of Night and his necklace didn't react at all.

"Did you take it off while we were at the viscount's manor?"

"No. I've worn it since Victoria gave it to me."

"Did you sleep after you ate the food at dinner?"

"Yeah, why?"

"Can divinum enchant an item without an alchemist?"

He stilled. "Yes."

The viscount could've enchanted it while he slept, but why? What would he gain from messing with Velo's necklace?

Unless it wasn't the viscount.

Benny used the serpent's blood to control the storm and strand us on the island. An alchemist or divinum could've helped him enchant the necklace. They could've snuck into Velo's room and enchanted it while he slept. Benny probably couldn't decipher the totem. He could be tracking the necklace somehow.

I scoffed and rose from the floor. "Unbelievable," I murmured and gently picked up the warm chain. "I think Benny's tracking this."

"A tracking item only works short distances. How could he track it from far away?"

"Anything could be possible with fresh divinum blood. If he caused the storm, it's possible he enchanted a tracking item with a long range. It's not a firm theory, but either way, whatever he did to it isn't safe. We need to get rid of it."

I walked toward the door, but Velo's grip on my arm stopped me.

"You can't." His voice wavered. "Please."

I covered his hand with mine. "He'll find us if we keep it."

"He'll find us anyway. He always does. Maybe that's not what Benny did."

"If not, then it's something else he'll use to stop us. For all we know, this could kill you." He opened his mouth to argue, then closed it. "Do you know how to undo an enchantment?"

His jaw clenched, and he released my arm.

I sighed. "I'm sorry."

He followed me up to the deck. When I reached the railing, he asked, "Can I do it?" My heart squeezed at the trembling in his voice. I nodded and handed it to him.

Stepping back to give him privacy, I watched as he gripped

the chain tightly with both hands. He pressed the pendant to his forehead and whispered something I couldn't hear with his eyes closed.

I folded my arms and blinked the tears away.

After a moment, he took a deep breath and dangled the last connection he had with his daughter over the side of the ship. Closing his eyes once more, he unclenched his fist, releasing it into the same waters that took her life.

His shoulders sagged, and his head drooped.

Standing before me was a man who once ruled the sea. Now, all I saw was a broken father saying his final goodbye.

Velo didn't look at me again. He turned and briskly crossed the deck, disappearing down the stairs that led to the sleeping quarters.

I scanned the water for Benny's ship, but only found the unblemished horizon that divided the sea and the clear blue sky. No item that I'd ever heard of could be powerful enough to track us this far.

"Making me do all the work while you follow my trail." I *tsked* as though Benny could hear me. "Lazy."

Chapter Thirty-Nine

The island was more humid than anywhere I'd ever been. The early morning air was thick and nearly damp enough to drink. The ship was too large to hide. If Benny managed to follow us, he'd spot it from far off the coast.

After the attack on the Isle of Night, it was too risky to leave anyone behind. Each of us was equipped with weapons, food, and gear. There was no guarantee we'd find the temple before dark.

We'd sailed all night, following the same sky on the totem, which was suspicious. Of the thirty-two possibilities, the chance we'd have that sky on the night we needed it most was slim. I hadn't considered that other forces might be involved in the hunt. Then again, it was becoming abundantly clear that I knew very little about enchantment. Anything was possible.

When I finally gave up on trying to sleep late last night, I snuck into the sleeping quarters to check on Kendra. The bite marks were bandaged, and her sleeping face was relaxed and worry-free. I felt a tinge of envy that she slept through the night. I had tossed and turned in my bed, unable to still my racing thoughts.

We walked in a line through the thick brush and made our way inland. The tracking crystal in my pocket glowed faintly from the corpus imperium dagger fixed to my belt, but not brightly enough to indicate a nearby artifact. When the land sloped upward at the foot of a mountain, I stopped to address the group.

"I need someone to climb a tree to search the area."

"Why can't you do it?" Indigo asked.

I ignored her. "Any volunteers?"

"I volunteer the youngins," Ushar said, pointedly making eye contact with Nelson and Finny.

"I'll do it," Finny said. Other than Velo, he was the tallest of the group.

The nearest tree rose over fifty feet, with no low branches to use as footholds. He unfurled a rope that was attached to his belt and tied it around his waist and legs. After throwing one end over the lowest branch that could hold his weight, he maneuvered up the tree with the deftness of a monkey.

My tension worsened the higher he climbed. Just as I was about to call him back down, he neared the top and peered over the surrounding trees.

"I see a clearing!" he shouted. "There's something lighter there, maybe the top of a building, but it's hard to tell!"

"Good work! Now come back down before you kill yourself!"

Finny made it back down the tree with ease. His cheeks were flushed, and I patted him on his sweaty back.

"Where did you learn that?" Jerma asked. He shrugged sheepishly.

"I grew up near a forest. There were a lot of trees and not much else to do."

Kendra smiled. "Well done."

We resumed our hike, and two hours later, we reached an opening in the trees. I squinted through the branches and gasped.

An enormous stone temple appeared before us. The sandstone structure was covered in moss and decorated with intricate patterns and details. The building dropped and rose in different sections, indicating an intricate inner layout. Crumbling stairs led to the entrance, which was framed by tall, worn columns. It was the most beautiful piece of architecture I'd ever seen.

The crew stopped behind me and gaped at its beauty.

"If there's an ancient artifact to be found, it would be in there," Ushar said. We all nodded in agreement. I turned and smiled at the group.

"Ready?"

We climbed the stairs in silence. The temple's details were even more intricate up close. Shapes similar to what we found on the totem were carved into the pillars and walls. Moss and ivy crawled up every surface, obscuring some of the finer details.

The temple's interior was even more impressive. I craned my neck to gawk at the tall stone ceiling. Pieces had crumbled, allowing the sun to filter into the dark cavernous room. Directly in front of us stood a statue taller than the entrance. It was a figure of a boy with bent elbows and what I imagined were cupped hands that had broken off long ago. The face was too worn to make out any details. Fallen stones lay at its feet and were covered with moss.

Halls were branching off in each direction.

"We need to stick together," I said. "Follow me."

I led everyone down the hall hidden behind the statue. We zig-zagged through the temple's interior, dodging puddles and climbing over collapsed walls. Designs and symbols were carved into every surface.

We followed the hallway to the right and entered a large room with a broken domed ceiling. More stone figures, smaller than the one at the temple's entrance, stood in a circle around a pool of sunlight. The faces were somber, and they each held a long staff. We split up and carefully inspected the statues and markings on the floor. The stones in the center of the room were organized in a spiral.

Indigo walked along the stones. "I don't know what we're looking for, but this might be important. Maybe—"

The center stone sank under her weight and she jumped backward. The next stones in the spiral lowered into the floor with a loud grinding sound until all the stones in the circle descended into a spiral staircase.

I peered into the hole and a gentle gust of chilled air brushed my damp face. Darkness swallowed the light several steps down. Kicking myself for not bringing lanterns, I pulled out the crystals, which had started glowing brighter the moment we entered the temple.

The stairs weren't wide enough to fit both feet. I handed the other crystal to Velo and took the first two steps with great care. My heart skipped. I forced my breathing to slow and focused on keeping my footing.

By the time I made it to the ground, I'd circled the spiral twice. Velo had a particularly difficult time balancing with his wide shoulders. Kendra came last. She gracefully tapped from one to the next without trouble.

A narrow arched tunnel led to the right and left. The glow of the crystal didn't reach far enough to tell us much about where they would take us. The gentle breeze drifted from the right, which meant it had to be coming from an opening somewhere.

"This way." I nodded to the right.

A familiar tension built in my shoulders. I marked the warning and strained my senses to pick up on any sounds or shifts in the chilled air.

We walked in silence. Our collective footsteps bounced off the simple stone walls. There were no carvings, ornaments, or statues. The tunnel bent to the left, and when I rounded the corner, torches sprung to life on each wall. We froze and glanced at one another.

"Anyone else getting a bad feeling about this?" Ushar asked from the middle of the group. Some nodded in response. I scanned the hall, then pushed forward with the crystal stuffed safely back in my pocket.

The familiar pressure of warning intensified.

Something was wrong.

A large stone shifted beneath my foot, sinking the same way the spiral had. This stone tilted forward and I gasped, swinging my arms to grab onto something. A hand yanked the collar of my shirt backward. I slammed into a strong chest just as three thick pillars shot up from the floor and crashed into the stone ceiling.

Velo jerked me further back, and I stumbled away from the trap. Had I taken one step further, the pillars would have crushed me against the ceiling. My heart thundered, and a cold rush swept through me.

"Holy shit!" Mora gasped with a hand over her mouth.

Velo released me, and I gave him a grateful nod. My hand pressed against my chest as though I could slow my pulse.

I straightened my shirt. "Well, I think it's safe to say that the Sands are well-guarded. We need to be extra careful."

"No shit," Indigo mumbled.

The pillars were large, but there was just enough room to squeeze between them. It took several of us to pull Velo through. As captain, it was only right for me to take the lead, but the fear of what other traps might lie ahead made my legs weak.

We kept moving, and the gust of cool air strengthened. My palms dampened with each tentative step. The tunnel turned to the right ahead, making it impossible to tell how much further we had to go.

Thunder rumbled from behind us, quiet at first, then growing louder with each moment. Everyone paused to listen.

"Footsteps!" Falrey gasped.

Shit.

"Run!" Kendra shouted. I spun around and did my best to search for any stones that looked out of place while sprinting through the tunnel. Our steps drowned out the rumble of our pursuers.

The pillars from the trap behind us would slow them down, but we couldn't spare a moment. I skidded around the corner and gasped. The ground disappeared into a pit full of sharp wooden spikes.

I launched myself over the wide trench, landing on my stomach on the other side. My body started to slide off the edge, and my feet scraped the trench's wall. I desperately clawed the stone to keep myself from falling.

"Stop!" I screamed. Velo had enough speed to vault just in time, clearing the hole.

Indigo was not so lucky. When she tried to jump, her footing slipped.

She fell face first.

Velo was helping me out of the pit, so I fortunately missed the tragedy. But I couldn't escape her short scream and the muted, wet sound of her body being impaled by the spikes.

She made no other sounds. I pushed myself onto my knees. Every part of me screamed not to look, but I had to know.

The bloody spikes pierced every part of her body.

She twitched once, twice, then went still.

Kendra slowed in time to avoid the fall and screamed. It was a chilling, shrill sound and I grimaced. I forced myself to look away. Velo had gone pale, and his face was locked in horror. The rest of the team slowed down and jogged around the corner. Each one of them cried out and turned away when they saw her. Mora grabbed Finny in time to cover his eyes.

The footsteps had paused, which meant they had reached the pillars.

We needed to move.

Velo and I stretched our arms out to the others at the same time. I pointedly avoided looking down.

"You need to jump!" I shouted.

Kendra forced herself to focus. Ushar moved next to her, and they jumped at the same time. Velo clumsily caught him, and my heart skipped for a moment. Kendra landed easily in my arms. One by one, each of them made the jump, clearing the hole. I didn't look back at Indigo's body. It didn't feel right to leave her there, but there wasn't time. I had to protect the others.

Velo took the lead, and we bolted through the tunnel. A shadow on the floor ahead indicated another pit. Velo hurdled across. This time, the ground on the other side crumbled under his weight. He scrambled to gain purchase as the stones fell away around him.

I charged forward, past the rest of the group.

One of his hands managed to hold onto a sturdier stone.

I bent my knees, ready this time, and launched myself across. I landed roughly on the other side, then grabbed Velo's hand with both of mine and pulled. Despite my strength, he was too heavy for me to lift. He maintained his grip on the rock, but his feet desperately scraped the wall, trying to find a foothold.

There were no spikes this time. Only bottomless darkness.

Ushar landed heavily beside me and scrambled for Velo's other hand. We pulled and my arms nearly ripped from their sockets, but I didn't let go. I ground my teeth and dug my heels into a crack between stones. There wasn't enough room for the others to jump over to help.

It was up to Ushar and me to save Velo.

Chapter Forty

I grunted and pulled with everything I had. Terror creased Velo's face. My muscles burned and strained. His skin was slick, and I struggled to hold on with my own damp hands.

Ushar and I heaved, and he finally began to rise.

Velo found a stone sturdy enough to step on. We heaved again, and he hooked his elbow on the ledge. We helped pull him the rest of the way up.

Velo laid on his back for a moment. His chest fluttered and sweat shined on his skin. My arms screamed when I pushed myself to stand.

The footsteps had resumed. They made it through the pillars.

"Come on!" I waved to the others, and they jumped one by one. Thankfully, Ushar and I managed to pull everyone to safety.

I tugged Velo, and he stood on shaky legs. We charged ahead, keeping pace with one another. I tensed at every shadow and misplaced stone. The tunnel cut to the right, and we slowed enough to make sure there wasn't a drop on the other side.

A hoarse scream echoed behind us. Unlike Indigo, whoever had fallen into the spikes was not granted a quick death. Another shrill scream rang out, and I flinched. Shouts followed, and the footsteps paused.

None of us slowed down.

The tunnel cut left up ahead, and soft light illuminated the wall. A surge of strength propelled me forward. We skidded around the bend and lurched to a halt.

The tunnel opened into a cavernous room. The floor abruptly fell away. We stood at least thirty feet above a mossy stone floor. Across from us sat an enormous statue of a woman sitting with her legs crossed and her hands cupped, as though presenting an offering.

Kendra carefully leaned over the edge, searching for a way down and finding none.

"What now?" Simon asked through ragged breaths.

The pounding footsteps resumed.

I bit my lip. Finny was shifting on his feet and hyperventilating.

The rope was still wrapped around his belt.

I grabbed it, startling him, and unwound it. A large stone slab, which might have fallen from the ceiling, was resting to our left. There was a deep crack that split halfway down the stone. I tied the end of the rope into a thick knot, slid it into the fissure, and knocked the rope with the hilt of my dagger to wedge it firmly into the crack.

I tossed the rest of the rope over the edge.

"Go!" I urged the group to climb down. The footsteps slowed again, likely because of the next pit.

The crew climbed over the edge. I positioned myself between them and the tunnel, dagger in hand.

Our pursuers were nearing the tunnel's final turn.

Velo stepped in front of me.

"Go, I'll hold them off."

"No fucking way; get down!" I tried to push him toward the ledge, but he wouldn't budge.

"I'm heavier than the rest; it might snap! Go first. I'll follow."

He grabbed my shoulder and shoved me away. I hesitated,

then gripped the rope to lower myself over the edge. I shimmed down as quickly as I could without falling. I joined the others, but when I turned around, Velo was still at the top.

The footsteps rounded the corner.

His eyes met mine, and he drew his daggers. "Go!" he shouted, then disappeared into the tunnel. The ringing of clashing steel echoed from above.

"Velo!" I screamed.

Kendra pulled on my arm. "Keep moving!"

I shoved her off me, then grabbed the rope to climb back up. She circled her arms around my waist and yanked me back to the floor.

"Velo!!" I screamed again, but he didn't answer. Men I didn't recognize peered over the edge. They grabbed the rope and started to climb down.

My crew drew their weapons.

"Go, Captain! We'll help Velo!" Falrey shouted over the sounds of battle.

Kendra tugged on my arm again, and I reluctantly followed. Mora motioned for Finny to follow us.

"There!" Kendra pointed to a slanted stone that jutted out from the floor beside the statue. The three of us sprinted toward it. "Don't look back!" she added.

The rectangular stone was about four feet tall and a foot wide. Finny examined a delicate design that framed it on the floor.

"I think it's a switch of some kind or a lever," he said. He pushed against the lower side. I joined him while Kendra pulled from the other side. I forced my body against the stone. After a moment, the lever gave way and flipped. The three of us kneeled on it to push it the rest of the way down.

A scream rang out from the ledge behind us. A man tumbled over the edge, flailing his arms until his body smashed against the stone floor. He sobbed and tried to move without success.

The crew was locked in battle.

A rumbling shook the room. The statue's hands began to lower. A shiver of warning snapped my attention to the tunnel.

Benny's crazed eyes locked onto mine from the ledge. His chest heaved with ragged breaths. Velo appeared behind him and slashed his dagger across his back. Benny's mouth opened with a scream and he spun around, swinging his blade. Velo ducked, then sliced Benny's leg. All sounds were drowned out by the roar of the grinding stone.

The massive hands halted a few feet from the floor. Kendra tugged me toward it, and I tore my eyes away from the fight.

Velo would be okay. Benny was no match for him.

We peered into the palms. Its surface wavered the same way heat warps the air on a scalding hot day. Kendra gripped one of the fingers to lift herself.

"Wait!" I grabbed her leg, and she paused. I skimmed the floor and found a pebble, then tossed it into the palm. Instead of hitting the stone surface, it vanished.

A deep scream split through the room. I spun around.

Benny's blade speared through Velo's stomach.

"VELO!!" My scream ripped from my chest, and I watched him fall to his knees. I tried to run, but Kendra and Finny grabbed my arms. I struggled against their hold and screamed his name again.

He collapsed on his back.

"Get up!!" I screamed.

He didn't rise.

Kendra grabbed my face and forced me to look at her. "Go, now! Find the Sands!" I tried to push her away from me, but she held me tightly. "Undo it, Louie!"

Benny was climbing down the rope.

I was hyperventilating. The room spun. My body vibrated.

She was right. I could turn back time and undo all of it. It was the only way to save him.

Finny moved in front of me with his dagger and crouched into a fighting stance.

"We'll stop him, Captain! Go!" he said over his shoulder without taking his eyes off the fight. His voice cracked, and his hand was shaking. I grabbed his shoulder to pull him behind me. I couldn't lose him too. But he pushed my hand away.

"Go!"

Kendra pulled me again. I reluctantly climbed the finger, and when I pulled Kendra up, she put her hands on my shoulders to steady herself. She forced a small smile.

"Don't wait for us."

Before I could reply, she shoved me backward into the palm of the statue's hand. We locked eyes once before I disappeared.

Chapter Forty-One

Water broke my fall.

The temperature wasn't hot or cold. When I gasped, my lungs filled with air instead of water. I opened my eyes and struggled to process my blurry surroundings.

I kicked hard, propelling myself upward. When I breached the water's surface, I scrambled to hold onto a nearby floating flat stone. I expected it to wobble, but it remained fixed in place as though it was resting on the floor. I lifted myself and paused to catch my breath.

I was in a tall stone tower that was halfway full of water. Arched windows stretched from the floor deep below to the pointed ceiling high above. Some were missing glass, yet the water remained inside. Sun-dappled trees swayed gently outside. Ivy and moss crawled up the sandstone walls, which were decorated with the same intricate designs as the temple.

More dark, flat stones rested in a circle. In the center, a steady column of sand fell with a quiet hiss from an opening at the highest tip of the pointed ceiling. Sunlight came with it, creating a golden spotlight. A wide bowl floated beneath the beam to catch the falling sand. It was made from the same dark stone as the ones that circled it and was decorated with golden lines and curves. Despite its fullness, it also remained still on the water's surface.

Birds flitted through the open windows. The hush of rustling leaves rode on the warm breeze that drifted from outside.

I searched the ceiling and walls but found no entrance that I could've fallen through. Kendra, Finny, and the rest were holding Benny off, but for how long?

I was close enough that I could reach into the bowl.

My body vibrated with warning.

Something wasn't right.

We didn't see a tower from the outside, which meant it must be concealed somehow. The room was enchanted as well. The traps slowed us down but didn't stop us. Whoever, or whatever, enchanted this temple made it difficult enough that most people would die trying to reach the Sands, but not impossible. Why didn't the inhabitants take the Sands with them? Why keep something so valuable unguarded? If I had to hide something, I'd make it as inconspicuous as possible. Not put it on display.

I dug the tracking crystal from my pocket. It was glowing just as much as it had when I entered the temple. Being this close to the Sands, it should be blinding.

Icy dread gripped my bones.

Whatever was in front of me wasn't the Sands of Time.

It was another trap.

A sudden splash of water startled me and I spun around. Benny plunged deep below. I pushed myself up and hopped to the next stone, then the next, to put as much distance between us as possible.

He rose and gripped the same stone I used. Blood stained the water around him from an unseen injury. He roughly wiped his face and tilted his head back to take in the room. I used that moment to hop to the next stone. His attention turned to me, then locked on the bowl.

His lips parted as he marveled at the sand. Then he lifted himself onto the stone with a grunt, and I hopped another stone away.

A wide smile split his bloody face. "Louie, we made it! Congratulations to us both." He drew a dagger from his belt and flung it at me. My dodge wasn't quick enough. It lodged deep into the fleshy area between my shoulder bone and ribcage. I screamed and nearly stumbled off the stone's edge into the water. He hopped to the next stone, and I did the same while pointing my dagger at him.

"You didn't come this far to die," I said roughly. I wasn't sure if the blade was safe to remove. If it hit something major, I might bleed out before he had the chance to do it for me. The pain was blinding. Every movement was torturous. I clenched my jaw to keep myself from screaming again.

He smirked and retrieved a second dagger from his belt.

"That's true. But I think you know how this is going to go. One of us is not leaving this room."

Our wet clothes weighed us down. Blood saturated his shirt at the chest, the right side of his stomach, his pant leg, and trickled from his forehead. More blood dripped from a gash on this upper left arm.

"You can't beat me at your peak. You think you can take me on with those injuries?"

"Says the woman with a knife in her shoulder."

If I had more daggers to spare, I would've tried to throw the one gripped in my hand. But if I missed, the only weapon I'd have left would be the dagger with the ruby, and I wasn't willing to risk it falling into Benny's hands.

His smirk darkened into a cruel scowl, and he jumped to the next stone. I couldn't keep running. I leaped to the stone between us and slashed my dagger at his calves. The movement made the skin around the embedded knife tear further. He hopped over my blade and stabbed his straight down. I jerked to the side, avoiding the strike by a few inches, and he lost his balance. I kicked him in the shin, and he stumbled backward, barely maintaining his footing.

The knife in my shoulder made it difficult to move, much less fight. Blood gushed from the wound. It wobbled dangerously every time I swung my blade, which increased the threat of it becoming dislodged. If this fight continued, Benny might finally succeed in killing me.

He prepared to charge again. I turned away, gripped the hilt of the knife firmly to keep it in place, and dove headfirst into the water. I kicked and descended as fast as I could using only my left arm.

Benny would need to choose between killing me or taking the sand. The choice would be obvious to him, but I needed to be clear of the tower before he touched it. I didn't look back. I pushed through the pain and stretched out my good arm to touch a glassless window.

My hand went through it. Warm air brushed my wet skin on the other side. I swam deeper to get as close to the ground as possible.

The water swayed and vibrated as I neared the bottom. A muted rumbling shook the tower. Grabbing the frame, I launched myself out of the window.

Chapter Forty-Two

I'd swam deep enough that the fall wasn't far, but it still hurt like hell. The ground shook with a thundering rumble, as though the earth itself was splitting open.

The temple was collapsing.

I forced myself up and bolted across the grass, still holding the knife in my shoulder. Large boulders of stone crashed around me. Sharp pieces shot out in all directions, pelting my body, and I used my free arm to cover my face. I squinted and pushed forward, rushing to the safety of the forest ahead.

No longer enchanted, the tower was exposed. A torrent of water gushed from the open windows and shattered what little glass remained.

The flood surged toward me.

I raced across the field, but I wasn't fast enough. The muddy wave swept me from the ground and carried me into the woods. My body smashed against thick trees, and branches shredded my skin. Water pumped into my lungs. My leg snapped against something hard, which sent me into a violent spin. I blindly tumbled out of control while feebly trying to cover my head with my arms.

Eventually, the flood slowed. The shallow water deposited me on the soaked forest floor. I choked and turned my head so the fluid could spill from my nose and mouth. My throat, lungs, and eyes burned. When I could finally inhale, I squinted through red.

Blood and water streamed down my face. The knife had ripped free from my shoulder, and while the bleeding was heavy, it didn't appear fatal. I wiggled my hands and feet, confirming that I wasn't paralyzed. The movement wasn't painless. The familiar ache of broken bones seared my arms and right leg.

Moans and sobs spilled from my torn lips. My body vibrated, and my teeth chattered. I tested my left arm, and the pain came from my wrist. The injuries in my right arm were far worse. No bones protruded from my skin, but the sharp lump in my forearm made it useless.

Lifting myself from the ground was impossible. All I could do was lie there and listen to the sounds of my crew being crushed to death.

It was difficult to tell how much time had passed, but the rumbling eventually quieted. The trembling forest stilled. My body numbed, and I closed my eyes. Darkness swallowed me, and I gratefully accepted the escape.

Blinding pain forced me awake. I squeezed my eyes shut and silently begged an unseen force to grant me sleep again. Instead, I lay there on the muddy ground, whimpering and shaking. The forest buzzed as though all was well and no tragedy had occurred.

I had to move. I couldn't tell how serious my injuries were. The pain was everywhere, all at once. If I didn't find shelter and tend to myself, I might not make it through the night.

A fragile thought whispered, *Would that be such a terrible thing?*

I was alone. My crew was dead. Kendra was dead. Mother

and Velo were dead. Finny was dead. I had no allies. No friends. No home. Nothing.

My physical pain wasn't enough to stop the grief now. A hellish, dark, bottomless sorrow seized me. I sobbed and screamed incoherent pleas and curses. Each movement intensified the pain.

We were together, all of us, moments ago.

They couldn't be dead. This couldn't be real. The Sands had to exist, somehow, somewhere. I could undo this. I could make it go away.

I can fix this. I can fix this. I can fix this.

But every time I tried to convince myself this wasn't real, the excruciating pain from my injuries forced me back to reality. The world was too sharp around me. Everything was too loud, too bright.

Too real.

When I was finally empty, the sun was setting. As much as I wanted to remain there on the ground until I rotted, self-preservation forced me onto my left elbow. I managed to sit. Thankfully, my hips, back, and chest seemed unharmed. While I could move my right leg, I knew it would be impossible to stand on it. My left leg ached, but I guessed my bones were still in their rightful place.

A broken branch rested beside me. I grabbed it with my left hand and used it to help me stand. I leaned on it to protect the right side of my body. Hobbling deeper into the forest, I wandered aimlessly, wiping blood from my eyes every few steps until it finally dried.

The sun brushed the horizon. Darkness was settling around me. When my broken body finally gave out, I crumpled to the ground in a painful heap.

My body and soul were shattered. The pain was unbearable, yet I was still alive, forced to experience it all.

Please, make it stop, I thought.

I watched the shadows stretch across the brush. When the sun completed its descent, I lay in total darkness.

A flicker of something ahead caught my eye and I squinted.

It was the warm glow of a flame tucked deep in the trees. I took a few shaky breaths, then forced myself to stand. I limped toward it.

A few minutes later, I stepped into a small clearing. The warm light came from inside a small stone building. When I finally reached the short steps, I collapsed again. Fresh tears stung my tired eyes and I let them spill.

"Hello?" I called weakly.

When I was met with silence, my heart broke again and I released another sob.

I promised to keep Kendra safe. Now she was dead. All for an artifact that didn't exist. I should've given up after the sea serpent. I was warned over and over about how dangerous this hunt was.

My late-night conversation with Kendra resurfaced. She was going to look for her mother. She had plans. Now she was nothing. The space she occupied had been swallowed by a void I couldn't escape.

I should've made her go first. I should've been the one to hold Benny's men back. A captain without a crew was a coward.

Eventually, my tears dried, and I was left feeling shattered and hollow. I wouldn't make it back to the ship with my injuries. Even if I did, I couldn't sail by myself. Where would I go?

"I know it hurts," a voice said from above.

Sitting on the stairs was a young boy, about nine or ten years old. His brown skin was taught on his skinny body. He wore white fabric around his waist and no shirt. I could count each rib. My sobs must have masked the sounds of his approach.

His black hair was shaggy and hung over his dark eyes. Something flashed in them. Small sparkles blinked.

There were stars in his eyes.

A tiny one streaked across the iris of his left eye.

"Who are you?" I asked with a stuffy nose and a hoarse throat.

He smiled softly. "That is a very long story."

Chapter Forty-Three

The boy helped me inside and guided me to a low bed in the corner of the room. The sandstone building was completely open with no inner walls, kitchen, or bathing area. Designs similar to those in the temple were scrawled across the walls.

He kneeled beside me and surveyed the injuries. I trembled and groaned. He held up a skinny arm, and a deep gash split his skin without being touched. Black blood leaked out from the wound, and he held it out to me.

"Drink."

My surprise was insignificant compared to my desperation. I accepted it and lapped up the blood. Drinking blood from a kid's arm should've felt weird, but it didn't. The air was charged. Nothing about him seemed like a child. He was a divinum more powerful than any I'd met so far.

After a few moments, the pain eased. When my bones and skin fused back together, I released his arm. The cut healed right away, leaving his skin smooth once more.

My head spun, and sparks tingled my skin. A peace I'd never experienced before stilled my mind the same way water cools a burn.

"It will feel strange at first. My blood is strong."

"Did you just hear my thoughts?"

"No. Every human feels that way after tasting it."

We were quiet for a moment, and I closed my eyes. The tranquility was a wonderful gift. The tornado of sorrow and devastation calmed inside me. When I opened them, the boy was watching me. His knowing gaze was comforting, and his presence felt like a warm blanket. He was more familiar to me than anyone I'd ever known or any place I'd ever been.

"You enchanted the temple, right?" I asked.

"I did."

"Why?"

"Why do you think?"

Talking to him felt like being in class again. He already knew the answer. I chewed my lip and considered my reply.

"To trap those who seek the Sands of Time," I guessed. When he didn't reply, I continued, "Nobody could find sand in the rubble of a massive temple. Hunters would give up searching for it."

He gave me an approving nod, and pride swelled in me.

"I have so many questions," I said. He stood.

"I have answers, though we must leave this place."

He walked to a chest in the corner of the room and retrieved another tunic and slippers. He handed them to me and went outside to give me privacy. I changed out of the wet clothes and wrapped myself in the soft fabric. I'd lost my regular dagger in the flood, but my enchanted one was fortunately still hooked to my belt. I strapped it around my waist.

The tracking crystal tumbled from the pocket of my wet pants and clattered to the ground, beaming brightly. I flinched and shielded my eyes. Spots danced across my vision as though I'd stared at the sun. I felt for it with closed eyes and when my hand wrapped around it, heat seeped into my skin. Keeping my eyes closed, I stuffed it into a tiny pocket on my belt.

The light was more intense than it had been with any divinum or enchanted item. Which meant either an artifact was hidden here, or the boy was an extremely powerful divinum.

Or both.

Clarity slapped me in the face. The threads of information connected to reveal the truth.

I found him waiting for me on the steps outside. The boy gazed thoughtfully in the direction of the destroyed temple.

"It's you," I said. He turned with one eyebrow raised.

"What am I?" he asked.

"You're the artifact. The Sands of Time."

He gave me a small, sad smile. Instead of answering, he said, "Come with me."

We walked unhurriedly through the dark forest, away from the fallen temple with the light from the crystal illuminating our path. I trailed behind, watching his small back.

When the reality of what happened threatened to resurface, I closed my eyes. A strange sort of infinite nothingness expanded inside me, as though I was floating in a lifeless ocean with only water in every direction. I wanted to stay there forever.

I opened my eyes. The boy had stopped and was staring blankly at something behind me. I spun around, and Benny's fist slammed into my face. I faltered but maintained my footing.

His wet clothes and skin were caked with crusted dust and blood. A demented smile twisted his face underneath the mess. He was breathing hard, and when his eyes locked on the corpus imperium dagger hanging from my belt, he lunged for it.

I wasn't quick enough. He yanked it through the loop before I could stop him and pointed the blade at me.

"Where is it?" he asked breathlessly.

"How the fuck are you still alive?"

He swung, and I lunged backward. His movements were sloppy.

"Where is it?!"

"You saw it. It's under the rubble."

"Liar!" His voice was rough. "You ran, which means you knew that was going to happen. Where. Is. It," he punctuated. When

I didn't answer, he glanced at the boy.

He darted around me. I lunged for him, but he dodged. He snaked his arm around the boy and held tight, forcing him to face me. The cold steel blade pressed against the boy's throat.

"Tell me, or this boy dies."

The divinum's voice spoke calmly in my mind.

"If he harms me with this blade, my body will die."

I put a tentative hand out. "Benny. I don't have the Sands. You'll kill a boy for nothing."

"I don't believe you!"

"If I had the Sands, wouldn't I use it to go back in time right now to hide before you found me?"

His jaw clenched. "Show me the map."

"What?"

"Your map! The star map! I lost my crew and nearly died. I'm tired of spying and getting nothing. My patience had run out. I'm not leaving empty-handed. Give it to me, and I'll let him go."

"What do you mean, spying?"

He scoffed. "I hid an enchanted whisper-ring in your quarters."

Of course.

He wasn't tracking us; he was listening. He heard everything about Vincent, the serpent, the Isle of Night. All of it.

"And Velo's necklace?"

He smirked.

A rumble of fury vibrated deep inside me, muted by the divinum's blood.

He used Velo's most precious item against us.

"Map, Louie. Now!" He pressed the blade harder against the divinum's skin.

"Velo should've been the one to kill you," I sighed and took a step closer. He tensed. "Benny," my voice was low and steady, "slit your throat."

The corpus imperium stone activated. His eyes bulged, and his hand shook from his resistance. He released the boy.

"What is this?" he stuttered.

"Your well-deserved death."

The power overtook him, and he did as he was told.

He dragged the blade across his flesh. Blood dribbled from the cut, slowly for a brief moment, then released in a torrent of red. He fell to his knees and reached for me. I stood motionless and watched.

I wondered if this avenged the lives he'd ruined. Benny wasn't responsible for Victoria's death, but she spent her last day with a broken heart when she should've been enjoying the precious final moments with her father. The sea serpent lost its life because of him. Velo's blood was on his hands. He'd killed indiscriminately. His crimes had piled up, and karma had finally come to collect.

My hands weren't clean, but I would never be as cruel as him.

When he finally fell face down on the ground and his choking silenced, I took a deep breath. The divinum had watched silently with an inscrutable expression.

"Am I a bad person?" I asked. The boy looked at me with starry eyes.

"Morality is a man-made concept."

"That's a yes."

The boy turned to continue our journey. "Come."

I nodded and retrieved the dagger that fell from Benny's hand. I wiped it on his wet shirt, then followed the boy. I didn't spare another glance at Benny's body. The island's creatures could have him.

Chapter Forty-Four

We walked for over an hour. Eventually, we reached a mountain slope. The boy led me up a narrow path that ended at the wide mouth of a cave.

"Are you going to explain?" I asked.

"We will rest here," he said, sitting cross-legged on the cave's damp floor. I joined him. The crystal glowed from inside the pocket of my belt. I pulled it out and rested it on the ground to give us light. Then, as though the sky waited for us to find shelter, the clouds released heavy sheets of rain. I could pretend that no world existed beyond the wall of water pouring over the cave's entrance. Only me and this strange boy existed.

Dozens of questions flitted through my mind. I took a moment to collect my thoughts, and he waited patiently.

"What are you?" I asked.

"What do you think I am?"

I rolled my eyes. "Can't you just tell me?"

He laughed. It was a light sound that warmed me. "I could, but it is more fun to hear your thoughts."

"This is fun for you?"

"With you it is." He gave me a fond smile. "You always surprise me, Louie. You found your way to me. You have opened your heart again, despite the pain you have suffered. You learned the secret of my stars before any other human."

"You created the sky shifts?"

He nodded.

Holy shit. Holy mother fucking shit.

He wasn't a divinum.

He was a god.

"Are you . . . Lex?"

"I am."

The god who tossed the stars across the sky for his entertainment. I shook my head numbly.

A god. A real, flesh and blood, divine being.

"You don't look like a god," I said.

"How should a god look?"

"I don't know. Big, glowing, floating around, lots of abs."

"Gods have no physical body of their own in this world, unless a human offers theirs upon their death, as this boy did." He gestured to his young body.

"This world?! How many worlds are there?"

"That is not for me to share."

"How many gods are there?"

"That is also something I cannot share."

"I thought gods were immortal, but you said your body would die if he hurt you with the dagger."

"Enchantment is the only thing that can kill a god's human body. Items, artifacts, and divinum." Lex lowered his gaze to the ground. "I was quite fond of this boy. He had a kind soul and a brilliant mind. An unfortunate incident left both of us severely injured, and he offered his form to me. For as long as I inhabit this body, it will remain preserved." A spark of sorrow cut through the calm afforded by the god's blood. I knew without a doubt that he truly loved the child.

More questions swirled in my mind. I didn't know where to start.

"Shall I share my story?" he offered. I nodded. "Gods are immortal, restless beings. Living forever can be quite lonely and, frankly, boring. About one million years ago, we collectively decided to create a new world. A masterpiece where we could play and come and go as we pleased. We took our time shaping it, carefully crafting everything you see around you. We breathed life into our creations using our energy, or enchantment, as you call it. We designed every flower, stone, and cloud. Divinum were born during that period." He hugged his knees to his chest.

"Humans are my creation. The other gods were not impressed, but I put great care into forming your species. There is a part of me in all of you, which you know as a soul. Slowly, your kind evolved. As time passed, darkness spread like a disease. A darkness so thick and poisonous that it rotted souls. Humans began destroying the beautiful world we worked so hard to build."

He paused for a moment with a distant expression. I remained silent and patiently waited for him to continue. Eventually, he sighed.

"Humans had too much godly energy. They were abusing it. I stripped away as much as I could without destroying souls, hoping that would solve the problem. Unfortunately, it did not. Without power of their own, humans sought to steal the energy from divinum. This infuriated the other gods. They demanded that I exterminate my creations. I refused. Souls rotted before my eyes, and I was helpless. Every time I interfered, it made things worse. I would end one war only for another to begin shortly after. I gave you guilt, love, compassion, and more, but it was never enough. The other gods cannot kill humans since you contain my energy. Only I can. Eventually, they abandoned this world, and I remained here."

"Humans have nearly wiped out the divinum," he continued. "They need my protection. I created the illusion of the sky shifts to disorient sailors and give divinum a safe home in the deep ocean and forests, such as this one. Wars also increased when humans discovered how to cross the sea. The world is more peaceful now."

"The sky shifts aren't real?"

"They are, but not in the way you are familiar with. What you have mapped are the skies from different moments in my existence. It is the same sky at different times. Your favorite sky, the one with your constellation of the animal you cared for, is what the sky looked like on a cool September night five hundred thousand years ago." He smiled with something akin to pride. "While you are not the only human who will recognize the patterns, you are the first."

I beamed with childlike pleasure, as though I'd impressed a parent. I tossed my braids over my shoulder. "I am the best, after all."

He chuckled. "You are indeed."

I bit my lip, then decided to ask the question that had been nagging me. "Why did the divinum trust me if humans have done such terrible things to them?"

"Since everything is made of the same energy, the divinum can see your soul. That is how they were able to trust you without knowing you. They know your intentions. The core of who you are."

I nodded, though his words were hard to process. I wasn't a good person. I knew that. I didn't understand what they could've seen in me that made them trust me. I shook my head and glanced around the cave. "Why live as a human in the middle of nowhere?"

He smiled fondly. "There is more life here than anywhere else in the world. I can assure you, it is never boring." His smile faded. "I lived with humans for a long time. Those who built the temple cared for me. When they died, I chose to stay and establish this place as a safe haven for divinum. When rumors spread that there was an ancient artifact here, I knew this place was no longer safe. I enchanted the temple knowing someone would eventually find it, then believe that the artifact was destroyed when it fell."

My pulse quickened at the mention of the artifact. I couldn't avoid it any longer. I'd been putting off asking the question because I wasn't sure if I could survive the answer. But I had to know. "Can you control time?"

"I cannot. I can create the illusion of non-linear time, such as the stars from many years past, but it is nothing more than an illusion. No being can control time."

His words were a punch to my gut. The air swept from my lungs, and I wrapped my arms around my stomach to brace against the fresh wave of grief.

All of this for something that didn't exist.

All the pain, all the death, for nothing.

He remained silent, and I hung my head.

There was no going back for me. I couldn't save Mother, Velo, Kendra, Finny, Ushar, Nelson, Mora, and all the rest. There was nothing I could do for Victoria or Finny's sister. I'd never be able to undo what happened fifteen years ago. There would never be a reality where I'd never met Nathaniel.

There was nothing left for me.

The peace afforded by his blood was fading. My earlier sorrow swelled once more. If I could have more of his blood, would it stop the pain again?

"I cannot hear your thoughts, but I can feel your despair. Your soul and I are made of the same thing. That is why you experienced the sea serpent's heartbreak and the magnapistris' disdain. But I cannot help you. If you keep drinking my blood, you will not survive without it."

Chapter Forty-Five

My chin quivered. I pulled my knees to my chest and buried my face. I cried silently, and the god did not try to comfort me. There was no shame or embarrassment. I knew I could be vulnerable in front of Lex. I couldn't help it.

When I was able, I lifted my head and saw the god watching me closely. Another star shot across his eye. I wiped my nose on the tunic.

He stood and said, "We must go. Prepare yourself, for your journey will not be a smooth one."

"What the hell does that mean?"

He turned and exited the cave without answering. I groaned and followed.

He led me through the forest with only the crystal illuminating our path. The rain had stopped, and the clouds were dissipating. I hadn't been paying attention to where we were headed. I followed Lex blindly.

The pain of Kendra's death wouldn't fit in the box where I'd shoved all the feelings I didn't want to face. I couldn't ignore the gaping void created by her absence. Even with Lex's blood, I swayed on the edge of that bottomless hole. Still, I clung to denial. If I let reality settle, I knew I'd collapse and remain on the forest floor.

I tried to convince myself that there might be hope. Maybe

she'd survived. Maybe we could make up for all the time we'd lost because I'd stubbornly denied my feelings for her. Maybe I could hold her again, feel her warmth in my arms, and witness her deep blue eyes bright with life. Now, all of this love had nowhere to go. If I'd been honest with myself and hadn't been such a coward, I—

I shook my head to silence the racing thoughts. It took every thread of willpower to keep myself from coming undone. I could release the pain once I was safe. I focused on the Lex to distract myself.

"What happens when a soul rots?" I asked.

"Souls are immortal. When a human succumbs to the darkness, that decay will remain when they are born again. The more rotted it becomes, the harder it is to repair. But just as a forest can grow from the ashes of a wildfire, so too can a human soul be healed. It is ultimately up to the human."

"What do you mean by darkness?"

"Hatred. Revenge. Greed. Self-loathing. Regret." He glanced at me over his shoulder. "A soul rots when a human holds on too tightly to the darkness."

I thought of Benny. Would he do better in his next life? Or would he feed that darkness until he becomes a shell of a person?

"Your love, Kendra, is a beautiful soul. In every life, no matter how much pain and abuse she suffers, she embraces hope. Time and time again, her soul has fought the darkness and won." He glanced back at me again. "And in every life, your souls find one another."

My heart squeezed, and a wave of grief rose again. I pressed my lips together to quiet the sobs but let the tears fall.

After an hour, the humid air cooled. I licked the salt from my lips. The hush of waves brushing the shore replaced the chirps and songs of the forest creatures. Once we stepped onto the sand, the clear night sky was revealed. Bonny was there, likely as a gift from the god in front of me. Before I could thank him, he nodded to our left.

The shadow of Nathaniel's ship towered in the water. Benny's abandoned one sat next to it.

My stomach dropped. I grabbed his arm to stop him.

"We need to hide! We can't let him find you," I exclaimed.

"That is not an enemy ship," he said, continuing along the beach. I hesitantly followed him while gripping my dagger.

The full moon cast a pale blue glow over the beach. We approached a smaller boat that rested on the shore. I took a closer look at the cove.

"Is that my ship?"

"It is the ship you arrived on, yes."

"I can't sail a ship that large by myself."

"I know. Row," he said, sitting in the jolly boat. I frowned but didn't argue. I was learning not to question an all-knowing nine-year-old.

I rowed us through the moonlight, tossing him pointed looks for not helping. The waves were calm. We glided and gently rocked in silence. Once we reached the ship, I noticed something I hadn't seen before.

A lantern was glowing softly from the deck.

"Are you sure this is okay?"

"Louie!" a high voice shouted from above.

A sweet, glorious sound.

I craned my neck and looked up. Staring back at me with a teary smile, waving excitedly, was a ghost. An impossibility.

Kendra cried out again. Her voice broke with a sob. "Get your butt up here!"

I swiveled back to the god, and he smiled softly.

"Is she real?"

"She is."

A surge of relief crashed through me.

She was alive. She was still here, existing, breathing, smiling, and living.

I covered my mouth and sobbed into my palms.

The lines spilled overboard, and I secured them to the jolly boat with trembling hands. We lifted into the air. Every second of our ascent was one I felt I'd burst through my skin.

When we reached the top, Kendra and Finny were there at the crank. I launched myself from the tiny boat into her arms. Her body was warm and very much alive. We sobbed together and held one another tightly. She stroked my braids, and I buried my face in her shoulder. After some time, she giggled through the tears and patted my back.

"You're squishing me," she said.

I reluctantly released her and held her at arm's length. Her clothes were bloody, but the stains were old and dry.

I wiped my face and asked, "How did you escape?"

"When the temple started to crumble, a wall fell. We slipped out before the roof came down."

Finny stood awkwardly nearby. I released Kendra and pulled him into a tight hug. He tensed, but let me hold him. When I let go, I patted him roughly on the shoulder and he winced. "See? I told you that you'd be okay."

"You never said that," he mumbled, rubbing his shoulder.

"Yet here you are."

My smile faded when I noticed the empty deck. I looked at Kendra, but she solemnly shook her head. My heart fell again. Velo and the others were gone.

"They fought hard. You should be proud," Kendra said. Then they both glanced at Lex. I spun to face him and opened my mouth to give him hell for not telling me she was alive.

"Do not tell them," his voice spoke in my mind. The same voice that warned me when I almost told Velo what I learned from the magnapistris. The realization that Benny would've heard us talking through the whisper-ring made me grateful that I'd kept my mouth shut. Lex had his reasons for wanting to keep his existence a secret.

"Respectfully, you're an asshole, but fine," I replied through the

mental connection. The corner of his mouth twitched. I scrambled for a name and gestured to him.

"This is Atticus. I found him in the woods."

Kendra and Finny nodded, accepting my simple explanation.

"I need to travel south. There is a small village, and I am hoping you can help me get there," the god said.

"How can we sail with only three of us? Plus, we need to get back to Mother," Kendra said. My heart sank. I should've told her when I had the chance. I still hesitated, not wanting anything to disturb the excitement of our reunion, but she deserved to know.

"Just a moment," I said to Finny and Lex. I pulled Kendra to the side and lowered my voice. "I'm sorry, but Mother is dead. Nathaniel killed her."

I watched closely as she processed the news. First, her eyes went round. Then her brow furrowed. Pink crept up her neck, and her eyes became shiny.

"He killed her?" she asked. I nodded.

She took a step back and shook her head. "No. That can't be true."

She looked at me imploringly, as though I might take back what I said. When I didn't, she fell apart.

"Oh, gods. No, gods, no!" She lowered herself to the ground. The scream that ripped from her throat shattered my heart. A dam of devastation was released. Mother was like an actual parent to Kendra. She grew up in her care. I always knew Mother had a soft spot for her.

I glanced at Finny, who was looking everywhere but at us, and said, "Prepare to ship off. The three of us will manage." He nodded and scurried away, grateful for an excuse to leave, and Lex followed.

I lowered myself beside Kendra and wrapped an arm around her shoulder. She leaned into me and cried. I held her until the sobs faded into quiet whimpers.

"It's too much," she said.

"I know." I rubbed her arm. "It's too much all at once. Let's process everything bit by bit. One thing at a time."

She nodded and sniffled.

Lex appeared before us. "We must leave now. I will help."

Kendra wiped the snot from her face and gave me a wary look. I stood and helped her up.

"He has an enchanted item. The ship will basically sail itself," I lied. Kendra's frown deepened, but she didn't ask questions.

Lex dropped the sails, raised the anchor, and shifted the currents and wind in our favor, pushing us south. I quickly changed into spare clothes that I found in the sleeping quarters before taking my place at the helm. Kendra leaned against the railing beside me.

"I was thinking we can go to Templan after we drop the kid off if you still want to."

"I would love that," she replied with a soft smile.

My body lightened at her happiness. But the peace was short-lived.

"Captain!" Finny called from the deck. I turned and followed his pointed finger.

A navy ship identical to ours was charging toward us. It sliced through the water at twice our speed.

I clenched my teeth and shouted at Lex, "Full speed ahead!"

The wind strengthened, and the ship lurched forward. We picked up speed, but it wasn't enough. The ship was gaining on us. At this rate, we wouldn't be able to lose it.

I cut the wheel sharply to the left. If I couldn't outrun it, maybe I could curve around it and head the other way. There were many dark coves. Maybe I could slip into one to lose it, or we could sneak off in the jolly boat.

But the other ship was prepared. It curved and barreled toward us. A sudden gust of wind caught our sails and pushed us forward just in time to avoid a total collision. The nose of the other ship skimmed ours with a loud crash. Kendra and I were tossed into the railing. It tore into our ship, ripping a large gash in the hull. I scrambled back to the wheel and straightened it.

There was a full crew on the other deck. Dozens of knights nocked flaming arrows. Nathaniel stood at the helm. His crazed eyes locked on mine, and his mouth was twisted into a murderous smile.

Chapter Forty-Six

We broke free from the other ship with a sharp jolt. Our sails caught another gust, likely of Lex's creation. I gripped the wheel to stay on my feet.

Someone shouted a command, and the arrows were released. Most lodged into the hull while a few made it onto the deck. Kendra and Finny rushed to stomp the flames out. The crew prepared for a second round of fire. Their ship was curving to the left to follow us. I kept us straight, desperate to get as much distance between us as possible.

"I need more wind!" I screamed. When the air didn't change, I skimmed the deck, but Lex was nowhere to be found.

Another round of arrows pelted the stern. Several whizzed over my head and lodged into the mast and deck. I stayed low and kept the wheel steady.

We were outmatched. There was no way we'd win this battle. With their ship being just as fast as ours and equipped with a full crew, escape would be nearly impossible.

Kendra and Finny frantically snuffed out the flames from the arrows, but there were too many. A wave rocked us, and water splashed onto the deck. Nathaniel's ship rocked too, which made the next round of fire less precise. Lex was tucked in a corner, watching the water with a focused expression.

The ship was closing in. I could hear their shouts behind me. Their bow collided with our stern. I dropped to the floor, narrowly avoiding being impaled by the bowsprit that speared the air above me. Wood splintered with an ear-splitting crack, no doubt damaging our rudder. We weren't going to make it. Not while he was at the helm.

I crawled on my knees to the lower deck.

"Kendra!" I screamed. She raced to me. The ship was backing off, separating itself from ours. I grabbed her hand and dragged her up the steps to the wheel. "Get distance. Keep going south. The rudder is probably damaged, but do your best."

Her face creased with alarm. "Where are you going?"

I cupped her face and kissed her deeply. When I pulled away, she was gripping my sleeves. I brushed her cheek.

"Watch the stars. You'll find me there." I pointed to the sky and gave her a sad smile.

"Wait!"

I pushed her hands away, turned, and launched myself from the shattered stern to the retreating ship. I grabbed the broken bowsprit, then swung myself on top of it. Kendra screamed and sprinted to follow, but Finny wrapped his arms around her waist.

I balanced on the beam and dove onto the deck.

Her screams tore at my heart. I stood and cupped my hands around my mouth, shouting once more, "Find me in the stars!"

Knights charged at me, and I drew my last dagger. In that brief moment, with the knights converging, my mind calmed. If she watched the stars, which she would, she'd eventually make the same discovery I had. She'd make her own star maps and find comfort in the illusions created by the god behind her, just as I had.

Swords were drawn.

I rushed forward and swung myself over the railing of the upper deck. Two men thrust their blades at me from either side. I ducked, and they both missed. Another came at me from the front and tried to spear me. I twisted to the side, then ripped my blade across the side of his neck.

Someone from behind wrapped their strong arms around me. He lifted me, but before he could slam me into the floor, I kicked him in the groin. He released me and crumpled to the ground, immobilized.

Four more men swung at me. One snatched my arm, trying to wrestle the dagger from my hand, while another grabbed my braids. I rammed my elbow into the stomach of the man behind me, knocking the air from his lungs. I punched the other in the face twice, and he released my arm.

Someone sliced their sword into my back, and I screamed. I fell into the chest of another knight, who gripped my shoulders to hold me still. I spun around him and plunged my enchanted blade into his back.

"Kill the knights," I ordered. The corpus imperium stone activated, and the man's eyes went wide. Another knight rushed at us, and the knight I held onto jabbed his sword at him. The blade pierced the other man's stomach. The other knights paused and watched their crewmate stab another man.

He slashed his sword wildly, and the knights backed away. I held onto the man's back and used him as a shield and a weapon.

A nearby man shook his head, then speared the knight in the stomach. I yanked the dagger from his back and twisted around his falling body. The knight tried to pull his sword from the man's torso, but my knife was already in his back.

I ordered him to do the same.

When another knight cut down the one I was controlling, I repeated my attack. They died by their own hands.

A sword sliced the back of my knees and I screamed. I spun around, still holding the knight. Nathaniel charged with the tip of his sword pointed at me. I staggered to the side, and it impaled the knight. I released him and jumped backward.

Nathaniel retrieved his sword, splattering blood on his uniform, and faced me again. Knights circled us.

"Back off!" he barked at them. "Assess the damage! I can take her."

I scoffed, out of breath. "You wish."

The gashes in my back and legs weren't deep enough that I couldn't fight, but I was still at a serious disadvantage. The remaining men backed away. We both lowered into a fighting stance.

I smirked and wiggled the dagger. "I guess you don't recognize this." He glanced at it. "It's enchanted with a beautiful red stone."

He paled and glanced at his fallen men. Then, his face contorted with rage, and he lunged.

I ducked under the first swing, but he anticipated the move and smashed his knee into my face. I stumbled around him and brought my hand to my shattered nose. Blood gushed, and I gagged.

He spun and swung again. I lunged backward and crashed my blade into his, throwing him off balance. He teetered, and I pushed forward, jabbing the blade at his chest.

He arched his body, and the dagger skimmed his jacket. He brought the hilt of his sword down on my hands. It collided with my wrist, but I maintained my hold. I used my momentum to duck and roll, then kicked his hand that held his sword.

It flew from his grip and skidded across the deck. He lunged for it, but I hooked my foot around his leg. He fell, and I pounced.

I landed on his back, but before I could run my dagger through him, he rolled us so he was on top of me. I did the same, and we tumbled toward the shattered railing.

I put my foot out to stop us from falling overboard, then rolled him onto his back again. He tossed his head, and it cracked into mine. Pain exploded in my skull. I tumbled to the side and rolled away.

I halted on my stomach and tried to crawl, but he grabbed my foot and dragged me toward him. I stabbed the blade into the wood of the deck to keep him from pulling me overboard. He threw his body over my legs so I couldn't kick him with my other foot.

He climbed on top of me. I twisted my body to face him before he could pin me down. He readied his arm to throw another punch. I pressed myself into him, swung my arm, and buried the knife in his back.

He screamed and tried to push off me, but I wrapped my legs around him and held tight. Our faces were close. Agony contorted his. Blood coated my mouth and throat. He continued to struggle against me. Footsteps of the remaining knights thundered toward us.

We were out of time.

We locked eyes and I smiled, issuing one final command.

"Throw yourself overboard."

Shock and terror seized him, and he strained to fight the power of the corpus imperium. He clawed at the dagger, but it was out of reach.

I tried to push out from under him. I pulled my legs away, but he grabbed them again. His face relaxed, and he wrapped his arms around me in a tight embrace.

I tried to fight, but his hold was too strong.

He lowered his lips to my ear and said, "As you wish."

He slid himself backward just as the remaining knights reached us. His legs went first, then his torso, taking me with him over the splintered side of the ship. My arms were pinned to my body. I couldn't reach for anything to hold on to.

We fell for a moment, then jolted to a stop. I looked up. Nathaniel had caught a splintered shard of wood that jutted out of the hull. He released me, but I had my arms and legs tightly wrapped around him. He reached up with his other hand and gripped the wood.

He twisted, trying to throw me off.

A few faces peered over the side. Two panicked knights lowered their arms to pull him up. Nathaniel couldn't let go to reach for them with me weighing him down.

"Let go!" he screamed.

If I managed to climb up his body, the knights would kill me.

I gripped him with everything I had and glanced behind me. My ship had vanished.

They were safe.

My panic cooled into calm acceptance. I looked up again. Nathaniel's grip was slipping. I tried to order him to let go, but the blood in my mouth garbled my words.

"Captain!" one of his knights shouted. A rope was being lowered.

The decision wasn't as difficult as I thought it would be. Maybe this was our destiny. Forever tied to one another, even in death.

I kicked the side of the ship and took three steps upward. I reached and grabbed the wooden shard. I dropped my full weight, pulling the wood down with me. It broke with a loud snap, and we dropped.

I was falling on my back and he was above me. We looked at one another.

For the brief moment we had during our final descent, I saw everything. The boy I loved. The man I hated. The nightmare and the weakness. The pursuer and the victim. The lives lived, and the lives lost.

If I had more time, I would've been pissed that his face was the last one I saw. But as Lex said, I could try again in my next life.

Maybe I would find Kendra sooner.

Maybe we could be happy together.

We collided with the moonlit water and vanished beneath the waves.

Chapter Forty-Seven

KENDRA

THREE YEARS LATER.

Louie's such an asshole.

Her last words were cryptic for no reason. No matter how hard I stared at the sky, there wasn't a single shape that resembled her. For someone who always said what she meant, she decided to be vague at the absolute worst moment.

I'd watched the stars every clear night for three years. How was I supposed to find shapes in a bunch of dots? There was one cluster of stars that kind of looked like a banana. I saw it during that first year, then again a few months ago. I drew it into a notebook and continued to look for any other repeating shapes. Maybe there was something tiny I was missing.

I took it as a good sign that there was nothing up there that looked like her.

Nathaniel's ship sank that night due to the damage it took from ramming into us. The king's guard reported no survivors, but that didn't mean she was gone. They didn't even know she was there, so how could they declare her dead?

When we returned, I discreetly spread the word that the Sands of Time were destroyed. The king sent men to search the rubble of the fallen temple, but they left empty-handed.

Finny and I bought a house together outside of Templan on a cliff by the sea. It was dark enough to see the stars clearly, and there were no buildings to block the view. I could watch the ships come and go and scan the decks for her. The last time we spoke, we talked about coming here. If she was looking for me, this is where she'd start.

Finny stopped trying to convince me she died. He put a tiny grave marker near the cliff's edge, which I ignored. It was just a rock. I left it alone because he would sit by it sometimes. I think it wasn't just for Louie, but also for Lyonel, Velo, and everyone else we lost.

He'd turned eighteen a few months ago and was dating a sweet girl who didn't care about his brand. While he hadn't said anything, I suspected he was thinking about proposing. They couldn't legally get married, but they could have a wedding and do everything else married couples did.

I had a feeling he was keeping it from me because he didn't want to leave me alone. I didn't bring it up either. Without him by my side, I wouldn't be able to ignore the suffocating loneliness.

The crisp air signaled the end of summer. Brilliant colors slashed across the sky, and the sun was partly hidden beneath the horizon. I set up my tea and snacks by the telescope Finny built for me. Hugging a blanket around my shoulders, I turned at the sound of footsteps in the grass. Finny approached with a rolled piece of paper and offered it to me.

"I ran into the postman on my way in. This is for you."

I'd received many letters from my birth mother. When I made it to Templan after delivering the boy to his destination, I found her in a dilapidated building at the edge of town. She cried when she saw me and fell to her knees to beg for forgiveness.

And coin.

At the time, it felt like a small price to pay to have her in my life. She was all I had left, other than Finny. After years of receiving letters and visits begging for more, I'd come to regret finding her.

When she showed up unannounced a few months ago, I finally had to threaten her to get her to stay away. I didn't want to get violent, but she left me no choice.

I sighed and unrolled the paper, then frowned.

It was covered with ink dots, as though someone flicked a quill and black ink sprayed the paper. A few letters were scrawled in the bottom corner.

L, TGPE

Finny peered over my shoulder. I raised a brow at him, and he shrugged. I handed it to him and unfurled the second page underneath. It was a map of the kingdom with one inkblot far off the coast.

I snatched the paper back from Finny and held it up to the darkening sky. The stars were beginning to reveal themselves directly above us. My pulse fluttered.

I tapped the paper. "What does this mean? What are those letters?" I shoved it back into Finny's hands. He squinted at it for a moment with bunched eyebrows.

"It's a letter, and there's a comma after the L. Maybe that's a sign-off, like—"

"Love," I finished for him. My heart thundered in my chest. I held my breath and searched my mind for possibilities of what the other letters could mean.

When the words came, the world fell away. The thin, fragile threads of hope I'd clung to for the past three years hardened. I put a shaky hand over my mouth and stifled a sob. Finny moved closer and put a tentative hand on my shoulder.

Love, The Greatest Pirate Ever

I wiped my face and slowly shook my head at the paper. "Making me wait three years. What an ass." I rolled the maps and sniffled. If I could've swam there in that moment, I would've. I tapped Finny on the chest with the paper. Beaming with a wide smile, I said, "Pack your things. We're going hunting."

MOTHER

I knew the man who hurt Louie was an idiot, but I didn't think he was this stupid.

One of Lenora's spies, who had been sailing with Commander Bartholomew since the destruction at Port Roche, reported that he was on his way to Bangor. I anticipated that he intended to raid the boarding house to search for Louie or any clues that might lead him to her and the Sands. His creaking footsteps up the old boarding house stairs confirmed my suspicions. If he was attempting to be quiet, he was failing spectacularly.

I remained in bed and feigned sleep. I'd already sent the girls away with the coin I'd been saving. The rest was tucked in a sack beneath my bed. I doubted his knights would stay long enough to search there.

Several sets of boots tiptoed along the hallway. Doors creaked open. Some of the men whispered. When they neared my room, my stomach flipped. I took a slow breath.

My bedroom door groaned loudly on its hinges, which was one of the reasons I made this room mine. Whoever held the knob startled at the sound and stopped abruptly. Fabric rustled, and it swung open without hesitation.

I sat upright and wore my best horrified expression. My eyes were well-adjusted to the darkness, more than most. The boy,

Nathaniel, stood at the threshold with a sword gripped in his hand. Four knights hid behind him.

"Who . . . who are you?" I stammered.

Nathaniel charged forward, raised his sword over his head, and speared it through my stomach.

There was no need to fake the pain. A shattering scream tore from my throat, and I clawed at the steel. He jumped onto the bed and stood with a foot on either side of me. He pulled the sword up. It yanked from my belly with a slick suction sound, and I screamed again. Tendrils of white-hot agony seared my body. Choked sobs locked in my chest. Tears stung and spilled freely.

He stabbed again, then again and again. I remained on my back, letting him eviscerate me until he was satisfied. He pulled the blade out one final time. I'd gone completely limp. My chest stilled, and my eyes went vacant. He was breathing hard.

After a moment, he jumped off the bed. I watched out of the corner of my eye. He pulled a handkerchief from his pocket and cleaned his blade. My black blood soaked the soft cotton. By the time he neared any light to see clearly, it would already be red.

He exited the room without a second glance toward me and instructed his men to search the house. Even if he had looked, the blanket that covered me would've hidden the wounds that were already healing.

I remained perfectly still while the brutish men trashed my office across the hall. They took everything. The chest of enchanted items, my weapons, and the black book. King Francis already knew of its existence. If I didn't leave a decoy, he wouldn't stop searching until he found it.

I wasn't concerned. The information was fabricated. Even if it was the original, he wouldn't be able to read the contents. The invisible ink could only be revealed by heating it with dragon fire. The original was tucked safely in the sack beneath the bed. Once it was safe, I'd send it to Lenora.

Every enchanted item we could find, every known alchemist, every captured divinum, the identities of the dealers, and the locations of the dungeons. Everything we needed to bring him down for good was in that book.

When the men left, I rolled onto my side and hugged my freshly healed stomach. I allowed a few moments to compose myself, then shoved the blanket off and stood. I briskly changed and retrieved the sack from underneath the bed.

I closed my eyes and visualized my destination. Fine sand. Inky waves. The soft glow from the swaying lantern hanging from the worn wooden porch tucked in the tropical trees. Every nerve in my body vibrated. As the image became clearer, the quivering intensified. My heart slammed hard against my ribs and my skin dampened. A feverish chill washed over me.

I reached for that familiar latching sensation and vanished.

Acknowledgments

Writing this book has been an experience that I will treasure for the rest of my life. I worked hard, but this wouldn't have been possible without all the love and support. Thank you . . .

To EJL Editing and my fabulous beta readers for helping make this story infinitely better.

To my big, wonderful, amazing family for offering me unconditional love and support since day one.

To my dear friend Lana for being my brainstorming buddy since middle school.

To Alan, who I miss every day.

To my dad for always listening to my crazy ideas until he finally became exasperated and told me to 'Just do it already!'

And to my mom, who will forever be my biggest fan.

Thank you.

ABOUT THE AUTHOR

Olivia Harlow is an American author born and raised on the east coast. When she's not writing, Olivia enjoys creating art, gaming, watching K-dramas, and of course, reading.

The Thief of Tides is her first novel.